Killer Routine

"Entertaining … Orloff does a great job of evoking some-time, struggling comedy clubs."   —*Publishers Weekly*

"Gritty and full of surprises, this is a fascinating glimpse into the world of stand-up comedy; it's definitely worth a read. Four stars."
—*RT Book Reviews*

"Well plotted, great characters, and a promising beginning to a new series."   —*Suspense Magazine*

"A fun book with a traditional feel, but also a page turner. More please."   —*Crimespree*

"You'll be seriously swept up in the story as author Orloff turns family tragedy into triumph."
—Reed Farrel Coleman, three-time
Shamus Award-winning author of *Innocent Monster*

"A wildly entertaining page-turner."
—David Bickel, author of *Creepiosity*
and TV writer/producer of "The King of Queens"

Diamonds for the Dead

"Alan Orloff's superior storytelling skills shine in his tension-filled debut."   —*Mystery Scene*

"Thought-provoking debut."   —*Publishers Weekly*

"Those who enjoy good characterization and characters with a strong sense of family will enjoy *Diamonds for the Dead*."
—*The Mystery Reader*

"*Diamonds for the Dead* has it all: compelling plot, great characters, and the kind of tension that keeps you screwed into your seat for a one-sitting read."

—John Gilstrap, *New York Times*
bestselling author of *No Mercy* and *Hostage Zero*

DEADLY
CAMPAIGN

ALSO BY ALAN ORLOFF

Diamonds for the Dead
Killer Routine

DEADLY

A LAST LAFF MYSTERY ———————————

CAMPAIGN

ALAN ORLOFF

MIDNIGHT INK
WOODBURY, MINNESOTA

FIRST EDITION
First Printing, 2012

Book design by Donna Burch
Cover design by Ellen Lawson
Cover illustration © 2011 Kelly Dyson
Editing by Connie Hill

Midnight Ink, an imprint of Llewellyn Worldwide Ltd.

Library of Congress Cataloging-in-Publication Data

Orloff, Alan, 1960–
  Deadly campaign : a Last Laff mystery / Alan Orloff. — 1st ed.
      p.   cm.
  ISBN 978-0-7387-2318-1
  I. Title.
  PS3615.R557D43   2012
  813'.6—dc23   2011033360

Midnight Ink
Llewellyn Worldwide Ltd.
2143 Wooddale Drive
Woodbury, MN 55125-2989
www.midnightinkbooks.com

Printed in the United States of America

ONE

"Politicians really chap my *tuchas*," Artie Worsham said, chewing on the stub of the unlit cigar he'd been gnawing for the past two days.

"Everybody chaps your tuchas," I said.

"Not true. Only people I dislike."

"You don't like very many people. That's a lot of chapping going on."

"I said people I *dislike*. Not people I don't like. There's a difference. Most people I don't have much of an opinion about."

I yawned, not much interested in Artie's semantics lesson. Usually I didn't mind politicians, as long as they were honest, hardworking, and dependable. Which, in fairness, narrowed the field considerably.

I surveyed the banquet room. The excitement of a crowd anticipating a good show never failed to make the fine hair on my arms tingle. Whether I was the one on stage, or a buddy of mine, or even some poor newbie on his first open mic night, the murmurs of the audience held a certain quality. Now, as we waited for Thomas Lee's nephew, Edward Wong, to stand up and make a speech, I had many of the same feelings.

About thirty of Lee's relatives and close friends occupied a private room in the back of his restaurant—Lee's Palace—Home of Very Famous Peking Duck. We were all there for a belated celebration of Edward's victory in the Democratic congressional primary.

"What is it with politicians anyway?" Artie asked me, words swirling around his stogie.

I wasn't sure if he was asking me a question or trying to jump-start a comedic riff railing against politicos. I fed him the straight line anyway. "What do you mean?"

"They all dress the same, they all smile the same, they all talk the same."

If that was his punchline, his routine needed some work. "I guess it's what the people want."

"Not this people," Artie said, thumbing himself in the chest. "I want liberty, truth, and justice from my public servants. And a little integrity would be nice, too."

"That all?"

Artie opened his mouth to respond, but Lee came up behind us and clapped him on the shoulder. "Hey, having a good time?"

"Sure," Artie said. "When do the dancing girls arrive?"

"No girls today, but we've got something even better. Edward's going to say a few words," Lee said.

"Oh, joy," Artie said, then slumped in his seat and crossed his arms.

Lee turned toward me. "How was the food, Channing?"

I patted my belly. "Excellent, as usual. You know how to throw a good banquet, that's for sure." It wasn't often I got the chance to eat my way through seven courses of Chinese delicacies, highlighted by some truly spectacular Peking Duck. Most days, I stopped after the third course. Lee was fond of his sister's family, always regaling us with stories of his nephew's exploits, right along with those of his own two daughters. One big happy family. "You must be very proud of Edward."

"I am." Lee extended his arms, taking in the whole room. "Everyone here is, too. Relatives, friends, the whole Chinese-American community. There aren't too many of us walking around the Capitol, you know."

"That's great. Whatever we can do, we're happy to help," I said.

Artie grunted his agreement.

"Thanks, guys. I know I can count on you." He smiled. "But it's nice to hear you say it. And Artie, when Edward gets elected, maybe he can keep the health inspectors off your back." He winked at me as he said it, then nodded toward the front of the room. "He's going to start soon. I'll catch up to you later." With a parting clap on the back, Lee set off to make sure his other guests were full and happy, too.

"Helluva guy," Artie said. Lee was one of Artie's closest friends, dating back fifteen years when he opened up The Last Laff Comedy Club next to Lee's restaurant. When I arrived on the scene some years later, Lee became one of my closest friends, too.

Someone clanked a knife against a water glass a few times, and the room slowly hushed as if someone turned down the volume on a radio. At the back of the room, a man stood and started fiddling with a small video camera. Footage of this little speech would probably appear on YouTube in a few hours as part of the requisite multimedia campaign.

Patrick Wong, Edward's younger brother, slid his chair out and stepped to the makeshift podium Lee had erected near the head table. With a graceful economy, he extracted a folded piece of paper from an inside pocket and laid it on the podium. Then he smoothly buttoned his jacket and licked his lips. He glanced around, seeming to make contact with every single person in the room, if only for an instant.

"First, let me thank Uncle Thomas for the wonderful food he provided this evening." He paused for some applause. "It's a good thing we'll be down the road in Washington next year, so we can come back whenever we want for some of this awesome duck." Another smattering of applause. "Thank you, Thomas." A third round of applause echoed throughout the small room, finally forcing Lee to rise from his chair and wave awkwardly. When he sat, the room hushed once again and all eyes returned to the dais.

Patrick cleared his throat, more for theatrical purposes than for any functional reason. Another trick of the professional public speaker. "You all know my brother, so I'll keep this very brief." He paused and glanced around, smile growing. "After all, I have to save my voice for some serious campaigning during the next ten weeks."

Next to me, Artie mumbled, "Get on with it, already."

"Help me welcome the next congressman from Fairfax County, and the very first Chinese-American representative from our district, my older brother, Edward Wong."

Edward strode to the microphone, and everyone in the room took their feet in a standing ovation, Artie and I included. Patrick put his arms around Edward, and they faced the crowd, soaking it in, huge smiles on their faces.

Artie had a point—about the cookie-cutter appearances of politicians, anyway. Edward wore a conservative dark blue suit, white shirt, and red tie, while Patrick wore a conservative dark blue suit, a white shirt, and a yellow tie, his small nod toward individuality.

Artie must have noticed me admiring the Wongs. "They *are* handsome and charming," he said, craning toward me so he could be heard above the applause. "Just like the you-know-whos."

Every time Artie talked about Lee's sister's family, he called them the Asian Kennedys. Never mind that he'd never actually spent much time with the Wongs—or any time with the Kennedys, for that matter. I suppose Artie felt comfortable drawing all his conclusions from what he saw on TV or read in the paper. I'd made him promise not to call them that today. Of course, referring to them as the "you-know-who" clan was even worse. I leaned over and spoke into his ear. "Yes, being handsome and charming helps in politics. Lucky for you those qualities are not essential for stand-up comedians."

The ovation continued until the two brothers broke apart. As the crowd settled back into their seats, Patrick returned to his spot at the head table, shaking a few hands along the way. Although the people were voting for Edward, they were also getting the services of Patrick, an accomplished lawyer in his own right. A 2-for-1 bonus.

If Patrick's presence was smooth and practiced, Edward's aura was commanding. He appeared reassuring, but there was something that told you not to turn your back on him. I imagined some people felt the same way about President Kennedy. I sat forward in my chair, waiting to be wowed.

"Thank you all for coming. It means a lot to me and to my family. Just as my family is always there for me, I want to always be there for you. It's about time our community had their voice heard in places that matter. With your support, we can make it happen." He'd probably practiced his speech—and a dozen variations—many times over, yet the words seemed spontaneous and heartfelt. I wish I could deliver my routines with such ease. I guess it helped to have an audience full of friendly faces, especially faces not looking for a laugh.

"We've grown as a community and yet many of our needs don't get addressed. We hold many positions of esteem—doctors, lawyers, business leaders—yet we are underrepresented in the corridors of power. I feel it is my obligation, my duty, to change that." As he spoke, he emphasized his points with his right hand. Not quite pointing, not quite shaking his fist. It was a gesture I'd seen Clinton use to perfection when he stormed the nation back in the nineties. He smiled at the back of the room where the guy with the video camera stood. "And I will change that, with your support. Together, we can do anything."

I could barely hear Artie muttering next to me as the crowd applauded. The applause died down slowly, but it was replaced by shouting coming from somewhere in the back. Three men, clad entirely in black with ski masks covering their faces, had burst into the room.

All three carried aluminum baseball bats.

One remained by the door and the other two split up, the taller one advancing toward Edward at the podium, while the shorter one headed for the back of the room. The butt end of a pistol peeked out from the waistband of his jeans.

My heart pounded and I felt Artie tense beside me.

The masked man closest to Edward stopped and brandished his weapon. "No cell phones. Remain calm and no one will be harmed. Do not scream. Now, cover your faces."

The voice, polite and calm, sent a chilling ripple up my spine.

Artie and I complied, covering our faces, but I made sure I could see what was going on between a gap in my fingers. Missing three on my left hand helped. Most of the other guests also covered up, but a few braver souls watched. Were the thugs going to beat each of us to a pulp with their bats?

The thought of that brutality—not just feeling it, but witnessing the carnage—sent another, larger, tremor through my body.

At the back of the room, the shorter guy walked up to the man shooting the video and grabbed his camera. He flung it on the floor and whacked it a few times with his bat, finishing things off by stomping on the plastic-and-metal carcass.

From the podium, Edward spoke. "Listen. Take what you want. We won't stop you. Please don't hurt us. We have done nothing to you." His voice cracked.

The taller intruder slowly walked toward Edward. He raised the baseball bat until the barrel was an inch from Edward's chin. "I said to be quiet."

Edward didn't respond, but a wild look passed behind his eyes for an instant. Then he went back to looking merely scared.

"Stop!" Edward's father sprang to his feet. "Do you know who I am? Do you know who you are dealing with here?" He didn't wait for an answer. "I am Hao Wong. I suggest you re-evaluate your plans for this evening."

The thug turned away from Edward and took a few steps toward Hao. "Sit down and shut up." He didn't raise his voice, but he got the message across. Hao lowered himself into his seat.

Next to me, Artie mumbled, "Goddamn punks."

The thug's head spun around toward us. "What? What was that?" He glared at us, two fiery eyes piercing the holes in his ski mask.

My heart stopped. I prayed Artie would keep his trap shut for a change. Across the room, terror painted Lee's face.

"Who said that?" the taller thug asked, walking slowly toward us. He held his bat with both hands on the grip. When he stood before us, he repeated his question. "Who said that?"

Neither of us opened our mouths.

"Somebody better answer me, or there's going to be *real* trouble."

Artie snorted. "Who do you think you are, coming—"

The masked man drew his bat back.

TWO

I sprang out of my chair, talking right over Artie. "I said it. I'm the one who said it."

The intruder turned his attention to me. He cocked his head one way, then the other. I braced for the impact of bat against skull. Thought of Artie witnessing the attack and shuddered.

I tried to come up with some clever rejoinder that would disarm this punk—literally—but couldn't. I simply closed my eyes, waiting for the end.

Instead of clubbing me with the bat, he rammed the barrel into my shoulder and pushed. I stumbled backward, smacking my head against the wall behind me with a muffled *clonk*.

"Anybody else have something to say?" the thug asked the crowd, done with me and my insolence, at least for the moment. Artie stared at me, lips trembling. I mouthed, "I'm okay," but he still didn't take his eyes off me as I collected myself and returned to my chair.

I glanced across the room into Lee's ashen face and felt his mortification at the turn of events, a palpable sock to the gut.

My feelings of sympathy were short-lived as the thug shouldered his bat again and screamed, "Now, cover your faces and get down on the floor!"

The sound of chairs scraping along the floor accompanied the flurry of bodies scrambling under the tables. I hit the ground, keeping my head up just long enough to see the intruders swing their bats, smashing plates and platters. Porcelain and glass shattered, sending shards sailing through the air like shrapnel. I ducked and covered my head, wincing along with the cacophony of breakage.

After three interminable minutes, the room quieted, demolition complete. I peeked out from my hiding place. The thugs had stormed off.

Gradually, all the guests got to their feet. Several people sobbed quietly, others held onto loved ones. I noticed a few minor cuts on some faces, but no one seemed seriously injured.

Artie poked me in the side. "You okay?"

"Yeah, I'm fine. Shook up is all."

"You sure? How's the noggin?"

"Okay." I'd have a small bump, but considering everything, I wasn't complaining.

"You didn't have to cover for me, you know."

"Yeah, I know."

"Well, thanks," Artie said.

I fought the urge to massage the bump on my head and settled for kneading my shoulder. "Sure."

"Goddamn punks," Artie said again.

The room looked as if a bomb had gone off. Broken china and glass covered the tables; traces of food dotted the walls. Lee stood near the door wearing an expression of astonishment.

I turned to Artie, still trying to absorb what had just happened. "Someone was sending a message."

Artie removed the unlit stogie from his mouth. "Shoulda sent an e-mail instead."

———

Two plainclothes detectives arrived and took our statements. After twenty minutes of recounting the story, in three separate recitations, Artie and I were dismissed—we still had a comedy club to run. Before we made it out of the restaurant, though, Lee caught up to us.

"Hey guys," he said. "You really okay?"

"We're fine," Artie said. "Just let me know when the cops catch those guys—I'm going to love testifying against them."

"Uh, about that," Lee said. He glanced over his shoulder. "Listen, those detectives . . ."

"Yeah?" I wasn't getting good vibes about this.

"They're not going to report it."

"What? After that attack? Why the hell not?" Artie said, face turning crimson.

"Hao decided that news of the attack would ruin Edward's image and cost him the election. No one wants that."

"That's bullshit. Those guys almost killed Channing."

"Just a bump, Artie."

"Well, it could have been a lot worse," Artie said. "I can't believe the cops went along with that. Don't they have a civic duty to protect us citizens?"

"They're friends of Hao's," Lee said, throwing air quotes around the word "friends."

"Ah, more political cover-up," Artie said. "Figures."

"What about all the other guests?" I asked. "Surely news of what happened will leak out."

Lee shook his head. "Unlikely. Hao and Edward are in there right now, along with Hao's brother Xun, convincing everyone to keep it in the community so it won't ruin Edward's chance to get elected. Hao and Xun are very influential men in those circles. This incident won't be leaked, you can be sure of it."

Artie piped up. "What about us? What if we told the press?"

"Please, Artie. Channing. Don't do that. For me. For Edward. This is his career. Don't screw it up," Lee said. "Obviously, what those goons did was terrible. But really, no one got seriously hurt. And I can replace the dishes."

Artie squinted at him but let me do the talking. "I don't know, Lee. It doesn't seem right, forgetting about what happened here."

"Please, Channing. Let it rest." Lee practically had tears in his eyes. "Please."

"Aw, shit." I shook my head, about to go against my better judgment. "Okay, we won't say anything. For now. Right, Artie?"

Artie frowned, then grunted his assent.

Lee exhaled. "Thanks, guys."

———

Four hours later, Artie and I sat at our bar, going over the night's take. We'd had a pretty good night financially, but I think both of us had something else on our minds.

"We could've been killed, you know," Artie said as he snapped a rubber band around a stack of twenties.

"Aren't you being a little dramatic?" I said. "They were obviously just trying to intimidate Edward. Politics is a rough sport."

"I thought sports had rules," Artie said. "I can't believe Lee wants to sweep it all under the rug."

"It's not Lee, it's the Wong brain trust. I don't like it either, but I can see their point. It's Edward's career, after all. And a lot of hope for that community."

"Shit, Channing, I'll say it again—we could have been killed."

"Who could have been killed?" Skip Gold, our bartender, had materialized at Artie's side.

Artie started to respond, then waved at me. "You tell him. I don't wanna think about it anymore."

I took a deep breath. "At that dinner Artie and I went to, at Lee's, a few a-holes in ski masks trashed the place. While we were all sitting there."

"H-h-holy sh-sh-shit," Skip said. He came by his nickname honestly. Unfortunately, the stuttering didn't help his stand-up comic aspirations.

"Yeah, it was bad. They took baseball bats to all the breakables. Lee will be cleaning up that mess for days. Luckily, no one got badly hurt."

"Did they make off with a lot of loot?" Skip asked.

"Nah. Didn't take a thing," Artie said. "Just your basic roadkill getting their jollies scaring the crap out of good people."

"I thought you didn't want to think about it anymore," I said to Artie.

"What? You think I can forget something like that?"

"What did they want?" Skip asked. He'd pulled a rag out and was polishing the bar, though it already gleamed.

"Hell if I know," Artie said.

"Hell if I know," I echoed. "If I had to guess, I'd say they weren't happy Edward was running for Congress."

Artie made a clucking noise, then closed the accounts book he was working on. "I'm heading home. After a day like today, I need some serious sleep."

"I'll walk out with you, boss," Skip said.

I followed Artie and Skip out. I could use some sleep myself.

———

The next day, I got to the club early for me, around noon, and after checking in with Donna McKenzie, our de facto manager, to make sure there weren't any fires that needed dousing, I wandered next door to talk with Lee to see if he knew what the hell was going on.

A hostess greeted me inside the door. "Hello, Channing. How are you today?" I came in so often, I wondered if some of the staff thought I was addicted to MSG.

"Great. Lee around?"

"Sure," she beamed, as if nothing terrible had happened yesterday. "He's in the kitchen. Go on back."

I made my way to the kitchen, detouring slightly to check out the private room. See how much damage had been done. I poked my head in. The room looked like it always had—before yesterday, anyhow. No broken dishes. No pieces of glass on the floor.

14

Not a mark on the walls. Evidently, someone—or some fairly large cleaning crew—had come in and scrubbed the place spotless.

Lee really *was* trying to pretend it had never happened.

I found him in the kitchen with his sleeves rolled up, fussing over a simmering stockpot. He noticed me and barked something at his cook, then wiped his hands on a dishtowel and came over to greet me.

"Channing, my friend. How's it going?" Like the private room, Lee's demeanor had been cleansed. Now he was Mr. Rogers.

"I'm okay. I came by to see how you were."

"Oh, don't worry about me, I'm fine." He glanced around the small kitchen, then grabbed my elbow and steered me toward the door. "Let's go for a little walk, okay?"

Lee wasn't the exercising type, so I knew something was up.

He stopped at a few tables to greet some customers—a more gracious and gregarious restaurateur you wouldn't find anywhere—on our way out. When we reached the sidewalk, we turned left, away from The Last Laff, toward the far end of the shopping center. Lee hummed a tune I couldn't make out until we'd passed the pet shop on the corner and were out of sight of the shopping center's parking lot.

He pulled me against the brick wall and glanced around as if he were a Russian double agent about to divulge some nuclear codes. "Listen, Channing, I was up all night. Thinking about what happened. And I can't just sit on my hands. I need to find out what's going on. For my peace of mind."

"Okay…" I cocked my head at him.

"I need you to do me a favor."

"Keep talking," I said, resisting the urge to tell him I'd help as long as it didn't involve bombing any foreign countries.

"I was told—quite directly, I might add—to keep my nose out of it. That it was a family matter." Lee swallowed, looking hurt. "Hell, I *am* family."

"Your sister told you to butt out?"

Lee's expression took on an icy hardness. "The words came from her mouth, yes, but they were not hers. She was simply speaking for Hao. Margaret wouldn't ever prevent me from looking after my family. Her husband put her up to it—hell, he was right next to her, practically pulling her strings. I had no choice but to agree. I could not shame my sister in front of her husband."

"So you're out of it?" I knew where this was headed.

Lee nodded slowly. I'd seen basset hounds with cheerier faces.

"You don't get along with Hao or his brother, do you?"

"They never liked me much. Think running a restaurant is a stereotype. Menial labor for the Chinaman. Or some such shit. Assholes. Of course, Hao didn't mind that I owned a restaurant when I hired his daughter, little Miss Joy, as a hostess." Lee shrugged. "On the other hand, he and Margaret have raised three fine children, so maybe I'm just being a little sensitive."

I didn't have any specific knowledge, one way or the other, but valuing Lee's opinion, I'd have to peg Hao and his brother Xun as assholes.

Lee leaned closer. "So this is the favor part. I need someone to snoop around a bit, ask a few questions. I'd do it myself, but there's no way I can. If Hao finds out I'm poking my nose into this, especially after I said I wouldn't, well . . . I wouldn't want him to get pissed at my sister for something I did."

I didn't say a word, trying to process it all.

"*Someone* has to find out why three punks with baseball bats came into my restaurant and attacked my guests. Root out some answers. And I'd like you to be that someone."

"What do *you* think is going on here, anyway?"

Lee's nostrils flared. "Not to sound too obvious, but I think some bad people were threatening someone. I'm not sure who the bad people are, and I'm not sure who the person being threatened is, not exactly. It's probably Edward—politicians are always riling someone up—but it wouldn't totally surprise me if they were after the man himself, Hao." Lee shook his head. "You saw how he got up and tried to tell off the goons. Arrogant jerk, he could have gotten us all hurt, angering the wrong people like that. And I don't want to even think about them going after Hao at home. Not with Margaret…"

I'd figured it had been a message for Edward, not even considering Hao as a possible target. But Lee made sense, and if the violence was directed at Hao, then it might be another reason why he hadn't wanted to make the attack public.

I drew in a sharp breath. I wasn't some kind of private investigator. I didn't even know Lee's sister or her family very well, with the exception of Joy. What information did Lee actually think I would be able to unearth? In my mind, I sifted through all the questions forming and picked the most obvious one to start. "Why me?"

"I know you, Channing. You're smart, resourceful. Conscientious. If you say you're going to do something, then you're going to do it. The way you discovered the truth about Lauren's…" He gripped my forearm. "Please say you're going to do this for me.

17

Something bad is brewing and I need to know what it is so I can stop it. My family's safety is at stake here."

"I don't know. I'm not sure how effective I'd be. I mean, if they don't want you, their own flesh and blood, snooping around, I can't imagine they'd want a stranger mucking about in their lives. Politicians are pretty sensitive about their secrets, you know. Hell, I wouldn't even know where to begin."

Lee reached into his pocket and pulled out a business card. Handed it to me. In red, white, and blue, in a fancy font, were the words: *Sanford Korbell, Congressman, Virginia's 11th District.*

"What does Korbell have to do with this?"

"Like I said, Edward was probably the target, and Korbell's his opponent, so that's probably where we should start, huh?"

I noticed the "we," but didn't call Lee on it. "You want me to walk right up and ask him if he hired some goons to send a message to Edward?"

"Come up with some excuse. Tell him you want to volunteer to work for his campaign. That his message has really spoken to your heart and you want to get up off the couch and participate in the great democracy that is Virginia."

I suppressed the urge to gag. "I'm a comic, not an actor."

"You can sell it. He'll believe what he wants to believe, and he wants to believe everyone agrees with him. He'll eat it up. An eager, idealistic guy like you comes in, gushing about his great message, and wants to help." Lee's head bobbed up and down.

"I don't know. This whole thing seems … underhanded and dirty somehow."

"It is. It's the world of politics. But I'll risk being a little underhanded if you can find out what's going on."

"What if Korbell discovers my—our—little ruse? He may use it against Edward."

"He won't. You simply tell him you changed your mind, after all. No harm, no foul." Lee smiled. "You worry too much. Look, I made a promise to my sister that I wouldn't get involved. But I didn't promise anyone that a friend of mine wouldn't ask a few questions."

I blew out my breath.

"Channing?" Lee's hand gripped my arm again, this time gentler. "So what do you say?"

"I don't know. I'm not really the snooping type."

Lee stared at me.

"I'm a comedian, not some kind of undercover operative."

Lee stared at me.

I owed Lee plenty for all he'd done for me and Artie over the past few years. Three years ago, he bailed Artie out of some financial difficulty, and he was by my side eight months ago, when my fiancée Lauren was killed. Plus there were several thousand free eggrolls to consider.

I found myself rubbing the knot on my head—from the thugs' attack—and I pictured Lee's panicked face and Artie's trembling lips. *Goddamn punks.*

"Okay. I'm in."

THREE

At a few minutes before ten on Monday morning, I cruised into Sanford Korbell's campaign office. I'd called his district office, wanting to meet with someone about his campaign, and they'd directed me here. Evidently, there was some kind of law that mandated keeping campaigning separate from the actual business of governing. Politics never failed to confuse me.

His campaign office was located in a plain office building off Route 123, midway between Vienna and the City of Fairfax. Not far from our club, not far from I-66, not far from Tysons Corner, where his district office was located.

As soon as I stepped into the office, a bubbly young blonde smiled brightly at me from her desk. "Good morning. Are you Channing Hayes by any chance?"

"Yes I am. Good morning." When I'd called about half an hour ago asking about the campaign, I'd been quite vague. Luckily, the lady I spoke to hadn't asked many questions.

"Very good, very good. Our Public Information Liaison, Nicole Benton, is expecting you." She punched her phone, announced my arrival, then hung up. "She'll be out to greet you shortly. Please, have a seat."

In the waiting area, I settled into a worn, but comfortable, chair. Several old campaign posters hung on the wall, reminders of past victories. All very rah-rah. The office even smelled like victory. A moment later, Sanford Korbell, dressed in a beige trenchcoat and gleaming burgundy wingtips, came rushing through. He nodded and smiled at me on his way to the door. One hand was on the handle when he whirled around and backtracked. He thrust his hand out. "Hello. I'm Sanford Korbell."

I hopped to my feet and shook hands. "I'm, uh, Channing Hayes."

A cleft chin punctuated his handsome, square face. Hazel eyes brimmed with confidence. "Nice to meet you, Channing. Do you work or live in my district?"

"Uh, both, actually."

"Excellent." He reached into his pocket and handed me a business card, identical to the one Lee had given me. "If you ever need anything, just give me a call."

"I did have a few questions."

His hazel eyes shaded a little greener. He tapped his wrist. "Sorry, but I'm late for a meeting. If Nicole can't satisfy you, feel free to give me a call, okay?"

"Sure. Thanks."

He nodded once and strode out of the office.

I sat again. Korbell was the first honest-to-goodness politician I'd ever encountered in the wild. It was always interesting meeting someone in person whom you'd seen on TV. I'd met plenty of comics I'd seen on the tube, and they always seemed smaller, less imposing in person. Not Sanford Korbell.

A few minutes later, another very attractive blonde woman— of the Midwestern girl-next-door variety—came down the hall and introduced herself. "I'm Nicole Benton. It's a pleasure."

We shook. She was about my height, in heels, and she was about my age, maybe a few years younger. But she was far perkier than I'd ever been. She wore a nicely tailored blue suit over a pink fuzzy sweater-blouse, and there wasn't a ring on her finger. "The pleasure is mine," I said, and it came out sounding way too smarmy, like Vic the Lounge Lizard attempting to seduce his prey. My cheeks got warm and I could only guess how red.

If she noticed my embarrassment, she didn't react. Maybe getting hit on by slimy horndogs was part of her job description. "Why don't we talk in my office?"

"Sure." We started walking. "I just met Congressman Korbell on his way out. He seemed different than what I expected."

Nicole laughed. "I hear that a lot. He's got a full slate of meetings and appearances today. I handle the re-election inquiries, so you're stuck with me. I hope that's okay?"

"Sure." There were worse people to be stuck with. I followed her down a short, thinly carpeted hallway to her office. Not large, but not small either, two windows looked out over the parking lot. The word *utilitarian* came to mind.

Instead of conducting the meeting from behind her desk, she took a seat in one of the two visitor's chairs. I eased into the other, trying to keep my eyes off her legs.

"What do you do for a living, Mr. Hayes?"

"Please, call me Channing."

"*Channing.* I like that name. Okay, Channing. What do you do?"

"I'm part-owner of The Last Laff Comedy Club. Mostly, though, I'm a stand-up comic."

Her eyes sparkled. "Seriously? A stand-up comic? Like Jerry Seinfeld?"

The typical reaction when I tell people what I do. "Well, not as famous."

"I don't think I've ever met a real live comedian before."

Some of my best friends know comedians. "Glad to be your first."

"That must be so fun!"

So fun! If only she knew the other eighty percent of not-so-fun things involved in making stand-up appear *so fun.* "It's pretty cool, but it's not *all* laughs, you know."

"Things rarely are. I think I've heard of The Last Laff. Georgetown, right?"

"No. We're in Vienna. In your district."

"Oh, right. Of course. I'll have to come by sometime. I think I'd enjoy that."

"Anytime. I'll give you a VIP pass—Very Important Politician."

"You *are* funny." She touched my arm. "And very sweet. Thank you so much for the offer." She smoothed her skirt and cleared her throat, putting all talk of VIP passes behind her. "So, why would a comedian be interested in joining Team Korbell? I imagine there are better places to find laughs."

"I've always been interested in politics." I resisted the temptation to reach up and feel my nose to see if it was growing.

"Really? Well, we welcome volunteers and we welcome donations." She laughed. "And we certainly welcome both."

I read that it's good to mirror someone else's mannerisms in order to build up a rapport, so I chuckled in response. "Why don't you tell me about your, uh, vision for the future?" I'd spent a few minutes last night combing through Korbell's website, absorbing buzzwords and familiarizing myself with his positions on the issues. Coming across like a complete dolt often was an advantage in the comedy business, but I thought it might help if I sounded a little more versed in NoVa politics for today's meeting. I had a fake image to uphold.

"I guess you could say it's more of the same. Congressman Korbell has had a string of very successful terms and we'd like to keep things going. Ease transportation congestion, continue to lower crime, emphasize family values. We truly believe in the power of the people. Just a sec." She got up and retrieved a framed photograph from the sideboard behind her desk and handed it to me. "I know you've seen him in person, but I believe you can tell a lot about Congressman Korbell from this picture of him and his wife."

A smiling Sanford Korbell was hugging a smiling Katy "KayKay" Korbell. He looked like your prototypical politician—graying, but distinguished, hair, white teeth, a bit of ruggedness about him. KayKay was ten years younger—at least. Blonde and very attractive, I had a feeling she was very perky, too. As for being known as "KayKay," I couldn't decide if the nickname was Old Southern-Cute or Sorority-Silly. Most residents of the Old Dominion probably went with cute.

"That's what we stand for," Nicole said, pointing a perfectly manicured fingernail at the Korbells in the photo. "They're the ideal couple. Civic-minded, willing to help anyone in need, putting their wishes on a back burner so they may serve others. Generous to a fault. That's why KayKay, uh, Mrs. Korbell, started the Family First Foundation."

"I've seen her on the news. A lot." She was a fixture on the society pages and in the charity event circle. An ex-Miss Virginia, KayKay photographed quite well, and her smiling face often graced the glossy covers of local magazines.

"Yes, she's taken a very visible role in fundraising for the Foundation. She really believes in the mission of keeping families together and strengthening the family bonds. Here at Team Korbell, we all do. It is so important for society to have a strong family foundation. Why, I know I wouldn't be where I am without the love and support of my family."

"Families are nice," I said lamely, only imagining how my life would have been different if I had been part of a real family, the kind with two parents, two kids, and a shaggy dog.

"Mrs. Korbell's a very inspirational lady."

I detected a bit of hero worship in Nicole's voice. "Is she working on the campaign, too?"

"Oh, not directly. Of course, she'll make appearances with the congressman and do photo ops and all the other things a good congressman's wife does. But the Foundation is her baby. It's a blessing she's been given, and she wants to maximize its potential." Nicole leaned in and whispered. "She's such a very nice person. So caring. The congressman is a lucky man."

"I bet he is." I was beginning to get the feeling Nicole wouldn't have minded stepping into KayKay's Jimmy Choos. Enough chitchat. Time to go fishing for some answers. "So how difficult a campaign do you think the Congressman faces?"

"You can never be too complacent about elections. Strange things can happen."

"Of course."

"But I'm very confident. Edward Wong has a lot going for him. He's charismatic, and he's well-funded. His father's got a big war chest, I understand, and he's not afraid to use it on his son's behalf. But I think he's a little too young and inexperienced. He may be a factor in future elections after he gets more seasoning. Our other opponent, Tom Harris, is far too liberal and, well, he's running as an Independent, which is always very difficult."

"You're not afraid of an upset?"

"Well, according to the polls, we're in good shape with about two months to go." Nicole touched my arm lightly. "We're going to run a fair, hard campaign, and get our message out, exactly like we always do. I think the voters in the 11th District will continue to support the most popular congressman they've had in many years. So to answer your question, no we're not worried about an upset. We'll make sure it doesn't happen. The congressman is very good at anticipating problems and cutting them off before they have a chance to damage us."

"Any problems in particular you're referring to?"

"Oh no, I'm just saying he's a very good politician, as well as being a very good person. If all elected officials were as conscientious as he is, this would be a much better country. People want a solid citizen to represent them. They're tired of scandals and dirty dealing and all those negative things. They want men like Sanford Korbell."

I hadn't ever heard Korbell's name associated with any improprieties. "He's got a solid reputation, that's for sure."

"Yes he does. Another terrific reason for working with him."

"How long have you worked for him?"

"About seven years. Seven very satisfying years."

"And before that?"

"Oh, so you want the whole rundown?" She laughed again. Maybe knowing I was a comic was making her more jovial. "I went to Yale. Interned on the Hill a couple summers. You know, the typical policy wonk's dream. Then I heard the congressman speak and I became an instant convert. He's very persuasive. The rest is, as they say, history."

"Sounds like you're happy here."

"Oh, very." She held out her hand. "May I?"

I handed the picture back to her and she returned it to its favored place on her sideboard. I wondered how often she used that prop in her attempts to recruit supporters.

I hadn't gotten any information, nor any hint of any information, nor any inkling of any hint of information that would lead me to believe Korbell was behind the incident at Lee's.

Nicole returned wearing a smile, a different kind of smile, a closing-the-deal kind of smile. "How am I doing? Have I enticed you to join the team? You know, we're always looking for venues to hold fundraising events. A comedy club might be fun. What do you think?"

"Well, it does sound—"

"Hang on a second." She reached behind her and plucked a BlackBerry off her desk. Punched in a few numbers. "Dan, you busy? Could you stop in for a minute? Thanks." She clicked off and returned her smiling attention to me.

"I'm not sure having a fundraiser at the club is such—"

A knock on the door interrupted me. "Come in," Nicole said.

The door swung open and a rangy man with a narrow face stepped in. He wore the most neutral expression I'd ever seen outside of a driver's license photo. "Channing, this is Dan O'Rourke. He's our Jack-of-All-Trades. Dan, this is Channing Hayes. He's interested in joining our team, and he owns a comedy club."

I rose to shake hands, and O'Rourke obliged. "A pleasure," he said, without any of the enthusiasm I'd seen from the other campaign staff I'd met.

"What do you think about possibly having a fundraiser at a comedy club?" Nicole asked O'Rourke.

He pursed his lips. "Might work. It's something we haven't done before. Could expose the congressman to a demographic he doesn't typically reach. And a few laughs might open up some pocketbooks."

From his dour demeanor, I wondered what O'Rourke knew about laughs.

"Okay, Dan. Just wanted to get your gut impression. You can get back to work now. I'll go over the particulars with Mr. Hayes."

O'Rourke tipped his head at me and left.

"He's a real sweetheart," Nicole said. I couldn't tell if she was being facetious or not, so I just smiled. "So, about the fundraiser. What do you think?"

"Well, I'm just the co-owner, and you make a good case, all right, but I think I'm going to have to think about it. I always get into trouble making rash decisions."

"I see." She reached into her pocket and pulled out a business card and a pen. "Here," she said, jotting on the back. "If you have any questions—any questions, at all—please give me a call. My cell number is on the back." She handed me the card, and I flipped it over. Next to her cell number, she'd written *Call Anytime*, and the "i" in *Anytime* was dotted with a little heart. Did they teach that in the Young Republicans club at Yale?

While I was reading her note, she grasped my wrist gently and leaned closer. I got a whiff of her shampoo, something floral, and if I had to guess, expensive. "Channing, I want you to think about what we've discussed. Think about how fulfilling it would be to join such a wonderful man on such a worthwhile mission. I'd love to work with you, and I hope you feel the same. So think about it, and get back to me, okay? Soon? There's really not that much time before the election, you know." Then she let go of my arm and stood abruptly. "Thanks so much for coming by today. It was absolutely great meeting you."

All the players from Team Korbell sure seemed friendly. Except one, that is.

FOUR

ON MY WAY HOME from meeting with Nicole, I ran a few errands—grocery store, Target, bank. I wasn't usually up and about this early and I felt a little like an extra in someone else's movie. An extra with no lines and no real direction. *Just blend in, look busy, and don't do anything to steal the stars' spotlight.* I didn't mind. After appearing on stage where everyone was hanging on each word, sometimes it was nice to be able to slip into the background and accomplish mundane tasks without the pressure of trying to make people laugh.

At lunchtime, I thought about going to the club early and popping in at Lee's for some Kung Pao Chicken, but the idea of returning to the scene of the smash-up was too agitating. Instead, I stopped at Subway and got a foot-long turkey sub, double-extra black olives, and ate it at my condo while I read the *Comics*.

I got to the club around four o'clock and settled in to watch some audition tapes. Every comic—aspiring, rising, established, or those exiled to the bowling-alley circuit—had an audition "tape," although nobody used actual VHS tapes anymore. Most auditions came in on DVDs, and more and more comics were simply linking to YouTube clips. I preferred the DVDs. To me, it indicated the comic expended some effort, either by editing or doing voiceovers or fancy transitions, instead of taking the lazy way out by having a buddy shoot some video while he hammed it up for a bunch of drunken friends.

The performance itself was the most important part of the audition package, but I still reviewed the comic's resume and headshots, just to make sure there was some legitimacy. Of course, if big-wig corporate CEOs lied on their resumes, I had to believe lowly comics did a bit of fibbing, too. Actually, I'd be surprised if I got *any* resumes where something wasn't exaggerated, fabricated, or misrepresented.

Artie was at the dentist getting a crown fixed, so I took the opportunity to sit at his desk. We shared an office, but he had a fancy wood desk, while I sat at a folding card table wedged between some file cabinets and a dilapidated free-standing coat rack. *When the cat's away…*

I opened a big white envelope and removed a black folder with a label on the outside that read Marc Perry. Inside, a resume and headshot were tucked into one flap, and a DVD—in a little envelope—was tucked into the other flap. Neat. Professional. Just the way I liked it.

Scanning the resume, I saw he'd played a few pretty good places, not as the headliner, but as the opener and middle guy. He'd been doing stand-up for about five years, moving to progressively better venues. Exactly the kind of career path I'd expect from a young up-and-comer. His headshot showed him in a smiling pose. Not too hammy, not too serious.

So far, nothing in the package to eliminate him.

Now for the moment of truth. I popped the DVD into the computer and hit the play button.

Marc Perry strode on stage at some unnamed comedy club. He waved to the crowd, grabbed the mic out of the stand, and set the stand to one side. Then he launched into his act. Out of the first ten "jokes," I'd heard better versions of nine of them before. Multiple times. The tenth joke I couldn't hear because the audience was heckling him too loudly.

Oh well. Par for the course.

I hit the eject button, removed the DVD, closed everything back up, and scribbled "NFG" on the envelope in red Sharpie.

Picked up the next package. The glamorous life of a comedy club owner.

Before I could open the next envelope, two pairs of eyes stared up at me from the side of the desk. The peepers belonged to Donna's little girl. Olivia or Penelope or Charlotte or some other princess-like name. She was about four years old. Or three. Or five. I wasn't always too good relating to people younger than voting age.

"Hi," she said.

"Hi there."

She clasped her hands behind her back and shifted her weight from side-to-side, as if she were a human oscillating fan. Maybe she just had to go to the bathroom. "Hi," she said again.

"Where's your mommy?"

She pointed at the doorway. "Out there."

"Is she coming in here?"

The girl nodded. "She's with Sean. I think he's a-scared."

Sean was Donna's older son. I was pretty sure he was eight. "Scared of what?"

She pointed at me.

"He's scared of me?"

More nodding.

"Well, I'm not very scary, am I?"

She shook her head and a few dark curls flopped into her face. She brushed them away, but didn't speak.

"It's a nice surprise having such a beautiful girl visit."

"Yes it is." Not a trace of a smile. Purely matter-of-fact.

Donna bustled into the office. "Hi Channing. Oh, there she is. I hope Olivia's not bothering you. Tony's stuck at a job, but he's coming by after work to pick up the kids, and…heck, you don't care about my childcare problems. But it's just as well. Sean has something to ask you."

I didn't see her son. "Okay."

"Sean?" Donna also noticed he was missing and ducked back out into the hallway. "Sean," I heard her say, tone more stern. "Come here. He won't bite. Hey, Seannie, come back here." Donna's voice receded.

I glanced back at Olivia. Still oscillating. "Can I see your hand?" she asked.

I held up my right hand, wiggled my fingers.

"Can I see your other hand?"

I hesitated then held up my incomplete left hand.

"You didn't find your fingers yet?"

I started to laugh, but didn't want to frighten the kid, so I shook my head. "Nope."

"Mommy said they were missing. You lost them in a accident. I hope you find them. Then you can put them back on." She shook her head and her curls bounced. "I don't mean you. I mean a doctor. A sturgeon."

"Yes, well, that would be—"

"Are you ever a glass pole?"

It had been a while since I'd been around kids. I wasn't up on the latest slang. "I don't know. What's a glass pole?"

"Somebody who does something Mommy doesn't like. When she drives, she always yells at all the glass poles."

Ah, the flaming glass poles. "No. I would never do anything your mommy didn't like. In fact, I don't like glass poles either."

Olivia nodded, evidently satisfied with my answer.

"Got him," Donna said, as she led Sean by the hand back into my office. She pushed him in front of her and nodded her head, hand now resting on the scruff of his neck. "Okay, son. Go ahead. Ask your question."

Sean stepped forward, partially propelled by his mom. "Um. Would you, um, come to my school and talk to my class about your job. Like what you do to be a comedian?"

Donna patted Sean on the head gently and raised her eyebrows at me.

"Come to your class, huh? Like career day?"

"Uh huh," Sean said. "My dad can't come that day. So …"

"So you want me to fill in? I'd be delighted."

His face lit up. "Awesome. Lexie's bragging about how her father is an FBI agent and he's coming, but now I can say I'm bringing a comedian. Will you tell some jokes?"

"Sure, I'll tell some jokes. I'll even try to tell some funny ones." At least some funnier than the FBI agent.

Behind Sean, Donna's face showed relief. "Thanks, Channing. Tony's got a big job that week. He'd like to do it, but...besides, who wants to hear a contractor talk about what he does all day? He bores me to death with that stuff, and I'm married to the man."

"Hey, no problem." I nodded my head toward Olivia, who was still staring at me. Probably enthralled by my imperfect hand. "Wouldn't want to be a glass pole about it."

A blush bloomed on Donna's face. "So you've been talking to Olivia, have you?"

"Glass pole, glass pole, glass pole," Olivia said, to herself, as if she were trying it out as her mantra. "Glass pole, glass pole, glass pole-y, pole-y, pole-y."

Donna's face turned redder.

Sean put a hand to the side of his mouth and said in a stage whisper, "She means asshole."

Thanks, kid.

"Bye, Channing," Donna said as she grabbed each kid's hand with one of hers and shepherded them out the door. I heard them squawking all the way down the hall.

"Glass pole, glass pole, glass pole," I repeated aloud.

Maybe Olivia was onto something. I could always use a new mantra.

———

Monday night meant open mic night. Last week we had twenty-two hopefuls show up for twelve slots, so we encouraged the spillovers to come back tonight. Some weeks you got eight; some weeks you got twenty-two. As Artie liked to say, comedy was a funny business.

Tonight's wannabes trickled in, and their first stop was always the clipboard hanging next to the stage to sign in. Aspiring comics, mostly, but we got a few experienced ones trying out new material or just getting a little stage time.

When I had poked my head out of my office at around six o'clock there were two people on the list. Now, an hour later, the roster had expanded to nine.

I read the names. We'd seen the majority of them before, in one incarnation or another, and knew their relative strengths. Although the slots were awarded on a first-come, first-served basis, Artie or I would usually shuffle around the order a bit to balance the evening. We had to be careful not to string together too many weak acts or the natives in the audience would get restless. Restless natives led to heckling natives, and heckling natives and newbie open-mic'ers didn't mix very well. The hecklers usually won that battle. Which could be amusing for us, except we had been newbies once, and we remembered how it felt to be heckled when your jokes weren't landing. Demoralizing.

I parsed the list again. It looked like we had a pretty good sampling of new and experienced, young and old, male and female, broad and slyly clever. Shouldn't be too hard to put together a lineup that would generate a few laughs and qualify as a success. On open mic nights, the bar was set pretty low.

Despite the inherent risks of putting complete novices on stage, they were the ones who captured my interest. You never knew what you were going to get. Ninety-nine times out of a hundred, they weren't very good and didn't show much upside, but it was the one time when some unassuming guy came in and brought down the house that made listening to all the uptight girlfriend jokes worth it. Unfortunately, it had been awhile since we'd gotten one like that.

I crossed my fingers, hoping tonight would be the night.

Twelve years ago, *I* was the comic with potential. Now, after a couple shaky performances in the past month, my confidence had taken a hit, and I'd begun to wonder if I was on the downward slope of my career. Peaked at thirty-four.

I felt Artie's presence next to me; an instant later I smelled his coffee breath. "Hey, kid. How does it look tonight?"

"Nine so far. Probably get a few more stragglers. Maybe we'll fill up again."

"Terrific," Artie said. He enjoyed open mic nights immensely, partly because he liked nurturing new talent and partly because he got to emcee the shindig. More comics meant more patter-time for him. Artie never met a microphone he didn't try to seduce.

"By the way, Lee called and told me to, quote, 'drag Channing's bee-hind' over for some egg drop soup and conversation. Sounds like he has something buzzing in his bonnet."

I'm sure he wanted to be debriefed about my foray into Korbell's camp. "When?"

"Now. Come on, we've got about an hour."

"He wants to talk to you, too?"

"Naw," Artie said as he smacked his lips. "But I've got a hankering for some egg drop soup."

"And I'm sure you wouldn't mind hearing about what's going on."

Artie turned and headed for the front door. "Wouldn't miss it for anything," he called out over his shoulder.

A few minutes later we were ensconced in a red-upholstered booth, steaming bowls of soup in front of us. Artie and I sat on one side; Lee faced us and the door. His bowl of soup contained a dark liquid and a tangle of Asian vegetables I didn't recognize.

"So?" Lee asked as soon as the obligatory pleasantries had been exchanged.

"You want me to discuss this with A-R-T-I-E sitting here?" I asked, nodding my head sideways.

"Hey," Artie said, after a slurp, "A-R-T-I-E can spell. Go ahead. I can keep a secret."

Yeah, and I can play concert piano with my missing fingers. Of course, I couldn't play piano before the accident. *Ba-da-bing.* I asked Lee again. "You sure you want to hear it now?"

"Oh, hell. Why not?" Lee pushed his bowl aside, soup barely touched.

I brought Artie up to speed with a quick sentence. "Lee asked me to see if I could find out the story behind Friday night's attack by infiltrating enemy lines and talking to people in Korbell's campaign."

"I never said infiltrating." He flashed a look of mock indignation, then leaned in. "Come on, what did they say?"

"I talked mostly to an aide. I got the feeling—no offense—they're not really worried about Edward's chances. I don't think they had anything to do with what happened."

Lee seemed deflated. "Yeah, okay. Makes sense. A guy as savvy as Korbell wouldn't be so obvious about things. Worth a shot asking."

Since I was the guy doing the asking, I guess it was. "I know you said you weren't going to get involved, but ... did you happen to ask Edward or Patrick what they thought was going on?"

"You know me too well, Channing. Of course I did. Talked to Edward."

"And?"

"Bottom line, he said it was a private matter, it's all over and done with, and not to worry about it."

Artie looked up from his soup. "What the hell does that mean? 'A private matter?' We almost got killed. I mean—"

I put my hand on Artie's arm. "Relax, nobody got hurt."

Artie yanked his arm away and homed in on Lee. "'Not to worry about it?' Three punks invade your restaurant and they don't want you to worry about it?"

"That's what Edward said." I could almost see the steam coming from Lee's ears. Maybe Lee and Artie should have a contest to see who could explode first.

"According to him, it's all over and done with," I said.

"Pretty much," Lee said, then started muttering under his breath. In Chinese.

"Politicians," Artie said, crunching some more fried noodles into his soup. "Can't live with 'em, can't shoot 'em. Of course, you can usually indict 'em."

"I don't believe him. Not one bit." Lee gave a little snort, as if his opinion needed emphasis. It didn't.

"I agree. But obviously Edward wants to see it buried."

"As long as I'm involved, that's not going to happen," Lee said.

"You're *not* involved, remember?" I set my spoon down so I wouldn't be tempted to point it at anyone. "If they're not talking,

39

I don't see how you can get more information. Maybe you should trust them. If they say it's handled, then it's handled. You've got to know they don't want anything like this to happen again. Hao was telling the truth when he said it would kill the campaign if news of this got out."

"What? Don't tell me you're quitting on me?" Lee asked.

"Well…" I shrugged. "I wouldn't call it quitting. I asked some questions, got some answers. Ran into a dead end. I don't think Korbell has anything to do with this. I've got nothing else to go on. I'm sorry, Lee, but I don't think I can help you anymore."

"Channing, please. We're just getting started here." Fear played on his face.

Again with the "we" pronoun.

"Yeah, you can't give up now. We need to find out the truth here," Artie said. Knowing what you were talking about was never a prerequisite of his for getting involved.

I exhaled. "I wouldn't even know who to talk to next."

The faint outline of a smile appeared on Lee's face, and I knew he had an answer for me. Why did I have the feeling that I'd just been played again?

"Hao's having a cookout at his place tomorrow for his employees and some other friends. Sort of a 'meet the candidate' thing. What do you say we drop in, ask a few innocent questions, and see what we can discover?"

"I wasn't invited," I said.

"I'm inviting you. It's my sister's home, too, you know. Besides, there'll be plenty of food."

I knew when I was fighting a losing battle. "Sure, Lee. Sure."

"Thanks, Channing. It means a lot to me. You're a true friend."

"The sap is running awfully high in here," Artie said, tossing his napkin on the table as he rose. "Now that we have everything ironed out, it's time to go." He jerked his thumb at me. "Come on, Channing. We've got a club to run. Thanks for the soup, Lee. You're a true friend to me, too."

FIVE

Hao Wong lived in McLean, on the Langley side, in a house one notch below "mega-mansion." Ornate gateposts flanked the long driveway, which led up to a four-car garage. White brick façade with stone accents. A fifty-foot flagpole right outside the front door, Stars and Stripes fluttering in the breeze. Next to the flagpole a fountain the size of my living room spouted water through the mouths of three dolphins standing on their tails. Understated, it wasn't.

Lee said to pull up into the driveway, rather than park on the street with most of the other guests, so I shoehorned my vintage RX-7—which I called Rex, much to the amusement of those who found out—between a Mercedes, a BMW, and some kind of fancy imported sports car I didn't recognize. Probably some limited edition German high-performance prototype or something out of an Italian gearhead's skunkworks.

Lee led me around the back of the mansion to the cookout. A huge, freshly mown lawn—more like a field, really—was dotted with tables. Three large gas grills, next to the pool, sent up plumes of smoke, and the aroma of charred meat filled the air. Off to one side, about twenty kids played a game of touch football. I half expected to see Edward and Patrick playing, too, with their sleeves rolled up, JFK-style. Maybe they saved that for the photo-op portion of the event.

"There she is," Lee said, pointing to a knot of people. "Come on, let's say hello to my sis."

We made our way across grass that looked like a putting green. When we got close to the nearest group of people, Lee's sister Margaret saw us, and a warm smile blossomed on her face. "Thomas!"

Lee gave her a big hug and a peck on the cheek. "You remember Channing. From the comedy club."

Margaret bowed her head slightly. "Hello Channing. I'm glad you could make it. Such a good friend of Thomas's is always welcome in my home." She winked at her brother and I swore I saw Lee flush, just a hair. "I want to apologize again for what happened at the restaurant. I trust you are okay?"

"Yes, I'm fine." My shoulder had stopped throbbing, although I still sported a nice blue-black bruise.

"Let's put all that behind us. Why don't you help yourself to some food?" She pointed to a long buffet table, groaning under the weight of overflowing platters.

"Go ahead, Channing," Lee said. "I've got a few things to discuss here. I'll catch up to you. Mingle, mingle." He winked at me. Time to embark on my fact-finding expedition.

To keep up appearances, I filled a plate at the buffet table and got myself a beer. Then I set off to find some answers.

———

"They've always been like that. Uptight, demanding, hard-charging. As if they were born with a stick up their butts and liked it." Joy Wong paused for a millisecond and sipped a bit of her soda before continuing her diatribe. "They never found a challenge they could ignore. And competitive, let me tell you. I remember them playing basketball against each other until midnight, on more than one occasion. Their games would always end up with someone getting a black eye or bloody nose. Or both."

We'd been sitting at a picnic table for five minutes, and I hadn't uttered a word to Joy aside from my opening quasi-question, "So, excited for your brothers?" Lee's niece was like a Krakatoa of information. I just wasn't sure if any of the magma bits were useful.

"Now all we hear about is the campaign. It's 'my campaign' this, and 'for the good of the campaign' that. Shit, two weeks ago Edward forgot our mother's birthday. What a skunk! And heaven forbid they should come and see one of Rojo's gigs. I mean, I totally support them—have for years—and they can't even take two hours out of their all-important schedules to see my boyfriend's band play? They're exactly like my father, who, by the way, thinks Rojo's a loser, but you know what? He's overcome a lot in his life. Poverty, growing up raised by a single mother. Yet he's turned out great. A real success story. Besides, when my brothers were younger, they went out with plenty of skanky girls. Did I shun them? No. Live and let live. And if you asked them, they'd tell you how open they are, how progressive they are. What a crock! I'd call them self-important, but that would be an insult to all those self-important people who actually are important. Look, there's the big cheese now," she said, pointing to Edward, who had just emerged from the back of the house.

44

He went directly to where Hao and Xun stood, and a moment later, all three of them almost fell over laughing at some shared joke.

"Get a load of them, fawning over the golden boy." Joy's words were tinged green.

"They're just proud of him," I said.

"Proud? Yeah, they're proud, all right." She laughed, a humorless one. "Daddy says he's proud of me, too, but you don't see him throwing me any lavish cookouts. Of course, I'm just a girl, and I don't have a high-powered job, and I'm the youngest, and yadda, yadda, yadda. I guess life isn't fair." Joy stopped and took a breath.

I spoke before she could regroup. "Actually, I had a few specific questions. May I?"

She nodded. I guess her voice was tired.

"If you don't like your brothers, why did you work for them?" On the drive over, Lee said Joy had done some graphics art projects during the early stages of the primary campaign. This was after she'd quit her job working as a hostess at his restaurant.

"Oh, don't get me wrong. I love my brothers and I'd do almost anything to help Edward get elected. Yeah, I did some work for them, but . . . Shit, now they piss me off a lot. Typical family stuff, I guess. But I still wish them the best. Although, ever since Rojo moved in, things have been a little more strained. Which I don't understand, he's such a doll. He would do anything for anybody, can't ever say no. You know how he is. He's a lot like Uncle Thomas in that respect." She batted her lashes and made a lovey-dovey face. "I just adore my Rojo."

"I know. You guys make a nice couple, too." I'd met Rojo a few years ago, when I was the emcee at a charity event where his band played. We'd hung out backstage after the show, formed a fast bond, and we'd gotten together from time-to-time—at concerts, at Nationals games, at the movies. In fact, I was the one who introduced Rojo to Joy one night at Lee's Palace. Ever since he'd been getting more serious with Joy, though, I'd seen less and less of him.

She checked her cell phone for the time. "He should be here soon."

I tried to get back on track. "Your uncle is worried about what's going on. He's pretty upset about the incident at his restaurant."

Her eyes dilated and all traces of the lovey-dovey face vanished. "Oh yeah. I saw those fuckers barge right in. Had one of them breathing down my neck for a moment. Thought about grabbing a chopstick and gouging an eye out—right through the hole in his ridiculous mask—but he moved away. Lucky for him, I guess. You know—"

I held my hand up. "So about your uncle. He's worried and he wanted me to ask around to see if I could find out what was going on. Have any ideas? Anybody you know that might be aiming to get your brothers? Anything out of the ordinary lately?"

Joy took a couple more gulps of soda, then picked up her pack of cigarettes and a lighter. "Mind?"

I did, but I wasn't going to say anything. I gave my head a little shake. She took one out, lit it, then took a nice long drag and gazed upward, as if the answer might be written in the clouds. Then she lowered her head and faced me. "Not really."

"Is that a 'no,' or is there something you aren't sure you should tell me?"

"Well … it's probably nothing." She blew some smoke off to her left, from the corner of her mouth. "For the past few weeks, my father has been leaving me alone."

"What do you mean?"

"He's been minding his own business."

I waited for more, but Joy had nothing to add. "That's it? Your father's left you alone, and that's unusual?"

"Ha. You don't know my father. Every other day he's in my business. Telling me to do that or not do this or do something else. Mostly, he tells me that whatever I've done is wrong. That's how he gets his jollies—harassing me about *my* craptastic life."

Joy's observation hardly qualified as something out of the ordinary. "Just you? Or does he ride your brothers, too?"

"Oh please. In his eyes, Edward and Patrick are blessed angels, sent from above to bring peace and joy to the world. I'm just a stupid girl, after all."

Somehow, I got the feeling Joy Wong could fend for herself just fine.

"Hey, there's my guy now." Her attention shifted to Patrick and Rojo angling toward us across the lawn, engaged in an animated discussion. Joy waved and called out to them. When they saw her, Patrick peeled off abruptly, and Rojo came our way, big grin on his face.

He wore baggy jeans with fashionable rips in the knees and a red-and-white-checked flannel shirt over a white t-shirt. Could be a farmer, could be a grunge musician. When he got closer, his red-dyed hair became evident. *Rojo.*

Joy popped out of her chair and gave Rojo a big kiss, lots of tongue. Then they hugged until Rojo broke it off and held out his fist toward me. I bumped it, gently.

"Hey buddy, how're you doing?" Rojo asked, voice barely above a whisper.

"Good, man. I'm good."

Rojo gave me a little nod, and with that small gesture, he expressed sympathy and support for what I'd been through in the last eight months, since losing Lauren. We'd always had a way of communicating without having to use all those pesky—and sappy—words.

"Excellent. You know, if you ever need anything..." Another caring look from him, and then we were just two friends again. His gaze stopped on my plate. "Hmm. Must be chow time. Need anything, hon?" he asked Joy.

"No, I'm good. Thanks."

"Okay. BRB," Rojo said, then set off in the direction of the buffet table.

Joy watched Rojo as he walked away, then turned to me. "When are you going to come see the band play again?"

"Soon." Every time I'd seen Dark Danger, it was a rocking time.

"They're doing a show Thursday night, at the Exx-Sight Lounge."

"Oh?"

"Come on, you don't want to be like my jerky brothers, do you?"

"No, I definitely wouldn't want that. I'll think about it."

Joy returned to rant mode for a couple more minutes—about what, I wasn't quite sure—until Rojo returned with his food. Two plates, full up.

"Did you say hi to my father?" Joy asked him.

"Not yet. Didn't want to ruin my appetite." Rojo leaned closer to me, and whispered, "Mr. Wong doesn't like me much. I'm not Chinese, you know." He patted Joy's arm. "That's going to change. You'll see, we're going to be good buddies someday."

Joy rolled her eyes.

"Never underestimate the Mendes charm," Rojo said, winking at me while he took a sip of Joy's soda. From earlier conversations with Rojo, I knew he wasn't on Hao's Christmas list. Nice to see he wasn't going to give up trying to fit in.

"How come you weren't at Edward's dinner the other night?" I asked.

"We had a gig. I heard about it, though. Must have been terrible." His voice cracked and he put his arm around Joy, patting her shoulder.

"Yeah, it was," I said.

Rojo gazed off into the distance.

"You've been talking about who wants to hurt Edward and Patrick, but do you think someone could be after Uncle Thomas?" Joy asked me.

"No way." The thought had crossed my mind, but I'd escorted it out after about three seconds. On that one-in-a-million chance Lee had been the target, he wouldn't have asked me to go snooping. He would have owned up to it. "Look guys, he's very worried something bad might happen, that those thugs might return and do some more serious damage."

"Really?" Joy said.

I glanced at Joy. "Yes, really. And not just to his restaurant. He's worried about his family. He's worried about you."

49

"That wouldn't be good," Rojo said.

"No it wouldn't be. So if you—either of you—have noticed anything that seems out of the ordinary in your family, you need to tell me. And sooner is better than later."

"You got it, man," Rojo said. "If we think of something, you'll be the first person we call." When he picked up Joy's can of soda to take another sip, I noticed his hand was quivering.

SIX

THE CONVERSATION VEERED OFF into a discussion of the local music scene, and Rojo and Joy did all the talking. I worked on my plate of food, and when I could see the word "Chinette," I politely excused myself. More people to question, more answers to seek.

But first, I had some business to attend to. My beer had gone right through me. The line at the pool cabana's bathroom was too long, so I wandered around a bit, looking for another restroom. Or Porta-Potty—I wasn't too picky. Finding none, I thought I'd try the big house.

I wound my way up a flagstone path toward the back door I'd seen the caterers using to ferry food to the buffet tables. It swung open very easily, as if it had been freshly oiled. Hao probably employed a team of maintenance workers to make sure every door opened without a squeak.

I walked down a short hallway, looking for a bathroom, figuring a house this large would have a dozen. At the end of the hall, on my right, was a large family room. A giant TV screen took up

51

most of one wall and about ten chairs—of varying size and plushness—were strategically positioned to see the screen. Movie room, perhaps.

Thinking about my mere forty-inch screen and trying not to feel inadequate, I kept going, deeper into the house. Past a gleaming mahogany bar and a pool table. A poker table. A foosball table. Dartboard. From the amusements and sterile décor—chrome and glass with ebony accents—I figured this was Hao's part of the house. The Man-Cave. Someplace where the Wong menfolk could gather and grunt and scratch and make bodily noises without the disapproving looks of women. The lingering aroma of long-ago-smoked cigars seemed to confirm my assessment.

I continued my search, finally finding a bathroom. I took care of my needs, hand-combing my hair in the mirror when I was finished, and headed back to the party. Before I'd taken five steps, however, I heard harsh words being exchanged behind a closed door across the hall. I ducked back into the bathroom and pulled the door closed. Not all the way—I needed a crack to be able to hear the argument.

One voice sounded like Edward; I didn't recognize the other, except that it sounded older. Probably Hao. The volumes of their voices rose and fell, and their cadences changed rapidly—exactly like you would expect in a passionate argument. Unfortunately, I couldn't tell what they were arguing about because the argument was mostly in Chinese, with a few choice English words thrown in by Edward. Those I had no trouble deciphering.

I listened carefully for a few minutes until the intensity level diminished. Then I quickly left the bathroom, hustled past the closed door across the hall, and left the house the way I'd come in.

I guess Joy was wrong; Hao had started harassing Edward about something in *his* craptastic life.

Back on the lawn, I spotted Patrick temporarily by himself, so I headed over. It wouldn't be polite to grill him while he schmoozed potential backers.

When he saw me approach, Patrick thrust his hand out. Maybe Artie was right, maybe all politicians were cut from the same handshaking, smiling Mr. Insincere mold. "Patrick Wong. How are you today?"

I shook with him. "Remember me? Channing Hayes?"

"Oh, yes, yes. Of course. My uncle talks about you all the time."

I doubted Lee had ever even mentioned my name to Patrick, but I'd already mentally prepared myself for whatever smarmy politician maneuvers I'd encounter.

"Nice turnout today," I said, glancing around. "All campaign contributors?"

Patrick chuckled, the "about-to-make-a-witty-remark" variety. "Not yet. But after they taste some of the ribs, I think they'll come around."

I chuckled back, getting into the mood of things. Unfortunately, an elderly man picked that moment to sidle up to us. Patrick welcomed him into our little impromptu conversation and unfurled the campaign rhetoric.

Patrick rambled on for ten minutes about Edward's campaign, barely coming up for air. Evidently, long-windedness ran in the family. He described Edward's dreams, visions, goals, and priorities. He might even have listed his favorite foods—I was only listening with half an ear, waiting for him to run out of steam. Nowhere in his ramblings did I hear anything about "enemies vicious enough to attack us with baseball bats."

"So, at the end of the day, what we really value are *people*." Patrick sucked in a deep breath and closed his mouth. His speech had been filled with a lot more details than Nicole's, but with far less personal connection.

I wasn't getting any younger, so I cleared my throat and chimed in. "Your mission sounds very exciting. May I ask a few questions?"

"Absolutely."

"What's Edward's position on education?"

"He's 100 percent in favor of having a top-notch statewide educational system. In these days of shrinking budgets, he's committed to providing the funds necessary—"

I held up my hand. "Perfect, perfect. I totally agree. And I assume he's in favor of reforming health care?"

"Edward realizes how vital high-quality, affordable health care is to every single man, woman, and child in this state, and he's committed—"

I interrupted again. "Outstanding." I leaned in and lowered my voice. "Now I have a question about the other night? At Lee's?"

For a second, it looked as if Patrick's eyes might pop out and go rolling across the manicured lawn like miniature bocce balls, but he recovered quickly. He gripped the man by his shoulder with one hand and shook hands with the other. "It was a pleasure talking with you. Unfortunately, something's come up that needs my immediate attention. Would you mind excusing us for a few moments? I hope we'll have your support in November." He waited for the old guy to shuffle out of earshot before turning to me. "So …?"

"Give me your take on what happened the other night at Lee's."

This time, no chuckle. Instead, I got a head tilt and a glare. "What's there to say? We got attacked. Terrifying."

"Any idea who did it?"

He shrugged.

"Three men in ski masks took a little batting practice on the banquet tables, and all you can muster is a shrug?"

He blinked a few times and I could practically see the gears moving behind his slick façade. "It was terrible. Horrible. Frightening. And I have no idea who did it. What more can I tell you?"

"The truth would be nice."

More blinking. "Look, Channing. No one got seriously hurt. But it's over with. Won't happen again."

I was sick of being dicked with. If this was any indication of how the Wong campaign was being run, then they'll have a long future in politics, where the truth is a moving and often illusory target. "How can you be sure?"

"I'm sure," Patrick said.

A very long future. "Somebody was sending a message. What do you think that message was?"

"No idea."

"Do you think Korbell had anything to do with this?"

Patrick fluttered his eyelids yet again, then regained his composure. "Sanford Korbell? Ludicrous. He's our opponent, sure, but he's a straight shooter. Not his style at all."

"Uh huh."

"It's done. Let it rest." He extended his hand and tried to paste on his politician smile, but it was a wan imitation. "Thanks for bringing your concerns to my attention. It was a pleasure chatting with you."

I'll bet. I reached for his hand, clearly defeated in my quest for some answers, but before I could shake it, Edward strolled up. A large beefy guy came up behind him, but didn't join us.

"There you are, Patrick. Got some questions for you." Edward stepped toward me and, copying his brother, stuck his hand out. "Nice to see you again, Channing."

"Ditto," I said, and the three of us stood there, no one speaking for a moment. I tried to think of some way to ask Edward about the argument I'd overheard, but couldn't find a way to casually squeeze it in. Instead, I focused on the incident at Lee's. "What happened the other night? Why did three men with baseball bats terrorize your dinner?"

Patrick spoke up. "I told him we don't know. I also told him it wouldn't happen again." Edward stared at me, but spoke to Patrick. "Pat, would you mind giving us a few moments?"

Patrick was about to protest, but then his features sagged. "Okay. Sure." He drifted off, a completely different person in the shadow of big brother.

"What Patrick said is correct. We don't know who was behind what happened the other night, nor do we know *why* it happened. But we've taken some extra steps to assure it doesn't happen again." Edward motioned for the large guy to join us. "This is Brad Ames."

"Hey," Ames said, stepping forward. He wore a blue blazer and khakis, and his beefy neck lapped over the collar of his white shirt. If I had to guess, I'd say ex-football player who'd kept up his caloric intake without keeping up the exercise. I'm sure there was plenty of muscle underneath the flab and I made a mental note not to find out firsthand.

"Brad's our logistics guy, handles our events, security, travel arrangements, stuff like that. Kind of behind the scenes," Edward said. With his bulk, it would be hard for him to be discreet. Of course, that might be the point. "Brad, this is Channing Hayes. He's a friend of my Uncle Thomas."

Ames nodded to me, then took a parade rest position, hands clasped behind him. "You could say I'm Edward's right-hand man," he said. Then he caught sight of my left hand, the one missing three fingers, and he blanched to a shade that approached the color of his teeth. "Uh, sorry, I didn't mean to…"

"It's okay. I could use a left-hand man, myself." I held my hand up and tapped my thumb to my forefinger. I've become accustomed to the different reactions my missing digits generated. Some people jerked their head away, as if staring at my misshapen hand would turn them to stone. Others stared with wide eyes, as if I were a circus freak they'd paid to ogle. Still others noted it, but carried on as usual, as if it were a mole or a scratch or a patch of sunburn and not some kind of grotesque monstrosity. Those people were definitely in the minority. In truth, most people looked away very quickly and tried to avoid looking at it again. "Nice to meet you."

"Uh, yeah. Likewise," Ames said, staring at my nose, not wanting to make that mistake again. Some color seeped back into his face.

Edward spoke up. "Channing was at the dinner on Friday. I have a feeling that Uncle Thomas asked him to do a little investigation." He turned to me. "That right?"

I nodded. "He's concerned about his family's well-being, is all."

57

"Everything's under control," Ames said. He puffed out his chest a hair, as if he'd just sacked the quarterback.

"Oh?"

"Nothing a little more, uh, security can't handle." Ames pointed at a large guy near the pool, also wearing a blue blazer and khakis, then he pointed at another hefty dude across the lawn, dressed alike. Looked like half the starting defensive line was now playing security for the Wongs.

"See? Everything's under control," Edward said.

In response, Ames's chest expanded a little more. Preening for his boss? Judging from my two minutes with the guy, it was tough to believe Ames was the best the Wongs could do.

Edward reasserted himself. "Please be assured, I've addressed the matter and put it to bed. And, of course, nothing like it will ever occur again."

"Of course," I said. "What did *the matter* concern?"

Edward flashed me a tight smile. "Simply a misunderstanding that unfortunately led to violence."

Did they teach *Advanced Stonewalling* in law school? "Why didn't you report it?"

"We did. Didn't the detectives talk to you?" Edward maintained his pinched grin.

"Sure they did. But I got the feeling they weren't going to act on it."

"I'm sure that's not true. I am happy they're keeping it quiet, though. Nothing to be gained by making a giant stink of it, except bad press. As much as I hate to admit it, I've got a fight on my hands in this campaign. If the news hounds got wind of what happened, well, my race could be dead in the water. Besides, like

I told you, it's settled. No more attacks. No more violence. I can concentrate fully on my march to Washington. I trust I can count on your support?" He started to move off, eager to schmooze potential backers. "Say hi to Uncle Thomas for me, okay?"

SEVEN

NORMALLY, THE BRIGHT STAGE lights didn't bother me. Over the years, I'd gotten used to them. But tonight, fifteen minutes into my routine, they were killing me. Unfortunately, they were the only thing killing—my act was going straight down the toilet. I unscrewed the top of my water bottle and took a nice long swig, trying anything I could to break up the bad momentum I'd gotten myself into short of yelling "Fire!"

I set the bottle back on the wooden stool. Gazed out into the audience. Amazing how time stood still when you were on stage crashing, burning, and laying a dodo egg. I took a deep breath and plunged into the last part of my routine.

"So I went back to my high school a few weeks ago, just to visit. You know what's weird about going back? In your head, time's stood still. Same parking lot, same building, same stupid sign out front. But for other people, time kept marching by. I had a giant crush on my English teacher, Ms. Moretti, and I thought it would be cool to stop in and say hi. See if she remembered me.

And to check her out, of course. She was smoking hot. So I consulted the school directory on the wall, and reported to the office for my strip search. Security is so tight nowadays. When *I* went to high school, the security was designed to keep us hooligans in the school. Now it's supposed to keep the bad elements *out* of school. Scary." I licked my lips, kept going.

"But things were different back then. When I went to high school, you could bring in weapons. Hell, you *had* to bring in weapons to protect yourself. Like mutually assured destruction, everyone brought them. Sometimes I'd leave some books at home just so I could fit my nunchucks in my backpack. Of course, I don't have to tell you who had the biggest weapons. The teachers. They weren't stupid. And you knew they were just waiting for some wise-ass student to start something so they could get their frustrations out." I pantomimed kicking the crap out of a student, but as I was doing it, and even with a few lame snickers, I knew I was bombing.

This audience was worse off than 1940 London. Best to wrap things up quickly and get the hell out before someone got injured. Especially me.

"Anyway, I found my way to Ms. Moretti's classroom, and there she was, exactly as I remembered. Hunched over her desk reading a book, long dark hair cascading over her shoulders. It was like my pimply ass was back in eleventh grade. My mouth got dry. I took a few steps into the room and she looked up." I paused for effect. Licked my lips, then bugged out my eyes in horror. "I was expecting Angelina Jolie; I got Andy Rooney. Oh no, the years hadn't been kind to Ms. Moretti. I started to pretend I was in the wrong room, but it was too late—she recognized me. 'Channing? Channing

Hayes?' Even her voice had gotten worse, like chalk on one of the blackboards she'd made me clean, back in the day."

I took a few steps backward and covered my ears, a look of horror still on my face.

"Then she stood up. Fifty extra pounds had found its way into Ms. Moretti's blouse. Not to be unkind, but her participles were definitely dangling. Of course, she'd made me—I couldn't just turn and run. Besides, I was an adult now. 'Uh, hi Ms. Moretti. How are you?' A weird gleam had come over her face. She took a few steps closer; I took a few steps back. 'I'm fine, just fine.' She lowered her voice into a throaty rasp. 'I know you had a crush on me. I was hoping you'd come back and visit sometime."

"She kept advancing; I kept retreating." I backpedaled a little more, pretending I'd been cornered. "Then she said, 'You were always such a big talker. So, let's see what you've got.' She turned her stare down toward my package. Well, I'd had enough. I slipped around her and dashed for the door as her parting words chased me. 'That's called irony, Mr. Hayes. It took me fifteen years to teach it to you, but at least it's finally sunk in.'" I paused a beat. "Thank you, and goodnight."

I took a quick bow and jogged offstage to a smattering of applause. Mercifully, there were a few polite people in the audience. If the positions had been reversed, I'm not sure I would have clapped for a routine as putrid as mine had been.

What the hell was going on with me?

Artie met me in the wings. He'd been nice enough to drive the two hours south to this Richmond club and lend his support as I tried out some new material. I could tell what he thought by his expression, so I steeled myself.

"That sucked. Big time," he said. "And I'm not just saying that to make you feel better. You were truly awful."

Sometimes Artie had all the subtlety of a neighbor's leafblower at seven a.m. "Yeah, I wasn't feeling it."

"We felt it. It didn't feel pretty." He glanced around the club. The audience was laughing now at the middle guy. I'd seen him before and my stuff was much better than his. Usually.

"Did you record it?"

Artie held up the video camera. "Turned it off halfway through. Then I accidentally erased what I'd taken. You'll thank me later."

I taped my shows whenever I could—to critique after the fact and to capture any clever ad-libs I might have come up with. Tonight, I was *glad* Artie had erased the evidence. He jerked his head toward the door. "Come on. Let's get out of here before people come after us demanding their money back."

We headed toward the exit, past a row of tables. A fat guy wearing a football jersey caught my eye, and I swore I saw pity. Averting my eyes quickly, I followed Artie out. We almost got away cleanly, but the owner, a nice woman named Lizzy Northcutt, fell in step next to us. She didn't say a word until we'd made it out the front door into the sticky August night.

"Not your best performance, Channing." She worked her way next to me and shouldered Artie aside. He had that effect on people from time to time. Artie got the message and drifted off, giving Lizzy and me a little privacy. "You doing okay?" She shot a quick glance down at my less-than-perfect hand. Since the accident, I'd gotten more used to those quick glances at my missing fingers. Gawkers didn't shock me anymore.

"Yeah, I'm getting myself together. The pain isn't as sharp any-more." Unfortunately, neither was my comedy.

"I'm glad to hear that." She'd been good to me over the years, and I knew I could try out my new stuff here without endangering the possibility of future gigs. Although that was before tonight's flameout. "Can I make an observation?"

"Sure."

"I'm telling you this because I care about you—I'm not trying to rub your nose in anything. Hell, everyone has an off night, you know?"

"Go ahead, I'm a big boy. I can take it."

"Well, I saw you perform a bunch of times before your acci-dent. Your stuff had a certain edge to it, a vibrancy. You really con-nected with the audiences. I didn't see that tonight. Tonight, I saw a guy pressing. Trying to force the issue with some mediocre mate-rial, hoping your stage presence would save the day. In the past, it might have. But tonight you seemed tentative. Afraid. And when people smell fear ... it's all over. You know what I mean?"

I nodded. She'd verbalized what I'd been feeling, off and on, since I'd gotten back on stage a couple months ago. Tentative com-ics didn't last very long.

"Don't worry, if Sammi calls to see how things went, I'll be vague."

"Thanks." Sammi Long was my agent. A bulldog in a sundress, masquerading as a Southern Belle. I loved her dearly. But there re-ally wasn't any reason to upset her, not yet. Of course, if I kept bombing, word would get around fast, no matter how vague my club-owning friends were.

Lizzy softened her tone. "I'd like to see the old Channing Hayes return. *He* was a funny guy. And more importantly, he wasn't afraid of anything. The old Channing Hayes always looked like he was having fun."

———

The next day, I arrived for my one o'clock appointment five minutes early, like I always did, and took a seat in the waiting room. I sorted through a few magazines on the coffee table but didn't find anything worth reading. You'd think after so many sessions, I'd remember to bring something along to keep me occupied.

At exactly one, the inner door opened. "Hello, Channing. You can come back now." We made our way down the hall, not speaking, waiting until we got comfortable before I spilled my innermost feelings. I guess there *were* some routines I picked up on after awhile.

I settled into my usual spot on the couch.

"So, how are you?"

I recounted the incident at Lee's, feeling my pulse quicken with fear as I told it, but this time I felt something else, too. Anger. After I finished my story, I brought that up.

"Anger is a natural reaction. You're angry because of the violation you felt. Sort of a 'who do those people think they are, coming here, threatening me and my friends' thing. I'd be surprised if you *didn't* feel some anger toward those men. Unfortunately, you might also feel fear that this could occur again. Do you believe that to be a real possibility?"

I mentioned the favor Lee had asked me to do and I described my talks with Nicole Benton and the Wongs for a few minutes, without answering her question directly. Then I changed the subject. My dime, my agenda. "I had a show last night. In Richmond." I paused. "I totally bombed."

"Really? According to whom?"

I stifled a laugh. "Me. Artie. The owner. Every single person in the audience. I'm sure there were homeless guys down the block who noticed the ominous silence after my routine."

"Knowing you, Channing, I think you're exaggerating. But the *perception* you bombed is what's important. How did that make you feel?"

"How did what make me feel? My bombing?"

A nod.

"Like shit. I'm a stand-up comic. If people don't laugh, if I bomb, then I need to go find a new line of work. And there aren't too many other lines of work I'm qualified for."

"So you're only worried about bombing as it relates to working? To making a living?"

I shifted on the couch. "No. Of course not. I want people to have a good time."

"Well, you don't just want people to have a good time. You probably don't get enjoyment if there are people right now somewhere in Kansas enjoying themselves. You want people to have a good time when you perform for them. You want people to like *you*."

I thought about that for a moment. It was the truth. "So I'm a self-centered jerk?"

"Not at all. It simply means you have a strong need for approval. A trait you share with many, many people. Haven't you ever seen *American Idol*?"

I cracked a small smile. My therapist was a great therapist, but I didn't usually get much humor alongside the therapy. "I hope I have more talent than most of those contestants."

"Undoubtedly. I have a little homework assignment for you. I'd like you to think about why outside approval—from friends and from strangers—is important to you. Can you do that?"

"Sure." I could work on that instead of replaying last night's godawful performance.

"Good. Now, if I recall correctly, you've had a handful of shows since, uh, you've come back from the accident. How many of those did you bomb?"

I thought back. Last night's show was the worst, but I'd delivered a few other shaky outings. "Well, not too many out-and-out disasters, but I'm nowhere as good as I was."

"Again, you might not be a totally impartial observer. But why do you think that might be?"

"Could be a million reasons. New material. A little rusty. The comedy scene has passed me by. I'm over the hill." I hated it when I drifted into woe-is-me mode.

"You've only been 'out of the game' for less than a year. I doubt if the comedy scene has passed you by. Or that you're over the hill. Don't you think it's reasonable to expect you would need some time to get back in the groove? Shake off some of that rust?"

"Yeah. Maybe."

"You've told me before how important confidence is in stand-up. Possibly more important than the material itself. Yet I noticed you didn't mention that as a possible factor. What do you think about that?"

"It's tough to feel confident when people aren't laughing." I tried to remember how confident I felt when I began my come-back. "After the first show—which I nailed—I felt pretty good. But maybe there was something under the surface, because since that show, I've felt kinda wobbly."

"Is there anything you think you can do to help regain some confidence, short of getting back on stage and, uh, killing?"

Watching bad audition tapes made me feel better in compari-son, but I'm not sure that's what my therapist meant. Nothing more constructive jumped out at me. "I don't know. I think I'm a lost cause. I've lost my mojo."

"Channing. We've gone over this ground before. You're too hard on yourself. Cut yourself some slack. Everyone bombs once in a while. Even Bill Cosby. You just need to get some confidence back. You'll find your mojo. You have to believe that."

———

Ty Taylor and I paid our cover charges and stepped into the dimly lit Exx-Sight Lounge, one of the many club-of-the-months that seemed to pop up like spring weeds on the music scene, only to die after a few months under the harsh sun of attention.

"Over there." I pointed to a couple seats by the wall, next to a table of guys wearing t-shirts emblazoned with band names. I followed Ty and noticed heads turning to watch as he made his way between tables. He carried about 275 pounds on his six-six frame and if I had to guess, I'd say his body fat percentage rivaled a telephone pole's. He worked as The Last Laff's bouncer on the weekends. During the week, he was a student at Georgetown Law.

Ty eased into his seat and I plopped down next to him. For a Thursday night, the place was pretty crowded. More crowded than our place, for sure. That's one reason Artie let me go tonight. Thursdays were good for us when we had a decent headliner, but this week, we featured a mediocre local impressionist who came across like Robert DeNiro no matter who he was trying to imitate. Even with good material, doing an impression of Oprah sounding like Robert DeNiro didn't fly.

I flagged down a server and ordered a beer; Ty got club soda and lime. He was a vegetarian and a nondrinker. Sometimes I wondered why he wanted to hang around with a bunch of demented comics. Perhaps that's how he tasted life on the wild side.

"What's the name of this band again?" Ty asked.

"Dark Danger."

"Dark Danger? That's not a commentary about my ancestry, is it?" Ty said, eyes narrowing.

"Easy, big guy. I don't think so."

He grinned. "Just messing with you." Not too much bothered Ty.

I'd told him we were there to hear a friend's band. Which was true. I hadn't told Ty that we were also there to see what had spooked Rojo. Which also was true. He'd seemed uncomfortable at the cookout when I'd brought up the incident at Lee's. As if he were hiding something. Now that I thought about it, Rojo had been acting strange lately—at least stranger than usual. I guess I just hadn't noticed exactly how different until I saw him at the cookout.

The server delivered our drinks and we relaxed, listening in on other conversations around us. The quarters were close so we had our choice of some good ones. Cheating boyfriends, cheating girl-friends, a three-way that slipped through some guy's fingers because he lost a phone number. The usual stuff I hear every day of the week at my club, but good stories nonetheless. I watched Ty's eyebrows rise and fall as he listened in. He wasn't around our club enough to be as jaded as I was.

After about five minutes, a tall man wearing all black stepped up to the mic on stage, Johnny Cash's younger brother. He tapped it once, then bent over. "It's shooooowtime. All the way from East Nowheresville, let's give it up for Dark Danger!"

The band hit the stage to some patchy applause and a few cat-calls. Toward the front, I saw Joy Wong jump up and cheer, the only one in the room giving the band a standing ovation before they'd even played a chord.

I'd been keeping an eye out, but I must have missed her entrance. Too busy eavesdropping. She sat as the band members played a few warm-up notes. In addition to Rojo, who played guitar, there was a bassist, a drummer, and a fourth guy who stood near a keyboard and a sax on a stand. Probably the musical equivalent of a utility infielder.

The band launched into their first number and Rojo danced and pranced and windmilled on his guitar for all he was worth. The song, an original composition, was pretty good, if a bit derivative of a thousand other songs I'd heard lately. But they sure put a ton of energy into it. The crowd showered them with some well-deserved applause as Rojo stepped up to the mic.

"Thank you," he said. "That was 'Set Her Free.' Our next number is 'Fifteen Beating Hearts.'" Dark Danger rocked out again and maintained their torrid pace through another three songs without any chatter in between. Even from where I sat, I could see sweat pouring off the musicians.

I dug their music. I dug their energy. I could do without their grunge attire, but I guess that was a small quibble. They'd seemed to step it up a notch since the last time I'd seen them play. Next to me, Ty's head bopped to the beat and he softly tapped his fingers on the tabletop. Looks like the band could count another new fan.

For the rest of the set, Rojo kept the pace humming with his high-energy jamming. The other band members left everything out there, too, and the audience, for its part, made quite a racket after every song. I could see why Joy was proud of Rojo, and I could also see why she'd be so angry at her brothers and parents for not coming to see him, for not sharing in the excitement for her boyfriend.

Just when I thought Rojo would pass out from exhaustion, he set his guitar down on its stand and took a bow. Then the band hustled off the stage.

The audience went wild, cheering and calling out. After a few minutes of bedlam, the band returned for an encore. They smoked through another five songs before calling it a night. After a final bow, the four band members ducked offstage as the houselights came up.

"Come on, let's go."

Ty followed my lead and we zig-zagged through the crowd, careful to avoid plowing anyone over. When we reached the main aisle, we swam against the tide, away from the exit. Time to see what information I could wring from Rojo.

Several women—barely older than girls, actually—gaped at Ty as we passed. How come no hottie's eyes sparkled like that when

I went by? We entered a narrow passageway next to the stage and the sound level diminished considerably. A couple band members emerged from a door marked "Private," and we flashed them a thumbs-up. They returned the gesture without much energy, having left it all on stage. We were about to knock on the door, when it opened again and the drummer came out. On stage, Rojo had introduced him as Seth Phillips.

"Hey. Great show," I said. "You guys get better every time I see you."

"Thanks." Phillips wore a red-and-white bandanna over his head and a big gold hoop earring in each ear. A dark Van Dyke beard covered his chin. I almost expected an "Arrgh, matey," instead of a "thanks."

"We're looking for Rojo. Is he in there?" I asked, pointing to the room he'd just left.

"Nope. He cleared out first. Was in a hurry, that's for sure." He found a smile for us, although it was a tired one. "Thanks for coming tonight. I'll check you guys later." He slipped past us, following his buddies down the hall, probably home to a cold beer and a hot shower.

"Now what?" Ty asked.

"Come on." We went deeper into the club, rounded a corner, and heard the sharp sounds of an argument. I recognized the rat-a-tat delivery of Joy Wong, followed by the more laid-back voice of Rojo. I stopped and grabbed Ty's sleeve. I didn't want to interrupt them.

I pulled him against the wall, where we both skulked, out of sight. I pressed my forefinger to my mouth. I'm not sure when eavesdropping on various members of the Wong family had become a hobby of mine, but sometimes you just had to go with the flow.

I turned and concentrated on their argument. The words were hard to make out, but I got the sense Rojo was planning to do something Joy didn't approve of. It sounded like Joy was pleading for him to stop, and I overheard the words "irresponsible," "dangerous," and "fucking dipshit." Of course, coming out of Joy's loose mouth, that didn't mean much—she could have been describing somebody she'd sat next to in the audience or the counter clerk at the dry cleaners. It was more the tone that had me concerned.

Something was going on. I doubted it had anything to do with what had happened at Lee's, but … it was possible.

Ty's stoic expression didn't reflect any such concern. He was generally less reactive than I was, which I suppose was a good quality to have as a bouncer. You didn't want to start manhandling customers at the slightest provocation. When we got to a place where we could talk, we'd have to compare impressions.

Rojo said something about a guy named Jimmy Fugano and Joy's cussing increased. Then, after a few more heated exchanges, Rojo raised his voice, too. "Stay out of it. I'm doing this for us."

Things got quiet.

Rojo stormed into view, angling toward us, but then he veered and banged through a rear emergency exit. He hadn't noticed us lurking. Ty and I straightened up and moved away from the wall, trying to appear less like suspicious eavesdroppers in case Joy came by.

I peeked around the corner. Joy sat on the floor, staring off into space. I ducked back out of sight.

"Come on. Let's follow him."

Ty started to protest, but I shushed him. "I thought you liked a little intrigue, a little adventure."

Again, he began to respond, but I took off and pushed through the same door Rojo had used, out into the night air. I spotted my quarry down the alley and set off in pursuit, walking fast. Ten seconds later, Ty fell in next to me. "Sure, I like a little adventure," he said, in a whisper. "But only a little."

We emerged from the alley onto Route 7, halfway between Seven Corners and Bailey's Crossroads. On the main drag, streetlights transformed night into day. Rojo had turned right, so we turned right. We spotted him about a block ahead, walking at a steady clip, a backpack on his shoulder bouncing with each step. Not speeding along, but not dawdling either. Foot traffic was steady—there were maybe a dozen bars and restaurants along the way, although the sidewalks weren't overly crowded. Most of the establishments looked kinda seedy, which made the ones that didn't stand out. Evidently, a few owners had seized the initiative and spruced up their properties in an effort to separate nighttime revelers from their disposable income.

Ty and I stayed on Rojo's tail, not talking, feeling like we were a couple badasses from some noir detective flick. Or at least I felt that way. Ty kept quiet. For all I knew, he was thinking about some torts exam on the horizon. We kept our distance but weren't worried we'd be "made," quite sure Rojo had no idea we were behind him.

At the next corner, a clot of people waited for the light to turn. Their destination, across the street, was the Good Fortune Shopping Center, which housed an independent grocery store, a bank branch, and a drug store. But I suspected the main attraction was a trio of bars clustered at one end of the commercial strip. Ty and I held back a bit, ready to hustle across when the time came.

The light changed and the mass of people swept across the street. Ty and I lagged behind, toward the back of the pack, and just made it across before the flashing "Don't Walk" sign turned solid.

Ahead of us, Rojo continued toward the far end of the shopping center, away from the bars. We followed. As we passed each bar, a different kind of music leaked out the front doors when they opened to let in more clientele. Ahead, Rojo slowed, then stopped in front of a Vietnamese restaurant advertising $5.99 lunch specials. He removed the backpack and set it on the ground, casually leaning against a store window, all while looking around as if he were being watched. Ty and I ducked into the nearest entranceway, a closed CVS store. I peered around the corner. Rojo's casual stance contrasted with his anxious glancing. The effect was almost comical. I wasn't chuckling, however. This was not the Rojo I was accustomed to seeing.

"He's meeting someone," Ty said, over my shoulder.

"Looks like it." I scanned the sidewalk, not sure who I was searching for. Anybody who seemed twitchy, to start. But that didn't narrow things down much—half of the people walking around here this time of night seemed twitchy in some respect.

Rojo pulled a pack of cigarettes from his backpack. Took one out and lit it. Leaned against the window, began puffing away. If he had a collar on his t-shirt, he would have turned it up. Was the cigarette the signal? Another trope from some awful B-movie?

Evidently, it was.

Two men approached Rojo from the opposite side. Both were Asian, both around thirty. The stocky guy had a blue Mohawk. The other guy was lamp-post skinny, with a pair of jeans that ended mid-shin. Either way-too-long shorts, or ready-for-the-flood pants. Some kind of swirling tattoo climbed the side of his neck. When Rojo spotted them, he tossed his butt onto the sidewalk and gave them a quick, furtive nod as they passed him. Then he snatched up his backpack, shouldered it, and followed them. They hadn't slowed a step, nor had they acknowledged Rojo's presence. If Rojo hadn't acted so suddenly when they passed, we'd never know what was up. What could be so mysterious that had Rojo acting as if he were selling state secrets?

Ty and I didn't have much time to think. The trio was headed our way.

I grabbed Ty in an embrace and pulled him farther into the CVS alcove, turning him so his back was to the sidewalk. Like hugging a tree trunk.

"Dude," he whispered, "is this really necessary?"

"Shut up."

I waited thirty seconds until I was fairly sure they'd passed, then released Ty.

"Don't think I'm easy."

"Come on." I sidestepped his large body and started down the sidewalk. Ty quickly caught up. We didn't see them at first, but when we got to the corner, we spotted them marching south along Route 7, on our side of the street. It wasn't too hard to spot a guy with a big blue Mohawk. Rojo followed the two guys, same as before. Not racing, but not poking along. Probably thought it made them less noticeable. If they wanted to be less noticeable, Mohawk should have worn a hat.

Ty and I kept pace, not talking. We were heading away from the hubbub of the bar scene where there were fewer pedestrians. Up ahead, the two guys turned right, and Rojo turned right, too, but not before glancing around to see if he was being tailed.

He didn't see us. The trio disappeared down the alley. Ty and I trotted down the street, stopping when we got to the corner. I peeked first. A security light shined on two Dumpsters, about fifteen yards away. Next to the Dumpsters, Tattoo had his hands around Rojo's throat, while Mohawk barked at him. Mohawk also had something in his hand. I couldn't be sure from this distance, but it looked like a knife.

EIGHT

"Shit." Ty and I sprinted down the alley. Ordinarily, I wouldn't go charging after guys with knives, but I had Ty by my side. Plus I wasn't planning on getting too close. "Hey, let him go," I yelled as I ran.

Tattoo let go of Rojo's neck; Mohawk held onto his knife. They both turned to face us as we came screeching to a halt ten feet away. Rojo gasped for breath and fear shone dimly in his eyes, along with what might have passed for gratitude.

The two guys didn't seem happy to have us intrude on their party. Mohawk spoke. "What do you two want? Get lost. This is private property. And it's a private matter." The knuckles on the hand holding the knife were white.

"You okay, Rojo?" I asked.

"Oh ho ho. You know Rojo?" He rolled the "r" for five seconds. You could hear the sneer in his voice.

"Yeah, we know him. Go ahead, let him go."

Mohawk took a couple steps toward Rojo, and Tattoo moved aside. "We're just having a little discussion. You heard him. He says he's okay. Right, Rojo?" The "r" rolled again.

Rojo squeaked out a "yeah," but his head shook from side to side.

Ty took half a step forward and flexed, but I did the talking. "We've already called the cops. Should be here in about a minute."

"We don't need the cops. Like I said, this is business. Tell him." Mohawk looked expectantly at Rojo and gestured with his knife. "Tell him."

Rojo licked his lips, clearly confused about what to say or do. "I, uh, well." The showman we saw on stage a little while ago was long gone.

Mohawk grinned, cold like an alligator's smile. "I'm sure none of us wants to be here when the cops arrive. Too many questions. Too much hassle." He hissed the last word. "That's okay. We know how to get in touch with Rojo. And Mr. D. won't be happy if things don't turn out right." He pivoted and feigned punching Rojo in the gut. Rojo's hands flew to his stomach to protect himself, and Mohawk let out a harsh laugh.

Even Mohawk's buddy shrank away a little.

Mohawk pointed the knife at Rojo's nose. "See you soon, Rojo." This time, the "r" roll lasted ten seconds. With a final sneer thrown our way, Mohawk and Tattoo jogged away, melting into the far shadows of the alley.

Rojo stared after them, massaging his neck.

"You okay?" I asked.

He nodded. "What are you doing here? You follow me?"

"You're lucky we did. What's going on?"

79

Rojo ignored my questions. "Why are you following me?"

"We were at your show, saw you take off out the back. Just curious."

He tilted his head at us. "Nothing's going on. A misunderstanding."

"Come on, man. It's me. No bullshit."

"It's nothing, really. Just a big misunderstanding."

"A misunderstanding is when you order decaf and get regular. This was a mugging. Could have been worse if we hadn't been here."

Rojo waved us off with a shaky hand. "Naw. They were only joking around."

My anger rose. Would it have been a joke if they had carved their initials into Rojo's forehead? I'd seen enough real violence in the past year to know it wasn't remotely a laughing matter. I got up into Rojo's face, like the other guy had been, except I didn't put my hands around his neck. "I want you to tell me what's going on. For your own good, believe me. Why were you meeting these guys? This have anything to do with what happened at Lee's?"

"Nope. Not a thing. This is my deal, completely." Rojo stared at me, pleading with his eyes. "Okay, it's not just a joke. Look, I owed these guys some money. An old debt. I gave them what they wanted. We're even. All this," Rojo paused and waved his hand in the air. "This was all for show. Teach me not to screw with them in the future. Believe me, that lesson's learned."

I didn't take my eyes off Rojo's face, trying to determine if he were dealing straight. I glanced at Ty who shrugged. "Okay, I believe you." I exhaled and backed away. Rojo exhaled too.

I tried to imagine what these two guys would look like with ski masks on. I tried to remember what the thugs sounded like, right before they started swinging baseball bats. Could these two have been there?

I wasn't sure, but I wouldn't bet against it. Like my buddy, Fairfax County cop Freeman Easter, was always saying, *I don't believe in coincidences.*

———

The next night, we gathered for our traditional pre-show meeting. We usually didn't meet before the weekday shows, but every Friday and Saturday evening we all took a break from what we were doing and assembled for a few minutes. Once the customers started coming in, we didn't always have time to compare notes. Of course it was Artie's idea, and he led the festivities, pacing the floor. The rest of us—me, Skip, Donna, and Ty—sat around the table trying to keep our yawns at bay.

"We're on a roll. We've had three really good weeks in a row. Great comics, lots of customers, lots of profits," Artie said, rubbing two fingers together. "I want to keep the streak going this weekend. We need to concentrate on providing the best experience we possibly can for our customers. Great food, great drinks, great service. Great comedy. When people come to The Last Laff, I want them to feel great. That's why I only have great people working for me. Strive to be great. I know you can do it. You've done it before and you'll do it again. You're all pros. Now, who's with me?" He was big into the Knute Rockne motivational speeches. I think they fired him up more than they fired us up.

"We're all with you, Artie. Like we always are," I said, trying to short-cut the process. I attempted to stifle another yawn and was only partially successful.

Artie nodded, then turned to Skip. "How about you? You with me?" He held up his hand for a high-five.

Skip reached up and grazed Artie's hand with his, eyes rolling. "Sure, I'm in," he said, voice lacking even the slightest hint of enthusiasm.

"Donna?" Artie asked.

"I've got work to do, Artie. Are we done here?" She had little patience for Artie's cheerleading.

Artie ignored her. "Big guy, you ready for tonight?"

Ty nodded. "Yes, sir. I'm always ready. Even when I'm chasing strange musicians down dark alleys, then facing dudes with Mohawks and knives, I'm ready."

"Great, great, then let's all—" Artie stopped mid-exhortation. "What the hell are you talking about?"

Donna sat straighter in her chair. She didn't brook Artie's blather, but she loved gossip. "What *are* you talking about? Something happen?"

Ty winked at me. "The fearless twosome. Super nighttime adventures of the dynamic duo on the mean streets of Bailey's Crossroads."

"Come on, spill," Donna said. She'd inched to the edge of her chair.

"Last night. Me and Channing. Keeping the streets safe for regular citizens." Ty grinned, happy to have an audience. Why was it Ty decided to open up now, in front of the others? I would have been content keeping last night's "adventure" quiet, at least until I found out more about what was going on.

"Mohawks and kn-kn-knives? Fill us in," Skip said.

Artie stepped up, trying to gain control of his meeting. "Okay. Let's have some details. What were you two doing?"

Ty explained what happened last night, sticking pretty much to the facts, except he omitted the part about our embrace. I saw no need to remind him. When he finished, Skip let out a low whistle.

"Man, all the exciting stuff always happens to you," Skip said. Then he blanched, realizing a lot of very exciting—very bad— stuff had indeed happened to me, and it destroyed much of what I held dear. "Sorry, Channing, I didn't mean ..."

I waved him off. "It happened. It's history. I'm trying to get past it." My mantra. At least it had been my mantra before Donna's daughter turned me on to "Glass pole, glass pole, glass pole."

No one spoke for an uncomfortable twenty seconds.

"Uh, okay everyone. Back to work." Artie clapped his hands once, like a quarterback dismissing the huddle. "Remember: be great!"

I rose, but Artie placed his hand on my shoulder and gently pushed me back into my seat. The others scurried off to get ready for the first show.

Artie pulled up a chair directly in front of mine and sat, our knees practically touching. "You guys didn't get hurt last night, did you?"

"No, we're fine. Just a little scary is all. But I had Ty as my wing-man, so I'm guessing the other guys were more scared." Not sure if this was exactly true, but I wanted to set Artie's mind at ease.

"Think this is related to what happened at Lee's?"

I shrugged. "Your guess is as good as mine. What I do know is that my friend Rojo is in some deep shit, and I need to help him out. Whether it's connected to Edward or the campaign, I don't know."

"Did you tell Lee what happened?"

"Of course. He was pretty shook up by the whole thing. Says that underneath Rojo's grunge musician shell is a really sweet guy."

"Feh."

I eyed Artie.

"Hell, Lee likes everyone, and even if he didn't he wouldn't say anything bad about them."

Artie had some revisionist history going on—Lee *didn't* like his brother-in-law Hao very much *and* he'd told me about it. "In this case, he's right; Rojo is a good guy. The Rojo I know wouldn't be involved with the goons we saw destroy Lee's. But there's something that doesn't seem right. I just have to find out what."

"Did you call Freeman?" Artie asked.

"I was mighty tempted, but I didn't. Rojo said it was all cool."

"You should call Freeman," Artie said.

"Lee doesn't want the cops involved. Edward and Patrick don't want the cops involved. Rojo doesn't want the cops involved." I jutted my chin toward Artie. "Seems the only ones who want the cops involved are us."

"Plus you don't want to get your friend Rojo into hot water," Artie said.

"There's that, too."

"I've been on this planet a lot longer than you, and I've learned sometimes—oftentimes—people don't want what's best for them."

"Maybe so. But this isn't really our business now, is it?"

Artie snorted. "Lee's my business."

"Then maybe you should do what he wants."

Artie snorted again.

"Lee asked me to look into this. Discreetly. I may not like where this is heading, and I might not have kept it quiet if it were solely up to me, but I made a promise to Lee."

"Promises, shmomises."

"Yeah, well, just because I haven't called the cops—the real cops—doesn't mean I'm done. I promised Lee I wouldn't call them, but I also promised him I'd nose around. I'll keep on prowling until I get some answers."

"I've got a bad feeling about this. You told Lee you'd ask a few questions. You didn't sign up for hazardous duty. I think it's time to call the cops. They're trained to catch crooks. You're trained to tell jokes. Big difference."

"Thanks for the lesson."

He sighed. "Just be careful, okay?"

"I'm always careful. Relax, I'll be fine." I started to get up, but Artie gently pushed me down again. I guess we weren't finished.

"You recovered yet? From your Wednesday night massacre in Richmond?"

"I guess. I'm just afraid it will show up on YouTube or something." That's all I needed, video evidence of my bombed performance going viral.

"Don't worry. Their standards are low, but they've got *some* standards."

And Artie was one of my *friends*.

———

We kept our streak of successful nights alive, which put everyone in a good mood. Except me. As I sometimes felt at two in the morning, especially lately, I was a little discouraged with my own career. I also had Lee's "investigation" nagging at me. But I think what was bugging me most was the loneliness. I missed Lauren.

What happened to her had been tragic, the kind of thing that never happened to someone you actually *knew*. Except it had. One night, about eight months ago, we were driving home after a show and an old boyfriend of her sister's had run us off the road in some kind of horrific game of chicken. Lauren died in the crash; physically, I'd only lost a few fingers and scarred my face, but emotionally I'd died right alongside Lauren. I captured the scumbag who did it—but not before he'd killed a couple other innocent people. He's now spending the rest of his life making new friends in prison.

I can only hope he's made a lot of very personal connections there with some very lonely inmates.

I drove home, listening to the radio, hitting the buttons, trying but failing to find anything good. The oldies were too old, the newer stuff too identical, and too many stations had shills pushing weight-loss programs featuring dietary supplements with names like "Fat-Ease," "Herbathin," and "BurnOff Supreme." Two a.m. radio sucked. I flipped through a few CDs, but couldn't find anything I felt like listening to there either, so I turned the car stereo off and drove in silence, alone with my thoughts. I wished I had better company.

I bid goodnight to Rex and trudged through the lobby of my building without encountering a soul. Took the elevator to my floor. I reached my condo at the end of the hall but didn't enter. Instead, I knocked softly on my across-the-hall neighbor's door. She worked late and I figured she'd be up.

She was. I heard her call out, and a minute later a shadow passed over the peephole. Then the door opened. Erin Poole, dressed in gray sweats, smiled at me. "Hi Channing. Come on in."

I followed her in to the living room where I sat on a recliner and she plopped down on the couch. "Working?"

She nodded at her laptop, open on the coffee table in front of her. "The usual. Plunking down the words." Erin wrote novels— mostly at night. She had several series going, all under different names. I wondered how she kept everything straight in her head. I had much less stuff to remember and I still botched a punch line here and there. "Glad you stopped by."

"Hey, my pleasure." I'd drop by sometimes after working at the club, so she wasn't really surprised to see me. Even though she always said she was glad when I visited, I often felt guilty interrupting her work. On the other hand, it was nice our night-owl tendencies coincided. Tonight, I could use the company.

"How's the comedy biz?"

I squelched a sigh. "Up and down. You know."

"Yeah, I know." She swept some long dark hair from her face. "You're a funny guy. What happened to you would knock anybody down. You'll get back in the groove."

She'd never seen me perform. That's okay; I'd never read any of her books. Lauren had always been urging me to, but I never quite got around to it. "Thanks. I'm sure you're right. I'll get my mojo back. Soon I hope. How about you? How's the writing?"

"Great. Just started a new series about a regular gal who settles the score with deadbeat dads who evade the law." She pointed at her clothes. "Hence the sweats."

Erin often dressed like her characters when she wrote. Maybe that's how she kept everything straight—whenever she got confused, she could glance in the mirror. With a two-inch scar on my cheek from the "accident," I usually avoided mirrors. Too many painful memories.

I'd popped in on Erin to buoy my spirits but wasn't doing a very good job. "Hey, I saw a good band Thursday night. Dark Danger. You should try to catch them sometime."

"Oh yeah? That's something I need to do more. Get out of this place for a change. Sometimes I feel like a hermit."

I thought about asking her out, but my stomach bucked. The three of us—her, me, and Lauren—had gone out a few times and we'd become good friends. I'm not sure why it freaked me out, but it did. I could only muster a limp, "Yeah."

Silence rushed into the void. Half my mind was in a different place, somewhere in the past with someone else. Coming here had been a bad idea.

"Hey, it's getting late. I'd better let you get back to work." I rose.

She got up, too, and if she harbored any disappointment, I couldn't see it on her face. "Sure. I need to crank out another thousand words before I turn in. Maybe I'll have Kara Worth waterboard some scumbag dad. That should be entertaining, huh?" A wicked grin lit up her face. Writers were a lot like comedians, I guess.

We said our goodbyes at the door and I shuffled across the hall into my condo. Went straight to the shelf next to the stereo that held my CD collection. I removed Lauren's favorite one from the jewel case and slid it into the player.

I didn't like the music very much. I just wanted to be with Lauren.

NINE

I SLEPT IN THE next morning, all the way *through* the next morning, rolling out of bed around one. I ate three bowls of Cap'n Crunch—hold the crunchberries—and did a load of laundry before heading to The Last Laff. It was going to be another busy night, which was good for us, but I somehow still had the feeling I was a kid at the circus, standing outside the big top peering at the main ring through a slit in the back of the tent.

I got to the club around 3:30 and settled in to do some paperwork. Forty minutes later, just as I was about to nod off from boredom, Ty burst into the office.

"What are you doing here? You're three hours early."

He tossed a folded-up newspaper on my desk. "Check it out." A small article, below the fold, had been circled in red. *Man Found Slain at Lake Barcroft.*

"Yeah, so?" Lake Barcroft was a lake in the eastern part of Fairfax County surrounded by nice houses. Although it wasn't as crime-ridden as Anacostia, where finding a body was a weekly event, bad stuff happened in the suburbs, sometimes.

"Keep reading," Ty said.

The article described the unidentified victim as an Asian male, about six feet, four inches tall, with a dragon tattoo on his neck. *Tattoo.* "Oh shit."

"Yes indeed, oh shit," Ty said. "We need to tell someone about what happened, don't we?"

"I thought *you* were the law student." I paused. "How about I give Freeman a call? See what he knows about the case. Why don't you go chill someplace? I'll let you know what I find out."

"Sure, boss. Sure." Ty disappeared out of the office.

I got Freeman's voice mail and left a message. *Call me ASAP.* He called back in four minutes. "What's so important, Channing?"

"Saw something in the paper about a guy getting killed at Lake Barcroft."

"Yeah?"

"You have any more information about that?"

"Why do you want to know?"

"I've got a friend who lives out there. She's feeling a little insecure. I told her I'd see what I could find out."

"You need to work on your bullshit, my friend." He sighed. "Tell *your friend* not to worry, unless she's a gangbanger. Looks like a rival gang hit. Some kind of turf battle. Three bullets in the back of the head. The vic, one Tony 'Lucky' Lin, ran with a very bad crowd. Now he's not running any more. And I guess you could say he's not 'Lucky' anymore either."

Leave the comedy to the professionals. "Okay. Thanks."

"You want to tell me why you care about this lowlife?"

"If it's a gang thing, then it's a gang thing. I'm sure my friend will be relieved. Thanks, man. I owe you."

"Damn straight," Freeman said, before clicking off.

As soon as Freeman hung up, I called Ty and filled him in. He seemed relieved. Then I called Rojo, who answered on the first ring. "Hello?"

"This is Channing."

"Oh, hey. Listen, I'm sorry about the other night. I didn't thank you and your friend for saving my ass." He paused. "And I'm also sorry about getting on your case for following me. After I had some time to think about it, I realized Thomas was just looking out for me and Joy. Which is a hell of a lot more than I can say for Joy's dad. That guy, he—"

I interrupted. "Lin's dead."

"Huh? Who's Lin?"

"Lucky Lin, the guy in the alley with the tattoo? D-E-A-D."

"Oh shit." There was a long pause, then he said, "Oh shit" again but in a much softer voice.

I told him about my conversation with Freeman—and about the three bullets in the skull—and got two more "Oh shits" in response. "Let's get together right now and discuss a few things. Joe's Joe?"

"The coffee shop? Sure. When?"

"As soon as you can," I said. "As soon as you can."

I made it there in fifteen minutes and bought two cups of coffee, one for me, one for Rojo. The least I could do. He came shambling along five minutes later looking like crap—wrinkled t-shirt, dirty jeans, two days stubble, long hair in a not-too-fashionable rat's nest. "Hey."

"Hey. Here's some coffee."

"Thanks, man. I could use it." He took a huge gulp, then slumped down in the chair across from me. "What did this cop friend of yours say, anyway?"

"I already told you everything I know."

"Who killed him?"

"He didn't know for sure. Some rival gang."

"Right, right. He think I have anything to do with it?"

"Why, did you join a gang and not tell me?"

"What? No, of course not." Rojo seemed offended.

"Yeah, I know. Just joking." I took a sip of my coffee. Lukewarm, if I was being nice. "I didn't say a word about our incident. Didn't think it was relevant."

"You didn't?" Rojo perked up a bit. "Thanks."

"Why would he think you had something to do with it? Where did you go that night after the, uh, altercation?"

He pursed his lips as he thought. "Let's see. I called..." He trailed off. "I went home. Joy was asleep."

"You called somebody?"

"What? No. I went home."

Were all musicians flaky? "Did she wake up when you got home?"

"No. She sleeps like a log."

"And the next morning?" I didn't know exactly when Lin had been killed.

"I slept late. Joy and I, uh, spent some time together, you know. Then, I just hung around."

"Did you tell Joy what happened?"

"No." Rojo kept fidgeting in his seat. Either he had a bad case of hemorrhoids or he was very uncomfortable with this line of questioning.

"What were you two arguing about?"

"When?" Rojo shifted in his seat. Ran a hand through his unruly mop, but the hair seemed to rebel, sprouting out in even more directions.

"The other night, after the show. Ty and I heard you two arguing backstage. Pretty loud."

"It was nothing. She wanted me to be done with Lin. She didn't want me to go meet him."

"But you owed him money, right?"

"Yeah, but …"

"But what?"

"Joy wanted me to pay him off at a different time. During the day. In public."

"Sounds like a good plan. Why didn't you?"

"Lin didn't want to wait. Said I'd owe him more unless I ponied up that night." Rojo shrugged. "So I went. When Joy saw me in the morning, safe and relatively sound, she was fine. She's a little high-strung."

No shit.

"I didn't kill him, you know."

"I didn't think you did."

"Then why are you asking me where I was?"

"Freeman's not stupid. He might somehow tie you to Lin. And that wouldn't be so far-fetched, would it? He did have his hands around your throat." I paused for emphasis. "They might like it if you had an alibi."

"I mean, why would I want to kill him? Because they roughed me up? Nah. I owed them some money, that's all. A complete coincidence he got killed that night."

"What have you gotten yourself into? This all seems out of character."

"Yeah, yeah. You're right. I've learned my lesson, that's for sure. No more messing around in stuff I shouldn't be." Rojo glanced around, head moving like a squirrel's. Might be his tenth coffee of the day, jumpy as he was.

"What exactly were you involved in?" I asked, keeping my voice calm and even.

He tried a smile, but it didn't work, so he went with a frown. "Nothing. Really. Nothing much. Water under the bridge now. Learned my lesson."

"I think you might feel better if you told me what was going on. Drugs? Gambling? Extortion? Loansharking? What? Maybe I could help somehow."

Rojo stared at me, trying to discern my angle. Then a cloud passed over his face and he waved me off. "Channing, don't get me wrong. I appreciate your concern. But don't worry. I've got this. Thanks, though."

I tried. "Okay. If you change your mind..."

"Yeah, thanks. Thanks." Rojo glanced all around, as if he were number one on the FBI's Most Wanted list at a brunch in Quantico.

"You might want to cut back on the coffee. I think it's making you a tad jittery."

TEN

THE DAILY ROUTINE OF a comedian, and certainly one who co-owned a comedy club, was a lot different than the routine of a normal—sane—person. Comics stayed up late and slept late, and we watched an inordinate amount of Comedy Central and the Cartoon Network. Or at least I did. Most days, I didn't get moving on anything remotely productive until mid-afternoon.

On Sundays, even more so.

That's why I wasn't very happy getting a phone call at 9:45, waking me from my slumber. "Yeah," I grumbled into the phone. It had to be someone I didn't know very well, or something very important. I was hoping for the former, then I could at least roll over and go back to sleep after I'd told them off.

"Channing? This is Patrick Wong. How are you today?"

I grumbled something about being semi-comatose.

"Hope I didn't call too early."

I bit my tongue. "What can I do for you, Patrick?" Shouldn't he and Edward be in church somewhere, smiling, kissing babies, and looking pious? Weren't they running for office?

"I've been thinking about our conversation the other day, and I'd love to talk to you about an exciting opportunity we have for you."

Exciting opportunity? "Thanks, but I'm pretty busy right now. Maybe some—"

"Please, Channing. At least hear me out."

Now that I was awake, what the hell else did I have to do? I guess my cartoons could wait. Besides, I'd like to take another run at Patrick. After the attack on Rojo, I had more questions. Lots more questions.

———

I assumed a politician's headquarters was like his car. It had to be functional, sure, but more than that, it had to deliver the right message about its owner. Korbell's campaign office reflected past successes. I wondered what Edward's would look like.

When I pulled up to the address Patrick had given me, I thought I was in the wrong place. A seedy strip mall in a low-rent part of the district. A check-cashing joint anchored one side of the shopping center. Next to it were two empty spaces, each with a *To Lease* sign plastered in the window slanted in opposite directions. Then came Edward's campaign headquarters, a storefront announced by a low-budget Wong for Congress sign hanging above the door. I parked and crossed the mostly empty lot. There was at least one saving grace about the location: a Peruvian chicken take-out joint a couple doors down sent the savory aroma of roasting chickens wafting through the air. Must be gearing up for the lunch throngs.

Even in the rundown shopping center, I was expecting something exciting, maybe ten or twenty enthusiastic volunteers working the phone bank or huddled up in a brainstorming session, trying to come up with killer campaign slogans. What I got was a room as big as a gas station mini-mart and a lone intern sitting at a beat-up metal desk working on a Sudoku puzzle. No troop of volunteers. No clever slogans being bandied about. A stack of campaign posters, stuck to thin metal stakes, leaned against one wall. A phalanx of folding chairs rested against another. Perhaps the volunteer brigade didn't report until later.

I walked up to the desk and waited patiently. A far cry from being greeted by name as soon as I entered, like I had been at Korbell's.

The intern jotted a few numbers into the blank squares of her puzzle without glancing up. She had stringy hair and a piercing through one cheek.

I cleared my throat until she finally noticed me. When she did, she stopped scribbling numbers and smiled a purely artificial grin.

"Hiya. Welcome to Edward Wong's Campaign Headquarters. A vote for Wong is a vote for progress. What can I do for you today?" The words of her overly rehearsed spiel melded into one long statement. I guess the opening "Hiya" was her way of making the lines "hers."

"Good morning. I'm here to see Patrick Wong."

"Do you have an appointment?"

An appointment? It was Sunday morning and I seemed to be the only guy in the place. "Yes, I believe he's expecting me."

She rolled her eyes at me and pulled out an iPhone. Hit a few buttons, then looked up at me, eyes narrowed. "What did you say your name was?"

"I didn't." I smiled, trying to lighten things up, but judging by her scowl, she wasn't amused. Unfortunately, I was getting used to that reaction. "My name is Channing Hayes."

A few more key taps, then she put the phone to her ear. "There's a Chandler Hayes here. Says he has an appointment." She paused and glared at me. "But I don't have one listed for him." She listened for another couple seconds, said "Whatever," then clicked off. She turned to me and shrugged. "He'll be right out."

The door to one of the two back offices opened, and Patrick Wong appeared. "Good to see you again, Channing. Thanks for coming."

In his office, Patrick sat behind a plain desk and offered me a chair—a metal folding chair. It looked like the Wongs had really embraced the "campaigning on a shoestring" angle. I didn't know if Nicole Benton was misinformed about Hao Wong's war chest, or if Hao was saving his money for a barrage of campaign ads closer to the election.

"Something to drink?"

A little early for a beer. "Water would be good."

He spun around in his chair and reached down to a dorm-sized refrigerator behind his desk. Pulled out two bottles of water. He handed me one, and raised his in the air. "Cheers."

I tapped his bottle with mine. "Shouldn't this be something like, 'To victory'?"

Like an experienced politician, his smile never wavered. He raised the bottle of Deer Park again and the plastic crinkled. "To victory." Patrick nodded at me. "How's your weekend been?"

"Fine, thanks." No need to drag the conversation down with unpleasant details.

"Good." He leaned back in his chair, pressed his lips together, trying to show me how much care he was taking with his wording. I knew better; he'd probably rehearsed his little speech before I got there. "If only more people got involved with our political process, this country would be better off. It's government *of* the people, after all." He hit me with a megawatt smile. "Don't you agree?"

"Sure. I'm also a big fan of baseball, Mom, and apple pie."

"Yes, well, we need conscientious, eager people on our campaign. People who aren't afraid to get their hands dirty, to go down those dark alleys to accomplish what's needed." When he said dark alleys, I thought I saw a twinkle in his eyes. "We also want people who are loyal and discreet. You never know what the other side is up to and, unfortunately, politics can be a shifty business." He softly tapped the top of his desk with evenly trimmed fingernails. "Of course, I'm talking about our opponent here. Sanford Korbell."

"Of course." If Artie were here, he'd have already *harrumphed* a half dozen times. I decided to save mine for later.

"Edward and I are very impressed by your efforts to help Uncle Thomas find out what happened. Even though we told you it's all taken care of, that there's nothing going on, you've continued to press on. Persistence like that should be recognized."

Patrick's head moved slightly from side to side; he probably wasn't even aware he was doing it. "My point is, you're tenacious.

And we'd love to have that tenacity working for us. Plus, we know you're a good guy because you've got Uncle Thomas as your friend. So, we'd like you to join our campaign staff."

I tried not to let my eyes bug out. "In what capacity?"

"Special projects. Punching up Edward's speeches. This and that."

"I don't know. I don't think I'm the political type." Why did I get the feeling this was a case of "*keeping your friends close and your enemies closer*"?

"It's good money."

"I'll think about it."

"That's all I ask." He propped up his smile and redirected the conversation. "So what *have* you discovered in your little investigation?"

"Not much. Nothing interesting, at least."

"Well, what might not be interesting to you, might be interesting to me. You know, politics is pretty strange."

"That's a good word for it." I nodded once and stared at the papers on his desk. Silence had a way of unnerving people who liked to talk. Politicians, for instance. My gaze stopped on a folded-up *Post*. Specifically, yesterday's *Metro* section. I'd seen that particular section not twenty-four hours earlier, when Ty threw it on my desk. "What do you know about 'Lucky' Lin?"

Patrick's mouth slowly hinged open. "Huh?"

I pointed to the newspaper. "Tony Lin. Murdered the other day. Lake Barcroft is in your district, right?"

"Oh, yes, yes. Tragic. Too many of today's young people get caught up in gangs. Just throwing away their lives." A thin sheen of perspiration covered Patrick's forehead.

"Do you have any special interest in this particular gangbanger?"

He wiped his forehead with the back of his hand, and when he realized how wet it was, the muscles in his face all seemed to contract at once. He'd transformed from a smiley politico-weasel into a fidgety wreck in the span of seconds. "The D.C. area is a rough place. People get hurt all the time. Reducing crime is a cornerstone of Edward's platform."

"I imagine that's a popular stance. Not too many people like crime. Outside of criminals, of course."

Patrick gave me an uneasy smile, not quite sure if I were joking or making some kind of point.

"Did you know Lin?"

"Not personally, no. But the Chinese community is very tight. Not much happens without everyone hearing about it. Unfortunately, this sort of thing reflects very badly on us." Patrick blinked rapidly. If I didn't know the root cause, I'd think he'd gotten some dirt in his eye.

"Did you hear who killed him?"

"No, I didn't. Another criminal, no doubt. I did hear he was into drugs, gambling, prostitution. The works." Patrick's forehead had turned into a veritable waterfall. He swiped it a couple times, but it was like bailing the *Titanic*. He collected himself, offered a sheepish smile. "I'm not feeling very well this morning. Please excuse me."

"Sure. Hope you feel better."

Patrick took a long pull from his bottle of water.

"Would you be surprised if I told you that Rojo knew Lin?"

For a second, I was afraid Patrick would do a spit-take right into my face. "Rojo? Joy's Rojo?"

How many Rojo's did Patrick know? "Yes, Joy's Rojo."

He picked up a paperclip from the top of his desk and ticked at it with a thumbnail. "Of course it would surprise me. How in the hell would Rojo be mixed up with that scumbag?" Patrick's expression was too forced, too phony. Maybe he should have taken one fewer Poly-Sci class and one more Drama class.

"Good question." I eyed him. "But you don't know the answer?"

"I have no idea. Listen, I get along with Rojo fine, but we don't really travel in the same circles."

"What circles are those?"

Patrick shrugged. "Rojo and Joy are a little on the bohemian side of things. You know, free spirits, musicians, the like."

"Comedians?"

Patrick opened his mouth to speak, then closed it. Then opened it again. "I suspect Rojo is quite a bit more unreliable than you are. I think Joy can do better, but she never really cares what her brothers think. Or her parents." He leaned forward. "Do you think Rojo had something to do with Lin's death? That Rojo's in a gang?"

"No, I don't. I've known Rojo for a few years, and he's always been a solid citizen, despite how he appears."

Patrick nodded, as if I'd just told him the secret to long life. "What makes you think Rojo knew this guy?"

"He was mugged by Lin and another guy the night Lin bought it."

"And you know this how?" Patrick asked.

"I was there. Lin had his hands around Rojo's neck at the time. We scared them off."

"We?"

103

"Me and a friend. A big friend."

"I'm sure it was just a random mugging. Wrong place, wrong time." Patrick leaned back, trying to appear casual and failing miserably. He still played with his paperclip. "Why was he being mugged?"

"Why does anyone get mugged?"

Patrick offered a tight smile. "What did Rojo tell you?"

"About the mugging?"

"About anything. We're talking about a guy who's living with my sister. If you know something, you need to tell me."

"I'm not sure what's going on here, but sooner or later I'll find out."

He faked indignation and once again, I bet he rued not taking any acting lessons. "I'm not sure I like what you're implying. My sister is involved with Rojo and I feel it's my duty to find out as much as I can about him. You'd do the same thing if it was your sister. So, what did he tell you?"

"Said he owed Lin money and things were now square."

"Did Rojo say *why* he owed Lin money?"

"Nope. Got any ideas?"

Patrick tossed the paperclip onto the desk. "Not a one. Sorry."

And I thought politicians were usually better liars.

———

On the drive back to my condo, I replayed my meeting with Patrick. Obviously he knew more than he was letting on. Obviously he wanted to "buy" my silence regarding the attack at Lee's. Obviously he was unnerved about Lin's murder. But that was as far as the obvious facts led me.

I didn't know why Lin was killed and I didn't know how the Wongs and Rojo were involved. It must have something to do with the campaign, but there were so many theoretical possibilities I'd need a lot more information if I wanted to come up with any plausible theories.

I didn't like being stonewalled, being played, like I was some kind of dim-witted dolt. I could see where Lee was justified worrying about this, and I could see why Artie was always complaining about cover-ups. And about politicians.

Right now, I wanted a nap.

I woke a couple hours later, body feeling refreshed, but my thoughts instantly reverted to Lee and the Wongs and Rojo. I considered going to the club, but it was still early and Donna would happily rope me into doing some kind of cleaning chore if I showed up with nothing to do. I didn't even need to go in tonight—Sundays were usually movie nights where I had nothing more pressing than hitting the button to bring the screen down from the ceiling and popping in a DVD or two. Even Skip could handle that.

I thought about catching up on some cartoons or going for a walk or knocking on Erin's door to chat—anything to take my mind off the Wongs. They'd insinuated themselves into all my thoughts and I needed a break.

I decided to call Skip—there wasn't much chance he'd gone in to work early, and I needed to mine his brain for a few nuggets of comedy gold. That wasn't quite correct; I wanted to bounce a few things off a juvenile mind.

Twenty minutes later, Skip ambled in. "Hey, boss. Hell of a weekend, wasn't it? Two great shows. Artie must be in hog heaven."

"Yeah. Artie likes a full house, that's for sure." I motioned toward the couch. "Take a load off." I slouched into the recliner as I watched Skip fidget for a few moments, trying to get comfortable. Like someone's puppy on an unfamiliar piece of furniture.

Finally, he stopped chasing his tail. "What's up?"

"I need a little help. With some material."

"And you asked me? Wow, I'm flattered." Skip beamed. "Shoot."

"I need about ten good minutes."

"Right. Ten minutes. Any particular topic or theme or anything?"

"Whatever eight-year-olds would think is funny."

Skip blinked. "Huh?"

"I'm going to talk to Donna's son's class about what a comic does. For career day. I thought I'd demonstrate by doing a few bits."

"And you thought of me?" Skip's face fell. "Thanks."

"Seriously, I need another fine comedy genius working on this. I thought maybe together we could come up with some suitable stuff."

His pout vanished. "Okay. Sure."

"Besides, you were eight more recently than I was." Although Skip was twenty-four years old, sometimes it was hard to tell.

He stuck his tongue out at me.

"Thanks, man. I owe you and little Seanie owes you, too."

"Yeah, yeah. Okay, I'll try to channel my inner runt."

"Good. What kinds of things do you think second-graders find funny?" I flipped the lever on the recliner and leaned the chair back until I had a good view of the ceiling. I often got some of my best ideas looking at ceilings.

Skip's voice floated through the air. "Farts, boogers, poop, pee-pee. Those are comedy go-tos for little kids."

"I see England, I see France, I see Bobby's underpants?"

"You can pick your friends and you can pick your nose, but you'd better not pick your friend's nose." Skip recited the line as if he'd been thinking about it just fifteen minutes ago. At least I had an excuse—I'd been recalling tiny tot material since Sean asked me to make an appearance in his class.

"I thought my nose was running but it's snot."

"Couldn't have said it better myself. Sounds like you don't even need my help, boss," Skip said, with a trace of disappointment.

"I was hoping to come up with something a little more, uh, original. You know, something that hasn't been around since J. Edgar Hoover was in a training bra."

"There's something to be said for old and comfortable. Like Artie."

"Old is okay when you're talking antiques, not comedy." With my legs, I pressed down on the footrest and the back of the chair straightened. I hopped out of it and went to an over-sized glass brandy snifter on the bookshelf, full of blue Penn racquetballs. I plucked one out and fit it between the remaining two digits of my left hand. For some strange reason, I always came up with better material when I squeezed a racquetball. A blue Penn racquetball. "Want one?" I asked Skip.

"Uh, no thanks."

"Suit yourself." I returned to my spot on the recliner and tipped it back again. Took a whiff of the familiar rubbery racquetball aroma. Waited for my mind to engage with the funny.

"How about a take-off of Captain Underpants? Or Sponge-Bob? Every kid is familiar with those two."

"Hmm." I squeezed the racquetball as I thought.

"How about something school-related? I mean, doesn't every kid hate school? Maybe you could riff on bad teachers and hard tests. Maybe something about bad teachers farting while they gave hard tests."

I thought back to the last routine I did about my old English teacher, which I booted in Richmond. Maybe joking about school wasn't such a good idea.

"What about a thing on teasing girls? Or psycho lunch ladies? Or a pet hamster that escaped?"

You couldn't fault Skip for trying, but he wasn't connecting. And he was distracting me from my own ideas. Time to cut bait. "Thanks, man, but I don't think we've got the vibe going today. Let's take a break and we can regroup at a later date." I tossed the racquetball at him and he bobbled it before it bounced off his knee and rolled across the floor.

Skip looked wounded. "Okay. Sorry, but I guess I don't think like a second-grader."

Maybe in a few more years.

ELEVEN

I wasted most of Monday morning puttering around my condo, not focusing on any single task long enough to get it finished. At around two, I left for The Last Laff, but as soon as I reached Rex in my condo parking lot, Lee's Mercedes rolled up. The window glided down to reveal his grinning mug. "Hey, how about going for a little ride?" His delivery made it clear he wasn't really asking.

I shrugged and went around to the passenger side. Hopped in. "Where to?"

"We got a little invitation. From Hao and Xun." He shifted into gear. "Let's go see what they want."

We drove for about twenty minutes, first heading south, then east into Annandale. Lee had the radio on and, uncharacteristically, kept the conversation to a minimum. His knuckles were white as he strangled the steering wheel in a deathgrip the entire time.

I thought about asking what was eating him but didn't want to induce a coronary.

A mile or two inside the Beltway, Lee left the main drag on Route 50 and negotiated a maze of sidestreets until he eventually came to an industrial area, full of warehouses and nondescript offices. He slowed as we approached a spiffy, freshly painted sign reading Elm Industrial Park.

Lee turned into the main entrance and we bumped along the access road. The surface was more potholes than asphalt. The buildings had been old in the sixties, and broken windows abounded. On one side of the vast parking lot, ten vehicles—a mix of cars and trucks—decayed, missing tires and various side panels, a visible indication of the site's ideal use: dumping ground. I was a little surprised some officials from Fairfax County hadn't descended on the property owners with threats of legal action.

The spiffy sign in front of the whole sorry place reminded me of an aging movie diva who'd opted for one final facelift, ignoring the rest of her dilapidated body.

Lee slowed the car to minimize the damage, and we wound our way past half a dozen buildings until we turned a corner and pulled up in front of a drab two-story building with yellow siding. At least it was yellow now—hard to guess what the original color might have been. In contrast to the other buildings we passed, this one looked like it actually was being used for something. A small fleet of vans occupied the back of the lot near a two-bay loading dock.

"This is the place. World headquarters of Wong Enterprises."

"Looks like the Wong place to me, all right."

"I forgot how funny you are," Lee said, completely deadpan.

"Okay, I won't use that in my routine." I pointed to the crappy building. "I thought the Wongs were successful."

"Ah, do not be deceived by outward appearances. The Wongs are very successful." Lee cut the engine. "Come on. It's rude to keep people waiting."

"They're expecting us?"

"Oh yes."

We entered the building through a heavy, brown-smoked-glass door and found ourselves in a small lobby. Half the fluorescent tubes were burned out and paint peeled from the cinder block walls.

"Maybe our definitions of successful are a little different," I said.

"Patience, my friend."

A small surveillance camera hung from a corner of the ceiling. It was pointed at the door. At us. Hard to believe there was anything in this dump worth protecting.

Lee crossed the lobby toward a fire door marked *Exit*. "This way."

I fell in behind him and we ascended the back stairway one flight. Lee pushed open the door to the second floor with a barely audible grunt. Instantly, we were transformed into another world.

All the lights worked. No peeling paint. Chrome and wood trim. Etched lettering on a pair of clear glass inner doors read *Wong Enterprises*. Lee turned to me. "See? Appearances can be deceiving."

Inside, we stopped at the receptionist's desk. Behind the counter-height podium, a very attractive—and young—lady smiled sweetly. Her pink fingernails matched her lipstick, as well as her eye shadow. Ditto the pink in her dress and the pendant around her neck. A small streak of pink running through her bleached hair drew everything together. "Hello. How may I help you today?"

Lee smiled back. "We're here to see Hao. I'm his brother-in-law."

"Oh, of course. He's expecting you," Miss Pink said. "I'll take you right back." She came around her desk and I caught Lee ogling her very short pink skirt. She teetered on five-inch platform shoes. Pink, of course. "This way, please."

We followed her down a long hallway, toward the front of the building. A few people worked quietly in cubicles we passed; others huddled in a small conference room. Large, framed close-up photos of mundane objects covered the walls: plastic forks in a variety of colors, plastic pens, and plastic mugs with cutesy advertising slogans inscribed on them.

"What kind of business is Wong Enterprises in?" I whispered to Lee.

"Plastics." He nodded at a picture of some plastic toys. "And a bunch of other stuff too."

Miss Pink minced along on her skyscraper shoes, then took a left and stopped in front of an open mahogany door. "Mr. Wong. Your brother-in-law is here. I'll let Mr. X. know they've arrived." She swept her arms and we entered, Lee first.

The Great and Powerful Hao rose from the leather club chair he'd been sitting in and greeted Lee with a formal handshake. "Hello Thomas. Thank you for coming." I hadn't noticed it before, but his words were slightly accented. Unlike Lee, Hao Wong had not grown up on Long Island. He moved on to me quickly and I got a similar treatment. "Nice to see you again, Channing. Please, have a seat."

Hao gestured to the casual living-room grouping where he'd been sitting. He sat back down in his leather chair while Lee and I shared the ox-blood leather couch. Across the huge office stood a gigantic mahogany desk, as big as a Ping-Pong table. You'd have to stand up and take a few steps to retrieve something from the edge. Intricate bas-relief designs had been carved into the wood, like an ancient Asian 3-D mural.

"Nice office, Hao," Lee said, voicing what I was thinking.

"Oh, you haven't been here before?"

"I was here once, a long time ago," Lee said. "It was nice then, too."

Hao opened his mouth to respond, but before he said a word, Xun Wong entered. He strode in and came to attention before us. Hao and Thomas both rose quickly; I followed their lead, a few seconds behind.

After we all greeted each other, we sat, and Xun took the seat opposite his brother. With a quick nod toward Xun, Hao took charge of the meeting. "Thanks for coming. We'd like to discuss what happened at Edward's dinner the other night. Very unfortu-nate." He paused, for what he must have thought was enough time to lend weight to the matter, then resumed his speech. "It seems that you think something sinister is going on. That something bad will happen. I assure you," he said, then tipped his head toward Xun and corrected himself. "*We* assure you the matter is taken care of. I believe my boys told you the same, did they not?"

"Yes, they did. But ..." I trailed off.

Xun took over. "But you persisted. Why?"

"I asked him to," Lee said, coming to my defense. "I asked him to get involved in the first place, and I asked him to keep going,"

Both Xun and Hao looked as if they'd been slapped in the face. "We asked you not to get involved, Thomas. And you promised you wouldn't." Hao squeezed the words out through clenched jaw.

I could feel shame radiating from Thomas, but I also sensed anger. I thought about politely excusing myself and letting the situation turn exclusively into a family affair, but there was no way I'd throw Lee to the tigers like that. I'd stay and we could get mauled together.

"Yes, I know what I promised. And I'm sorry I broke my word. But I wanted to make sure no one got hurt. I got some bad vibes, and then when Channing—"

Hao interrupted. "Bad vibes? You sound like Joy's musician." He scoffed, then shifted back into attack mode. "Thomas. I will ask you again. Please stay out of this. Even if something were going on, it does not concern you. I know you would feel very, very bad if you destroy Edward's career." Hao let the words hang there, hoping the guilt trip would force him off their tails.

Lee didn't answer, just stared straight ahead with his mouth shut. Fury burned in his eyes, and it occurred to me the Wong-Lee family Fourth of July picnic probably didn't need firecrackers.

"Thomas? Margaret would not approve of your behavior," Hao said.

In a soft voice, Xun said, "Thomas, listen to Hao. You do not need to be involved with our little misunderstanding. You have a restaurant to run. A beautiful family to take care of. Let us handle this. We are more than capable."

Lee remained mute, but his face had now taken on a deeper shade. Something approaching burgundy.

"Then it's settled. You will stay out of this," Hao said, then glared at me. "Both of you, of course. And there's really nothing going on." He rose. "I trust our position is clear."

Lee got up, still not speaking. He drew deep breaths through his nostrils, so loud he sounded like a teakettle warming up. I half expected him to erupt in an expletive-laden ball of fire. But he just stalked from the room without as much as a glance behind him, leaving me with the two Wongs. I started after Lee, but Hao stepped in my way, blocking the exit.

In a low voice he said, "This is the second time I find you meddling in my life. First, you put Joy together with that musician. Now this. But I can tell you are not a foolish man. Your interference in this may ruin Edward's political career. Ruin his life. I am sure you do not want that on your head. I'd hate to have this talk with you again. I hope you are better at knowing your position than my brother-in-law. He thinks he means well, and he does not want anyone to get hurt, but I am afraid it is he who will get hurt, if he keeps sticking his nose where it does not belong."

He stepped even closer to me, and I caught a whiff of peppermint. "Please try to impress upon Thomas what I am telling you. I'd hate for him—or for you—to get hurt." Then he stepped sideways. "Goodbye, Mr. Hayes."

Hao and Xun both glowered at me as I hustled out the door.

I found Lee waiting in his car, motor already running. I hopped in and fastened my seat belt. I'd had enough threats and intimidation and I didn't want to end up in a headlock down some alley like Rojo. Or worse, in a bodybag like Lin. "Well, I guess that's that."

"What are you talking about?" Lee's eyes narrowed.

"End of the line. *Finito*. Mind our own p's and q's. I'm getting the pretty clear picture they don't want you—us—snooping around. That it's none of our business. Maybe they're right, maybe nothing is going on."

"If there's nothing going on, why would they care if we ask a few questions?"

"Okay. It's obvious something's going on. But it's their bed. Let them lie in it." The operative word being "lie."

"How do you think they found out you were poking around?"

I sighed. "Could be anyone I talked to. Edward or Patrick. Their security guy, Ames. Joy." I gave a little laugh. "Somehow, I don't think it was Rojo."

Finally, Lee cracked a smile. "Sorry to put you through that."

"No sweat." We drove through the ramshackle office park and I thought about Hao's fancy office. Lee was right, appearances can be deceiving. As we negotiated the potholes, I wondered what it would be like if I had any living family members. Would I get along with them, or would I be at their throats? Despite what I was witnessing with Lee's family, I would have relished the opportunity to find out.

We left the Wongs behind as we merged into traffic back on the main drag. "So, I guess that's the end of that," I said again, hoping Lee would agree with me now.

Another smile formed on Lee's face. This time, though, it was the kind of smile the villain in a James Bond movie flashed, right before telling ol' Jimmy he was about to die. "I know you're not a quitter, Channing. Not by a longshot."

I was afraid he'd say something like that.

———

Later that day, Artie and I sat in our shared office. He chewed on an unlit stogie as he reclined at his desk, feet up. I took my usual position in the very uncomfortable metal folding chair at my card table. Artie was too cheap to buy a desk for me, but I guess nothing was stopping me from buying a desk myself. Except my own cheapness. Maybe we were more alike than I wanted to admit.

"So my boy, how was your visit to Mr. Hao-Bad-Am-I Wong?"

Artie liked to give wise-ass nicknames to those he didn't care for. "How did you know I met with Wong?"

"I know all." He tapped his temple. "Plus I talked to Lee. He might have mentioned something. So, how was it?"

"About what you'd expect. Hao and his brother Xun weren't too keen on our meddling. Said they preferred to take care of things themselves."

"I'm sure they do. All those guys are alike."

"Those guys?"

"Control freaks." He plucked the stogie from his mouth and pointed it at me. Shook it twice for emphasis. "Bet they have some serious skeletons in their closets."

"What makes you say that?"

Artie tapped his temple again. "Just an old comic's intuition is all. Plus I remember Lee joking about it a few years ago. His brother-in-law seems like he has a pretty big ego he needs to protect."

"Thanks for the bulletin. They kept saying they were afraid we'd somehow screw up Edward's political career. Ha, like we have that much power."

"If our Asian Kennedys are anything like the real Kennedys, it'll take more than you two knuckleheads to screw up their careers. Just don't go driving across any bridges with them, okay?"

I ignored Artie's Chappaquiddick reference. "They do seem pretty uptight and controlling. Interesting to note that Joy found a boyfriend exactly the opposite of her brothers—and her father—isn't it? And, if Hao hates him and Lee likes him, then so much the better."

Artie got a funny look on his face. "You really like this guy, Rojo, don't you?"

"What?"

"Admit it. You like the guy."

What was this, seventh grade? I identified with Rojo. Hard-working performer, raised by a single mom, heart in the right place. If I had gotten a bad roll from the Luck Gods, I might have been in his shoes. "Why do you care?"

"Kindred spirit, perhaps?"

I hadn't thought about it like that, but … maybe. I shrugged. "Okay, I like Rojo."

"See? I knew it," Artie said.

"Yeah, you're a real genius."

"Now you're catching on."

"So tell me, genius, does the name Jimmy Fugano mean anything to you?" I asked.

Artie froze. Slowly the features on his face thawed into an expression of concern, and he expelled a breath. "Jimmy Fugano? Where'd that come from?"

"You know him?"

"Answer my question. How did his name come up?"

I recounted the argument I overheard between Rojo and Joy. "Rojo implied he knew the guy and Joy didn't seem to like it much. Now you answer *my* question."

"Shit." A long, deep sigh wended its way up from Artie's diaphragm. He massaged his forehead for a minute with his eyes closed.

When they opened, he was the picture of the sad clown. "I know Jimmy the Raisin. We go way back."

"Jimmy the Raisin? He a comic?" I moved my chair around with a screech.

"No, he isn't. And there's nothing funny about him."

"Where do you know him from?"

"From another time of my life. A time I'm not very proud of."

Something loosened inside of me. I had the unpleasant feeling I was about to learn something I would have preferred not to. But I couldn't *not* know—that would have been worse. "Go on."

"If his name came up, we've got a problem," Artie said.

"What kind of problem?" Why couldn't Artie ever get to the truth? If he had as much trouble getting to his punchlines, he never would have made it on stage.

"Let me make a few calls, my friend." He picked up the phone on his desk and stared at me.

I stared back.

"Give a guy a little privacy?"

Since when did Artie need privacy?

He pointed to the door. "Vamoose. But don't worry, as soon as I find out something, I'll get back to you."

TWELVE

ARTIE GOT BACK TO me the next day. He was waiting by the hostess stand when I got to the club, shifting his weight from one foot to the other. From the tired scowl on his face, I figured he'd been waiting a long time. Of course, sometimes Artie just scowled for the heck of it. "Glad you decided to come to work today. We got plenty of it, you know."

"Well, it beat scrubbing my toilet with a toothbrush while I listened to Pink Floyd."

"Come on, Jimmy the Raisin is waiting." He grabbed my arm and guided me toward the door.

"I thought we had work to do," I said.

"Always a wise guy. You want some info, or not?"

I offered to drive, but Artie said he felt cramped driving around in my RX-7. So we took his Cadillac. Upholstered in fine leather, plenty of headroom, an abundance of legroom. You could hold a card game in the back seat and still have space for the bar. No wonder he felt cramped in my little two-seater. Compared to mine, this was like driving a rumpus room around town.

Between Lee's ride the other day and Artie's chauffeuring today, I wasn't getting enough behind-the-wheel time. Maybe I'd take Rex for a long drive some afternoon to clear my head.

As Artie drove, I held on tightly and kept my eyes closed, except for a squinty peek now and then. I knew from experience that was the best way to keep from seeing my life flash before me. When the car finally came to a stop some twenty minutes later, we were in Falls Church, in front of a small Cape Cod with crooked shutters.

Just one of dozens of small houses with small yards in the neighborhood. A surprising number also had crooked shutters, but no nefarious conspiracy jumped out at me. "This is the place?"

"This is the place." He unlocked the doors with a click of a button.

"Before we go in, could you at least give me a hint about what we're getting ourselves into?" I'd had enough surprise meetings. If Jimmy Fugano was big trouble, I'd like to know about it. Why the hell couldn't anyone deal straight with me, anyway?

"Sure. I could." He opened his car door. "But you'll find out soon enough."

He got out, slammed his door, and trotted across the narrow street to Fugano's house. I scrambled from the car and jogged after him. Without looking back, Artie hit the lock button on his keychain and the Caddy gave a little honk.

I caught up to him on the porch. Two faux-ceramic planters flanked the front door. Whatever had been planted in them was now desiccated, like plant mummies. Or maybe Fugano had taken a short cut and planted dried flowers.

121

A dingy straw mat lay on the ground, except instead of the word "Welcome," it read "Go Away."

All in all, charming.

Artie smacked the big brass doorknocker—in the shape of a cow—against the door. Four times in rapid succession. Then he stepped back and took a deep breath. "Might as well get some fresh air now, while you can."

I took a deep breath in case Artie was being literal and not metaphoric.

The door swung open and a short, skinny guy, at least as old as Artie, glowered at us for a second. Then his eyeballs fixed on Artie and his entire face changed. "Holy fucking shit on the floor. Artie Fucking Worsham."

Like I said, charming.

"The fuck you doing here?" Fugano's right cheek twitched. "For some action? After all these years?"

"How about we come in?" Artie said, already pushing through the door. Artie wasn't much bigger than Fugano, but he seemed to throw a bigger shadow.

"Sure, sure," Fugano said, retreating. "Who's your friend?"

"This is Hayes," Artie said. "And this is Jimmy the Raisin."

"Nice to meet you." It didn't take a detective to see where he'd gotten his nickname. His face had a million creases in it. Wrinkles radiated from his mouth. Wrinkled forehead, wrinkled cheeks, wrinkles around the eyes. Even his nose had wrinkles. If someone had come up with a nickname *other* than Raisin, he would have been laughed out of town.

"You look the same as you did twenty years ago," Artie said. "Too bad."

"You always were a ball-buster," Fugano said. "For the record, you look older. A lot older."

"Got a place to sit?" Artie said.

"In here." Fugano stepped aside to reveal the room behind him. TV monitors and computers lined the walls, at least eight of each. All were turned on, all were tuned to different channels and websites. The place reminded me of a cross between a Best Buy showroom and the bridge of the starship *Enterprise*. A single chair, a swivel recliner, sat in the middle of the room—the Captain's console.

The weird thing was Artie didn't seem nonplussed in the least.

On the other hand, I was plenty "plussed." What the hell was going on?

"Let me get a couple chairs. I'll be right back." Fugano disappeared down the hallway toward the back of the house, which was pretty dark. The room we were in would have been dark too, except for the three thousand watts of light emanating from the video screens.

"What is all this?" I asked.

"Control center. Jimmy's a bookie," Artie said, matter-of-factly. "A two-bit, piece-of-shit, good-for-nothing punk, slimy low-down skunk."

Shel Silverstein, Artie wasn't. "And how do you know him?"

"We used to do business together."

"What kind of business?"

"Bookie business."

I opened my mouth to interrogate him further, but Fugano entered the room, schlepping two kitchen chairs with avocado-and-yellow-striped vinyl seats. Forty years ago they might have been

123

fashionable—if you were color-blind. "Here you go." He set them down next to each other, then shuffled over to command central and plopped down in the recliner. He pressed a lever on the side and a footrest popped out, the perfect picture of an old geezer. Was that how I looked when I sat in my chair? "Been a long time, Artie."

"Not long enough. And if it wasn't for Channing here, it would have been never."

"I always liked it when you sweet-talked me." Fugano swiveled in my direction. As he did, a large, holster-like contraption swung into view, hanging off one side of the chair. It held four or five remote controls. He fingered them absently while he spoke. "So what can I do for you? My associates usually handle the day-to-day business at my office. It's closer to the customers, you know." He jutted his chin at Artie. "But for an old friend, I'll take your action. What sparks your interest?"

"I think you have the wrong—" I said.

Artie interrupted me. "I don't want any action, and he doesn't want any action. He wants some information."

Fugano's cheek twitched again, and he looked like a chipmunk with something caught in its teeth. "What kind of information?"

"Do you know a guy named Rojo?" Artie asked. I guessed he was going to do all the talking, which was fine with me. I was still trying to wrap my head around the idea Artie had dealings with this guy. And Rojo, too. My world might not be shattering, but it *was* shaking a bit.

"Why do you want to know?"

"A very close personal friend of mine is concerned for his family's well-being. Your name came up in his investigation of some

124

unpleasant matters." Artie perched on the edge of his vinyl seat. I knew he wanted to jump up and start pummeling Fugano. I could tell by the stultified language and his bright red cheeks, as well as his clenched fists. I'm sure Fugano felt some of the "love" too, but it didn't seem to change his demeanor in any noticeable fashion.

In fact, Fugano seemed to relax more. "Hmm. Rojo. Lemme think a minute." He stroked his chin absurdly.

"How 'bout we cut the shit? How many Jimmy 'The Raisin' Fuganos are there around here? He knows you and you know him. How long has he been a client?" Artie was getting wound up and I'd witnessed Amped-up Artie before. Fugano better watch out.

Fugano ignored Artie's question and turned to face me. "Your friend here was a big boxing fan. Back in the seventies. Ah, it was a good time for the sport then. Ali, Frazier, Foreman. Sugar Ray Leonard. Those were the days."

Out of the corner of my eyes, I caught a glimpse of Artie. His lips were pressed together, a thin white slash of anger. It wouldn't have totally surprised me to see the top of his scalp shoot off, followed by an eruption of gray matter.

"Yeah, Artie was an underdog man. Liked to bet on the little guy. Ain't that right?" Fugano smirked in Artie's direction, clearly enjoying his torment.

"What about Rojo?" Artie managed, through clenched teeth.

"What was it? Four or five years? Every week you'd come by. We'd shoot the shit for a while, talk about stuff. We were pretty good pals back then. And you were a steady customer, too. I appreciated that. Loyalty means a lot to me. Some weeks it was only a hundred bucks, other weeks it was five bills. Sometimes you won. Sometimes you lost. You sure seemed to enjoy it, that's for sure."

He snapped his fingers. "Then all of a sudden you stopped coming by. Quit cold turkey. In a weird way, I was kinda proud of you. I missed you, but I knew it was the right thing for you to do, at the right time."

"It might have taken me awhile, but I saw the light," Artie said.

I didn't know what to say. Watching this chucklehead dredge up Artie's unpleasant past made me squirm. And it was sure making Artie uncomfortable. But I knew Artie would hold it together, for Lee's sake. He wanted the information and if he had to suffer some indignity, then that was the price of doing business.

"Now, about Rojo," Artie said. His cheeks had muted from red to pink. Maybe we were over the hump now.

"What would it do for business if I told stories about my clients?" Fugano said.

"What would it do for business if I told the cops about your business?" Artie countered.

Fugano's lips parted slightly and the tip of his tongue poked out. Then he smiled, a broad one. "Touché. I don't think you'd actually follow through with that, but I admire your chutzpah. Reminds me of the good old days. Really, I guess it doesn't matter. Rojo's not a client anymore."

"But he was?" I asked. I'd never had an inkling that Rojo liked to gamble. Of course, I hadn't known about Artie either.

A reluctant nod. "Yeah, was, was, was. Pity, too. Seemed like an okay guy, hate to lose him. Why do you want to know, anyway?"

Artie waved him off. "What happened? Why is he a *former* client?"

"He'd been doing business with me for about a year. Sporadic at first, then more regular. More action, too. He probably lost more

126

than he won, but you know I don't track that too closely. It doesn't matter much to me. I make my living off the vig."

The vigorish was the bookie's cut, win or lose. Most books liked to minimize their risks and have equal amounts of action on each side of the bet. That's why point spreads were invented. This whole gambling thing fascinated me, more so now that I knew Artie had been heavily involved. "What did he bet on?"

"You name it. Like Artie, he never met a bet he didn't like."

"Let's get back to Rojo," Artie said. "Did he quit?"

Fugano caressed the leather armrest as he spoke. "Not exactly. Let me see if I can remember the chain of events—my memory isn't what it used to be, you know. He'd fallen behind on his payments, so I sent out my usual little encouraging reminder. He didn't—"

I practically jumped off my chair. "Did your reminder involve masked men and baseball bats?"

"What? No, of course not. I'm more compassionate than that. Jesus, who do you take me for? If I went around breaking kneecaps, who'd want to do business with me? Shit, I just texted him." Fugano actually looked offended. "I didn't hear back right away, so I texted him again. Still nothing. Which was unusual. Like I said, Rojo was a good guy—always paid up. Often late, but there was never any big problem. Anyway, he owed me a little more than normal, so I was beginning to wonder." He stopped talking.

"And then . . ." Artie prompted.

"And then I get this phone call. Some guy wants to pay Rojo's debt off. Can you believe that? Don't get too many anonymous donors around here." Fugano did the chin thing toward Artie again. "Ain't that right?"

Artie didn't answer, just gave a limp nod. He'd slumped in his chair, all the fire in his belly now quenched. Evidently, the interrogation had been ceded to me. "Who was it?"

"How the hell should I know? Anonymous is anonymous. I don't care if it's the Pope of England as long as he's pushing money in my direction."

"When was this?"

"About a week ago. More or less."

Right around the beginning of this mess. "So some anonymous guy paid off Rojo's debt? About how much are we talking here?"

Fugano's head slowly tilted down, as if he were consulting a ledger on the stained carpet. "Eighteen grand. Give or take."

A significant chunk of change. Especially for a starving musician.

"And get this. Mr. Anonymous threw in an extra two large if I promised not to take any more action from him." He shrugged. "I took the payoff. Rojo was a nice guy and all, but I got the feeling something was up. I don't need that kind of hassle. I run a nice, clean, friendly book here. Just like in Vegas, only more convenient. And it's not as hot, either."

"What gave you the feeling something was up?" I asked.

A nervous grin appeared on Fugano's craggy face. "Well, this guy gave me two grand to cut off Rojo, but he also said if I didn't, he'd have to make a house call. And this sure wasn't no doctor. I don't like house calls, present company excepted, of course." He winked at Artie, and every crevice in the Raisin's face seemed to deepen.

———

We left Fugano in his command chair and, as soon as we got outside, we both took deep breaths. Maybe there *was* something about the air in there.

Once we made it to the front seat of Artie's car, I started in on him. "Why didn't you ever mention your gambling?"

He stuck the keys in the ignition, but didn't turn the engine on. "Channing, it was a long time ago. Who wants to dredge up bad memories? I was a different person back then. Unhappy. Looking for something. Not sure what, just … something. I don't know …" He stared through the windshield into space.

I'd known Artie for years, and I thought I'd *really* known him, but every once in awhile, I found out something that shook me. Earlier this year, I'd learned about his partnership with another comic and rival club owner named Reed. I guess everybody had times in their lives they weren't especially proud of. I knew I had my share. "Why'd you stop cold turkey?"

"I wish I could say it was my idea, but it was Sophie's. She saved me from all that by delivering an ultimatum. I remember it well. We were at Stu's Super Sub Shop, sitting in a booth in the back, when she delivered the knockout blow."

"So to speak."

A wry smile. "Yeah. It wasn't only boxing I bet on. Football, baseball, basketball. Cards. Craps. If you could bet on it, I'd be interested. Didn't you ever notice I never gamble when we go to AC or Vegas?"

"Yeah, I noticed." I just figured Artie was too cheap to risk losing. He loved his money more than anyone else I knew, and I figured he couldn't bear the thought of parting with it.

"It was a dark chapter in my life, but luckily for me, I married a very forceful—and forgiving—lady. Now the only gamble in my life is The Last Laff. Speaking of which, we'd better get back there before Donna and Skip decide to turn it into a smoothie shop." He started the engine. "Do me a favor, will you? Don't mention this to anyone, okay? I'd hate for people to think Artie Worsham has a weakness."

"Sure thing, Artie." I pondered all my weaknesses as we drove back to the club.

THIRTEEN

I LEFT THE CLUB early Tuesday night, got home around midnight, and fixed a peanut butter and jelly sandwich. With surgical precision, I trimmed the crusts off two slices of white bread, then slathered one with Skippy and the other with strawberry jam. Slapped the two halves together and I was in business. Being a waste-hater, I balled up the crusts and popped them into my mouth as an appetizer. *Dee-lish.*

I grabbed a Sprite to wash down the whole gooey mess.

As I ate, I flipped on the tube, caught some of Leno, then switched over and caught some of Letterman. Most people had a preference, but I liked them both. Usually, I chose based on who their guests were.

With two bites left in my sandwich, my cell phone rang. I scooped it up and glanced at the number. Didn't recognize it. "Hello?"

"Channing, thank God, this is Joy Wong. You've got to come right over." Her words shot out of the phone, but she spoke in a whisper.

"What's wrong?"

"Please, you've got to come over. I don't know who else to call."

"Joy, slow down and tell me what's going on."

"I can't call my parents, and I can't call Uncle Thomas. They'd just explode. You know where we live, right? Please hurry."

"Look, Joy, if it's an emergency, call 911. Otherwise—"

"Please, it's important. And hurry." She clicked off.

The call for help reminded me of one I'd gotten months earlier when a comic who was performing at our club got handcuffed to the bedframe in our comedy condo as part of a sexcapade. That hadn't ended well. Hopefully, this episode would.

I debated calling 911 myself, but something about Joy's pleading led me to believe that, while important in her mind, no one was in real danger. At least that's what I told myself as I grabbed my keys, threw on my shoes, and raced out the door.

I made it to their apartment and zipped into a parking space. Rex seemed out of place among all the pickups and beat-up American sedans. I supposed it wouldn't hurt him to mingle a bit. I locked the door and jogged through an arched walkway toward the rear of the building. I found the back stairs and took them two at a time, feet clanging on the metal treads. Second door on the right. I knocked softly on the doorjamb, figuring Joy would be listening for me.

She was, because the door cracked open five seconds later and she peeked out. A security chain pulled taut. The door closed for a second, followed by the rattle of the chain being undone. Then the door swung open fully.

"Thank you for coming." Joy's eyes were red and she sniffled between words. She backhanded away a few tears. "In here."

She led me past the kitchen—sink full of dirty dishes, crumbs on the counters—and down a short hallway to a bedroom. Rojo sprawled on the bed, still in his clothes, a bag of frozen peas covering his left eye. When he saw me, he turned to Joy. "I told you I was fine. We don't need him. Jesus, I'm okay."

"You don't look okay. In fact, you look like shit," I said.

"I told you not to call anyone." Rojo tried to raise himself higher in the bed, but winced and clutched at his chest as he did. He slumped down again and his good eye closed.

"Somebody beat him up," Joy said.

Rojo remained inert.

"You should take him to the ER," I said, taking Joy's cue and stating the obvious, but hoping my opinion might have a little weight. After all, she called me over for some reason. I watched carefully, making sure Rojo's chest moved. Up and down, up and down.

"No!" Rojo's functioning eye reopened. "I'm okay. Just need a little rest is all."

"What the hell happened?" I asked.

"I fell," Rojo said, at the exact time Joy said, "He got his ass kicked."

"Cut the shit, Rojo. Next time, they might kill you," Joy said, her frustration evident. This wasn't the first time they'd been through this.

"*Who* might kill him?" I asked.

"Nobody. I told you. I slipped and fell down some stairs. Banged up my ribs, got poked in the eye. I'm a klutz."

"Who did this to you?"

"Please, can't you leave me alone?" He pulled the bag of peas away from his face. His eye had completely shut and looked almost purple. That had to smart. It hurt me, just looking at it.

"Can you talk some sense into him? He's as stubborn as my father," Joy said. With an exasperated sigh, she fled the room.

I took a seat on the edge of the bed, careful not to make waves on the mattress. "This is the second time you've been attacked in the past week—that I know about. What gives?"

"Look. I can tell you a few things, but you've got to promise you won't tell Joy. She worries." He shifted positions and it looked for a moment like he might pass out from the pain. Cracked ribs can be very painful, if that's what he had. Bruised organs could be painful, too.

"I don't think she's buying your story about falling. I think she's pretty worried, as is. Maybe the truth would make her feel less worried. The devil you know, and all that."

"Just don't tell her, okay? I'll get around to it." He gave me a pitiful look. "Please?"

"Why don't you tell me and trust me to exercise my own judgment about telling her?"

He chewed on that for a moment, then sighed. Then winced again. "Okay. Do me a favor, will you? Hand me that water."

I got up and handed him the glass of water from the nightstand. Next to it was an economy bottle of Advil, cap off. He'd need something a little stronger than that for broken ribs.

He downed some water and handed the glass back, arm trembling with the effort. "Thanks."

I returned to my position at the foot of the bed. "So?"

"So I didn't fall. Joy was right; I got my ass kicked."

No shit. "Who did it?"

"I don't know. Two guys jumped me from behind. It was dark. They wore ski masks."

I might not be Sherlock Holmes, but I knew a clue. "Guys in ski masks? Like the guys who busted up Lee's?"

Rojo shrugged, which was followed quickly by a grimace. Those guys had done quite a number on him. "Did they use baseball bats?" I asked.

"I don't think so. That might have *really* hurt." Grimace, grimace, wince.

"Anything else about those guys you can remember?"

"They smelled bad."

I couldn't tell if he were joking, so I just ignored him. "I talked with Jimmy the Raisin today."

Rojo's good eye flashed. "Who?"

"Jimmy Fugano. Your bookie. As Joy said, cut the shit. I know about the gambling."

He stared at me, a silent Cyclops, for what seemed like a minute. "Okay. So you know. I place a few bets now and then. It's under control. I could go to AC, but this is more convenient. Sue me." He glanced at something over my shoulder, then something off to the side.

I wondered if he knew his debts had been paid and Fugano had cut him off. "Is that what was going on the night in the alley? Paying off a gambling debt?"

Rojo gave me the stink-eye again. If I wasn't so grounded, I might have been put off, but I simply waited him out. After a minute he cracked. "Something like that. That business is done with."

"So who would want to beat the crap out of you?"

"Nobody I can think of. Mistaken identity perhaps. All us Mexicans look alike."

All Mexicans had red-tinted hair? "Believe it or not, I'm trying to help you. And so is Joy. But we can't if you don't tell us what's going on."

"I told you, it's all taken care of. Tonight's attack was just a random mugging."

"And I'm Chris Rock." I rose. "If you change your mind and really want some help with your mess, let me know. Otherwise, I'm outta here. Take care, Rojo."

I left without looking back, waiting for him to call my name, to reach out to me asking for my assistance. But I made it out the bedroom door hearing nothing but silence. In the living area, Joy sat curled up on the couch holding a bottle of Corona to her forehead. She wore a Dark Danger t-shirt and jeans, barefoot. She eyed me but didn't speak.

I walked over and sat on a chair next to the couch. "Thanks for calling me."

She tipped the bottle in my direction. Clearly, she was upset. Maybe she feared I'd notice her wavering voice if she spoke.

"Do you know what's going on here?" I asked, keeping my voice soft and smooth.

She shook her head, then spoke. "Not really. Something about gambling. I don't suppose he ever talked to you about it?"

"Nope. You have any details?"

Another head shake.

"Any idea who's using your boyfriend for a punching bag?"

"No. Every time I try to ask, he shuts me out. Like whenever I ask about his family or about him growing up."

I sat back. I'd asked some of the same questions, here and there, about Rojo's background and gotten the same vague, evasive responses. "He never talked to you about his childhood?"

"Not much. Had a drunk for a father and a mouse for a mother. Father told him he wanted a son who would be better than 'just a guitar player.' What an asshole." Joy sipped from her beer. "Do you know how Rojo got his name?"

"Tell me."

"When he was fourteen or fifteen, he highlighted his hair red, as a goof. His father saw it and went ballistic. Told him no son of his dyed his hair. That was something girls did. Demanded that Rojo either get the dye washed out or cut his hair off. Rojo refused. In fact, the next week, Rojo got his whole head dyed red. Really red. Then all his friends and everybody started calling him Rojo. His mother, his aunts. Everybody thought it was cute, and the name stuck."

"Seems relatively harmless to me."

"I know, right? But his father refused to ever call him Rojo, even after the initial stink had died down. Rojo thinks that every time his father saw the red hair, he fumed inside. I guess that was part of the reason Rojo kept it that way." Joy finished her beer and set the bottle down on the floor by the couch. "Funny what shapes a person."

"Is Rojo still in touch with his parents?"

"Not really. Calls his mom once in awhile. She has trouble keeping a job. Rojo sends her some money now and then."

"Father?"

Joy smirked. "Dead. Ironic. He was killed last year by a drunk driver on one of the rare occasions *he* was sober."

"How did Rojo take it?"

"Said he was okay with it. Deep down, though, I think he was a little miffed he didn't get the chance to show his father he would be a success in life."

"Maybe he's trying to impress your father, as a substitute." One benefit of being in therapy myself was an improved insight into other people's motives.

"Well, that's some more irony, because my father treats him like shit, too. Rojo doesn't deserve that."

"Maybe you father will come around."

Joy looked at me like I was a Martian. "Yeah, right. Guess you don't know my father very well." She looked away, eyes moist.

"Listen, Joy, I'm sorry—"

"Did you know Rojo volunteers at a music camp for disadvantaged youths?"

"No."

"Well he does. When we told my father about it, he just asked Rojo when he was going to get a paying job. Like a real man."

"That's rough," I said.

"Rojo's trying so hard to fit in with my family. I keep telling him not to worry about it. It's futile. There's nothing he can do to win them over, at least not my father. Too old-world. Too fucking stubborn." A few tears leaked out. "And now. This gambling thing… it doesn't sound like Rojo. I'm afraid he's gotten himself mixed up in something he can't get out of. I'm afraid he's not going to come home one day."

We agreed on one thing—this didn't sound like Rojo. "I'd like to help. I've got a friend who's a cop, and I can get him involved if you want. Or I can talk to your Uncle Thomas—I'm sure he can help somehow. I've seen this before with some of my comic friends. They get into something over their head and they don't know what to do about it, who to trust. I'm saying to you, right now, you can trust me to do what I think is right for Rojo."

Joy swallowed, and in a very tiny voice said, "Thanks."

———

Donna, Skip, and I crowded around the computer on Artie's desk. Skip sat in Artie's throne, I'd pulled up my folding chair, and Donna stood behind us breathing down our necks, figuratively as well as literally. Artie had exercised good sense and bolted when he heard we were going to update the club's website. I think he was still a little rattled about our visit to Jimmy the Raisin yesterday. Truth be told, I was too.

Working on the website was a team effort. None of us knew how to do everything that was needed; we were the three-headed dog Cerberus with a keyboard and only slightly less of a collective temper.

"What if we moved the title from here," Skip said, pointing to the upper portion of the screen, "to here?" His finger tapped the lower right of the monitor.

"That's just plain stupid," Donna said. "That's the title. By definition, a title tells people what to expect on the page. Putting it at the bottom defeats the purpose."

Skip grunted. He knew some of the HTML formatting stuff but had no sense of design. I knew how to manipulate images using Photoshop, but didn't have much sense of overall design either. Donna, on the other hand, had a pretty good eye, but was something of a techno-phobe. Plus she never passed up a chance to boss us around. That's why the three of us got together once a week and turned the twenty-minute chore of updating the website into a two-hour insult-fest. I guess it beat mopping the floors. Usually.

Right now, we were trying to update the performance schedules for the next two months, which meant Skip had control of the mouse. He clicked on this and that, testing out new fonts and colors, taking full advantage of his time in the driver's seat. It irked me a little, but I know it *really* pissed off Donna.

"Come on. Type in the new dates and let's be done with this. I've got real work to do."

After Skip did his thing, Donna would need my help to tweak the online menu, and then I'd fiddle with the graphics. Artie wasn't too keen on what we'd done last month and I needed to futz with it a bit.

The font Skip was working with now looked like it belonged on a funeral home's website, not a comedy club's.

Donna grabbed at the mouse, but Skip yanked his hand away. "What is it with you guys, anyway? You know, I have to pick out all of Tony's clothes so he looks presentable. You should get in touch with your inner woman. Be stylish, yet assertive."

"I'm still looking to get in touch with an outer woman," Skip said. "And the more touching the better." He clicked a few times, then started inputting names and dates and times of future performances on our Events page. "Hey, I didn't know The Laugh Machine is booked for next month. Nice."

"Yeah, Artie has a thing for them." They were an improv group consisting of two men and two women, all in their twenties and all quite attractive. They were Squeakies—Artie's generic term for comics who worked clean—and they performed like they mainlined Red Bull. Best of all, they were funny.

"Are the rumors about them true?" Skip asked.

Donna perked up. "What rumors?"

"Didn't you notice, the last time they played here? How they were always leering at each other and playing grab-ass when they thought nobody was looking?"

"Can't say I noticed," I said.

"Me neither." Donna exhaled and her breath tickled the top of my head. I leaned forward a little.

"I think they had a *ménage a quatre* going. We should start calling them The Sex Machine." Skip glanced at me to get my reaction, but I maintained a poker face. It took more than a little fooling around to get a rise out of me. This *was* the world of comedy we were talking about.

"Oh for Pete's sake," Donna said. "You're just jealous they didn't invite you to join in."

"I don't know the meaning of the word *jealous*," Skip said.

"You don't know the meaning of half the words we use around here. Of course that doesn't stop you from trying to use them," Donna said.

"Hardy har har." He went back to the next name on the list and started banging the keys.

Even if The Laugh Machine was more freaky than Squeakie, who cared? Their personal lives didn't matter to me, and I'm sure Artie didn't give a whit either as long as they brought in the crowds. The kind of people who cared probably weren't among our core group of customers.

Donna tapped me on the shoulder while Skip hunched over the keyboard. "Any more showdowns in alleys?"

I wasn't sure if Donna had heard about Lin's death yet, but I didn't want to get into it now. Or ever, for that matter. "No more showdowns. I think I'll be staying out of alleys, too." Some advice Rojo should heed.

"You're smarter than you look."

"Uh, thanks." I scooted my chair a little to the side to give Skip more elbow room, and Donna inched forward to fill the gap. I was curious if she knew about Artie's gambling history but wasn't quite sure how to broach the subject. *Hey, did you know Artie is a reformed gambleaholic?* didn't sound right. I'd have to figure out a way to finesse it sometime when Skip wasn't within earshot.

Skip mumbled a name, then typed it in.

"See? I knew you could do it," Donna said to Skip. Then she turned to me. "Ready for your Career Day appearance? Seanie's been talking about it nonstop to whoever will listen."

Skip stopped typing. "Channing's all jammed up on that. He even asked me to help him."

"Help him? With what?" Donna's voice took on that cautious quality it got sometimes, usually when Artie was about to spring some new scheme on us.

"His routine." Skip started typing again, but the fingers seemed to move more slowly on the keyboard.

"Your routine? What routine?" Donna asked. "Don't go crazy with this. All you need to do is tell the class what a comic does and tell a few jokes. You don't have to put on a show for them. The attention span of most second-graders is less than Skip's, and you never know what mood they'll be in. Just smile, tell them you try to make people laugh like that sweet Carrot Top, and make Seanie proud."

"Relax. I'm not going to mess this up. I want them to like me. But I think it's better to show them what I do rather than tell them." I turned my head just enough to see Donna's worried expression. "Besides, who doesn't like to laugh?"

"These are seven- and eight-year-olds. Do you even *know* any clean jokes?"

"Funny." Compared to most comics, my act was pretty clean. I wasn't a Squeakie by any means, but no one ever called me blue, either.

"That's what he wanted my help with. Clean, wholesome jokes," Skip said, as he stopped typing again. No wonder it took us forever to get the update done. Skip got distracted by every comment—those directed at him and those directed at anyone else, too.

"Having Skip help you out doesn't make me feel any better, Channing. If Sean gets suspended, I'm coming after you. And when I'm through, Tony will…" She didn't have to finish her thought. Her husband knew his way around a nail gun.

"Don't worry. How hard can it be to make some kids laugh?" I asked, picturing the class's response to the best fart joke I could muster. Thirty cherubic faces contorted with giggles. *Awesome.*

———

An hour and a half later, we'd finished updating the website. Donna and Skip left the office to do whatever it was they had to do, and even though Artie wasn't around, I sat at my card table desk. I pulled out my notebook and flipped it open to the last page

I'd been working on. I'd ditched the "returning-to-high-school" bit. Too hacky. I needed something fresh.

I sat there, biting the end of my pen, staring at the wall.

I sat that way for a long time.

I grabbed a racquetball from a pencil cup I kept on my desk and squeezed it while I thought. Closed my eyes.

Nothing.

My fruitless meditation was interrupted by a ringing cell phone. Mine. "Hello?"

"Channing? This is Nicole Benton. From Congressman Korbell's office. How are you?"

"I'm fine. How are you?"

"Good. I haven't heard from you, and I was wondering if you'd decided to join our team."

"Do you call all your prospective campaign supporters?" I pictured her in front of a big whiteboard, going down a list of names and checking them off after each follow-up phone call.

"Which would impress you more? If I said I did? Or if I said I didn't?"

Artie might call me dense at times, but I knew flirting when I heard it. "I'm just impressed you remembered my name."

She laughed, a throaty one, the kind I used to get when I landed a good punch line. "So? Have you given it some thought?"

I felt a little like a jerk maintaining my ruse, but until I got some answers about what was going on with the Wongs, I didn't want to burn any bridges. "Well, I brought it up to my partner, Artie, and we're still talking about the possibility of doing an event here."

"Excellent! We'll toss around a few ideas about it on our end—you know, so we'll be prepared to move forward quickly—while you keep thinking about it. Don't forget, not only will it be good for the Congressman, but it will be good for your club too. Being associated with a winner never hurts."

"Right. Artie likes winners, that's for sure."

"Artie sounds like my kind of guy." She paused. "You know, I'd like to take you up on your offer to come to your club. I can always use a good laugh, and I can probably manage to take one night off before the election."

"Well, let me consult the schedule, find a good comic." I made some noise shuffling papers on my desk. I'd love to show Nicole the club, but it would have to wait until I didn't feel guilty being some kind of double agent. "I think we've got someone good coming next month. Can I give you a call?"

"You're not just blowing me off, are you? I've got powerful friends, you know." She laughed softly.

"Not at all. I'll make a note of it on my calendar. *Show Nicole the club*. There, all set."

"Okay then, Channing. If I don't hear from you in a few days or so about the fundraising event, I'll give you a call, okay?"

"Sure," I said. Hopefully, I'd know what was going on with Rojo and the Wongs by then.

"Goodbye." She clicked off.

Another friendly exchange with Team Korbell.

I returned to my comedy notebook, but before I could even come up with an excuse to procrastinate further, a knock on the door startled me.

"Hey there." An old guy, hunched over, leaned against the doorjamb. He must have been loitering in the hallway, waiting for me to finish my call.

"Hey."

"Artie around?" he asked, in a gravelly voice. He wore a pair of old khakis, dirt around the pockets, and old-man sneakers, the kind that fastened with Velcro. Liver spots covered his hands like polka dots.

"Nope, I haven't seen him yet. Sorry."

"Well, I'm early. He said to meet him at seven."

It was only about 5:15. Early for Artie, late for the Early Bird Special. "Come in. Have a seat."

The old guy limped in and plopped down in Artie's chair.

I closed my comedy notebook. "I'm Channing Hayes."

He nodded. "Nice to meet you. Artie's told me a lot about you. I'm Wendell White."

Wendell White! Holy shit! I'd heard stories about him, from other comics, mostly old ones, and from Artie himself. White was a legend who'd made his name as a "club comic." Great performing on stage at clubs, but TV had passed him by with nothing more than a couple spots with Johnny. I'd seen pictures of him, although nothing taken in the last forty years. I jumped up and shook his hand. Pumped it like a well handle, actually. "It's a true pleasure. I've heard great things about you." I know I sounded like a fanboy, but I didn't care. *Wendell White!* "I can't believe you're here."

His twinkling eyes reflected my adulation. "Artie and I go way back. Spent a couple summers touring the Borscht Belt together. A few years ago that was..."

146

"I've heard stories."

"Knowing Artie, some of them might even be true." White started coughing, and his jag lasted a full minute.

"You all right?"

"Sure, sure. Must be allergic to something in here. Artie got a cat in his desk?" He winked at me.

"So, uh, what brings you to town?" Wendell White wasn't on the schedule, as far as I knew. Of course, Artie didn't always keep me apprised of what he had planned.

"Just passing through on my tour. You know how it is."

Wendell White had to be at least eighty, maybe eighty-five, and I hadn't heard he was still working. "Sure. Where are you scheduled next?"

"Let's see. I'm doing an old folks' home in Baltimore tomorrow night. Actually, it's tomorrow evening. They can't stay up too late, you know." He winked again. For a split-second, I worried the eye wouldn't open back up. "Then I'm going to emcee a talent show in Ocean City. Next weekend, I'm doing a Bar Mitzvah."

A Bar Mitzvah? Was he kidding?

He must have read my mind. Or my astonished expression. "I'm not kidding. My time in the big spotlight ended decades ago, but I still hit the road. No job too small. You know why I still do it? It's not the babes, although they're nice—thank God for pharmacological advances. And it's not the money. I barely make enough to keep me in Big Bites and Slurpees. No, it's because I have fun doing what I'm doing. Fun is the key. As a kid, I was uptight and anxious, always worried about how I was performing and how to climb the next rung on the ladder. But I finally learned. Youth is wasted on the young. And the stupid. It's all about having fun." He eyed me. "You are having fun, aren't you?"

"I try. I mean, sure, I have fun." First Lizzy Northcutt told me I didn't seem like I was having fun, and now Wendell White, whom I'd never met before, was giving me the "have-more-fun" lecture. Was I wearing a hangdog expression around town? Were my on-stage struggles affecting my day-to-day moods?

"Look. If you're not having fun with what you're doing, it's time to do something else. Life's too short." White coughed again. I hoped he didn't have a stroke in the office—Artie would be pissed at me for sure.

"Most of the time, it's great. But … you know. Sometimes you're just not in the zone."

White chuckled. "Ah, the mystical zone. You trying to tell me you're blocked? In a slump? Coming up dry?"

"Uh, well …"

"Hogwash. Sit your ass down and keep writing. Most of what we write is shit anyway. It's a numbers game. Write enough material, and some of it is bound to be good. You can't wait for those gems to fall into your lap or you'll be waiting forever." He pointed a polka-dotted, bony finger at me. "Artie speaks very highly of you. Says you've got a lot of potential and a good head on your shoulders. Not unhinged, like a lot of young comics these days. You've got to keep at it and great things will come your way. Now, I've got a burning question. Which way to the men's room?"

FOURTEEN

ARTIE LEFT ME TO close the club that night. He and Wendell White had departed hours ago, no doubt off to a quieter place to rehash—and revise—old adventures. I didn't mind; in fact, it was kinda nice not to have Artie peering over my shoulder. I suppose there was a late, late night party scene somewhere in the D.C. Metro area, but here in Vienna, Virginia, things were stone-cold quiet and had been for hours.

As usual, I went straight home. Last year, that would have meant home to Lauren. Since her death, I'd been coming home to an empty condo. I preferred coming home to Lauren.

But life has its own plans so I sucked it up the best I could, and every day and night was getting easier. Tonight, I walked down the hall to my apartment at the end, tip-toeing out of courtesy to my neighbors, many of whom I'd never met.

I thought about seeing if Erin was awake, but I chickened out. I fell asleep watching some old, stupid movie on Comedy Central.

When I woke up, that mystery nibbling at the back of my mind had finally been solved. Or at least I thought so. I had a darn good idea who paid off Rojo's debt to Jimmy the Raisin.

It was almost noon by the time I got showered and dressed, and my stomach was delivering its *feedme* monologue, consisting mostly of gurgles and groans, when I called Lee and asked him what he was doing for lunch. Of course, I knew the answer, and I also knew he'd invite me to the restaurant to join him. He always did.

I told him I'd be there in twenty minutes.

When I got there, the hostess ushered me back to Lee's table. A few dishes of appetizers were waiting for me, along with Lee. I flopped into the booth and touched a spring roll with the tip of my finger. Still hot. "Hey, thanks for inviting me."

"Anytime. You know that. I thought we might have a few things to talk about." He leaned across the table and whispered. "Like what you've found out?" Sitting back, he picked up his spring roll and took a bite.

I decided to omit the part about Rojo getting the snot beat out of him, at least until I had Rojo's okay. Besides, I needed to get the answer I came for. "You're a generous guy, Lee."

He put his spring roll down and cocked his head at me.

"I know what you did for Rojo."

"What did I do?" Lee asked. "Exactly?"

"Paid off his gambling debt."

Lee's jaw dropped. "I don't think I'm going to like this explanation. But you have to tell me what's going on. I didn't pay anything to anybody."

"Come on, man. Don't play innocent with me."

Lee stared at me. "Channing, I'm not the one playing around. Please tell me what's going on."

I'd been so sure Lee was Rojo's white knight. I hadn't wanted to divulge Rojo's business, but I'd opened the door, and I couldn't leave Lee hanging. I took a deep breath and recounted what I'd learned about Rojo's gambling.

Lee ran a hand through his hair. "Whoa. I never would have guessed. You sure?"

"Got it straight from his bookie's mouth."

"His bookie? Rojo has a bookie?"

"Yes he does, complete with a bookie name. Jimmy the Raisin."

Lee let out a whistle and a diner at a nearby table glanced in our direction. "I ... I don't know what to say." He slumped against the back of the booth and pushed the plate with his partially eaten spring roll away. I swabbed mine through some duck sauce and took a bite while Lee re-adjusted his thinking about Rojo. Crispy on the outside, chewy inside. Perfect.

"How'd you find that out?"

No need to drag Artie's name into this. I was pretty sure Lee didn't know about that connection. "Kind of stumbled upon it. I'm good at stumbling onto things."

"Jeez. I wonder if Margaret knows. I wonder if *Hao* knows. Maybe that's why he dislikes Rojo so much."

I didn't point out it was a genetically ingrained trait that parents dislike any underemployed guitar players cohabitating with their daughter.

"Doesn't necessarily mean Rojo's a bad guy, just that he has a problem," I said as Artie's face floated before me. "Doesn't mean he's a bad guy at all."

151

Some of the color in Lee's face had drained, leaving behind a gray mask.

"It gets more interesting. Someone paid off Rojo's gambling debt, behind his back, and threw in a bonus if the bookie didn't take any more of his action." I paused. "I thought it was you."

Another whistle from Lee, another—longer—glance from the lady struggling with her chopsticks one table over. I took another bite of spring roll, then wiped a smear of sauce from my cheek.

"Who would do that?" Lee asked.

"That's the twenty-thousand dollar question." I leaned in. "So who do *you* think would do that?" Lee certainly had better knowledge of the Wongs than I did.

He mulled it over. "I never heard talk of Rojo having any friends who could come up with twenty grand. Hell, they're all starving musicians, too."

"Me neither. From what I understand, his mother's broke and he doesn't have any siblings. I also don't see Hao bailing him out, but what about Joy's brothers? Looking out for little sister's beau?"

Lee scoffed. "Edward and Patrick are so wound up in their political aspirations, they wouldn't even think to give Rojo the time of day, unless they were asking for his vote. Besides, politicians—especially those running for office—wouldn't want to get mixed up with bookies. Voters tend to frown upon things like that." He held his hands out, palms up. "Sorry, but I got nothing."

"Okay. Let's think about this. Rojo was involved with Jimmy the Raisin, and somebody paid off his debt. Then how was Lin involved?" The more I thought about this mess, the more questions I came up with.

"Could he have been one of this bookie's enforcers?"

"The bookie says no, says he doesn't use that kind of muscle, so let's assume not. What other shenanigans could Rojo be into?"

Lee's attention shifted as the server brought two platters heaped with food, a plate of stir-fried vegetables and some kind of pork dish. Steam rose from both. She set them down on the table, followed by two bowls of white rice. "Enjoy."

"Thanks, doll," Lee said, and the server gave us a parting smile as she left to go help paying customers. If I had called her "doll," she would have given me a dirty look, but somehow Lee could pull it off. "If I didn't know he was into gambling, I sure wouldn't know what else he was into." Lee scooped some rice onto his plate. On top of the rice, he piled a hefty helping of vegetables, followed by the pork. When he finished, a mini-mountain of food sat before him.

I thought aloud, using Lee as my sounding board, hoping we'd gain more insight working together. "Evidently, Lin was into a lot of bad stuff, loansharking included. Maybe Rojo borrowed some cash from Lin to gamble with. His tab came due, but he only had part of it to repay. That could be why Lin was roughing him up in the alley when Ty and I trundled along. You know, maybe he was trying to spread what little money he had around, trying to appease everyone, stalling until he could come up with the rest of the nut."

"And now Lin is dead. Convenient." Lee picked up some food with his chopsticks, but didn't put it in his mouth.

"For Rojo. Not so convenient for Lin," I said.

He put his food back down. "So those thugs with bats who attacked us were sent by Lin, figuring Rojo would be at Edward's dinner. They wanted to remind him of his obligation. That whole thing had nothing whatsoever to do with Edward's campaign."

"That might be stretching things. Wouldn't there be better ways to send that message without getting a lot of innocent people involved?" I forked some pork into my mouth and the spicy, sweet, and salty sensations warmed my body. Lee sure knew how to run a restaurant.

"Hard to figure the minds of criminals, Channing."

"True." I swallowed my food.

"With Lin dead, I guess Rojo is off the hook with him. And with his bookie paid off, Rojo can breathe easy. Assuming he lays off the gambling," Lee said.

Again, I didn't bring up the fact that Rojo's most recent rough-ing up had occurred *after* Lin had been murdered. There was no sense alarming Lee until I had more information.

FIFTEEN

I was sitting at our bar, waiting for Skip to return from the storeroom with some supplies, when Freeman Easter strolled in, wearing his usual brown suit. "Afternoon, Channing."

It wasn't like Freeman to drop by in the middle of the day like this. Had Artie called Freeman and filled him in on what was happening? I thought we'd agreed I was going to keep looking into things for a while, sans police involvement. "Afternoon, Detective Easter."

"Oh, so now it's Detective Easter?" He chuckled. "Well, I guess that beats Schmucko the Clown."

"Tonight's not open mic night, you know," I said. That's how I first met Freeman; he did some open mic nights at The Last Laff, back when this was "just" my home club, before I'd bought in financially. Good material, good delivery, but he never showed any desire to give up the day job. Too many perks, I guess. Most comics didn't get to carry guns—legally, anyway. A damn good thing.

Skip emerged from the back, carrying a bag of cocktail napkins. "Hey boss, we're running short—" When he saw my cop buddy, he seemed to stand a little taller. "Oh, hello Freeman. Come to beat a confession out of me? Hey, is that a nightstick in your pocket, or are you just happy to see me?" He held out his hands in front of him, touching at the wrists. "Okay, you can cuff me and take me away. I did it. I'm guilty."

"Last I checked, telling bad jokes isn't a crime." Freeman shook his head. "You'd think someone who worked in a comedy club would have better material."

"You get what you pay for," Skip said.

"Let's find a private spot, shall we?" Freeman said, rolling his eyes at Skip.

We went back to my office; luckily Artie wasn't around. I let Freeman sit at his desk while I lounged in my rickety folding chair.

"How's Artie?"

"He's fine." I didn't elaborate, but I wondered if Freeman knew about Artie's gambling history. Was I going to wonder if every one of Artie's friends and acquaintances knew about his gambling problems of the past?

"Good to hear." With his tongue, Freeman worked at something caught in his teeth.

"You didn't come down here to ask about Artie."

"You're a bright bulb, you know that, Channing? Unfortunately, I'm here on official business. Sorry to be a downer."

"You're never a downer, Freeman." I put a sarcastic spin on the delivery, but my stomach clenched. I'd had enough police involvement in my life catching Lauren's killer. No offense to Freeman, but I'd hoped never to deal with a cop again on *official business.* "What's up?"

He stared at me for a beat before speaking. "Know a guy by the name of Sam Chun?"

"Nope."

"Also known as 'Big Chief'?"

"Not ringing a bell."

"Sporting a blue Mohawk?"

Damn Artie! I pretended to think. "Hmm. Blue Mohawk. You'd think I would remember that, wouldn't you?"

"This is serious, Channing." His stare intensified. "Do you?"

"Artie call you?"

"No." Freeman's left eye twitched. "What does Artie have to do with this?"

"Uh, nothing. Never mind," I said. Freeman was one of the good ones. Very smart, conscientious, and open-minded, at least for a cop. But he didn't like being dicked with. That I knew from experience. "Why are you here?"

Freeman sighed. "You called me the other day, remember? That friend of yours was asking about the death of Lucky Lin?"

"And?"

"Seems that Lin and Chun ran together."

"Really?"

"You want to tell me what's going on here, Channing?"

"I thought you said it was a gang thing."

"It is. So why does *your friend* care about it?"

"A concerned citizen, I guess."

If looks could kill, the one Freeman hit me with would have put me six feet under. He took out his pad and rifled through it.

"This came to my attention. A witness stepped forward after he recognized Lin from a news report. He saw a scuffle in an alley involving Lin and Chun and a few other guys, including quote, 'a man missing fingers on his left hand,' 'a big, black dude, cut like a bodybuilder,' and 'a guy with reddish hair,' endquote. One of my cop buddies knows I have a 'digitally challenged' friend and called me. Now, got something to say?"

Trash talk like that coming from anyone beside Freeman might have gotten a rise from me. But facts were facts, any way you tilted them. I *was* missing a few digits. "Nice to be known."

Freeman glared at me.

I was so busted.

Withholding information from the police probably wasn't a good long-term strategy. Or a good short-term one, for that matter. I hoped Lee would forgive me for breaking my promise not to blab to the cops. "Yeah, I met a guy with a blue Mohawk. And by 'met,' I mean he almost knifed me."

"When was this?"

"Thursday night. Possibly early Friday morning, if you want to get technical. They ran off."

"And you didn't think to report it? Goddamn it, Channing. You know better." Freeman cocked his head, like a dog hearing something beyond a human's ability.

I shrugged. "Seemed to resolve itself. They didn't take anything. Besides, I know how overworked you guys are."

Freeman focused his laser sights onto me, evidently deciding whether to read me my rights. Then his features unclenched, and he pulled out a pen and flipped to a clean page in his pad. "Okay. Give it to me from the top."

I'm a comic; I make up funny stories for a living. So I could have fashioned a humdinger of a tale involving dope dealers and prostitutes and car chases and barking dogs. But I gave Freeman the truth, with only a minor alteration. In my version, the three of us—me, Ty, and Rojo—were going out for a drink after the Dark Danger show, minding our own business, when we got jumped. No need to tell Freeman that Ty and I had been following Rojo, at least not yet.

"You say this was a completely random mugging?" Freeman tapped his pad with his pen.

I shrugged. "I really don't know what those guys were thinking."

"I find it a little hard to believe two guys jumped three of you, especially when one of you was Ty."

I swallowed. "Uh, yeah. Kinda hard to believe. But what do you expect from a guy with a blue Mohawk who calls himself Big Chief? Not the sharpest arrow in the quiver." I'd have to remember to tell Ty and Rojo about my little modification so our stories would match.

Freeman eyed me. "This the truth?"

"Would I lie to you? An officer of the law?" I wasn't into the nitty-gritty; I was more of a big picture guy. And since I was the artist of this particular big picture, my truth was close enough. "What did you catch Big Chief doing, anyway?"

"We didn't catch him 'doing' anything, unless you consider being deceased 'doing' something. We found his body. From the looks of things, he'd been murdered."

———

Freeman grilled me, and I answered his questions to the best of my knowledge. I gave him Rojo's full name and connected the dots about how I knew him. I still didn't feel the need to disclose the incident at the banquet; I figured if it were relevant, it would come up sooner or later. And it wasn't me who was trying to keep things under wraps. It was those involved: Edward, Patrick, Rojo, and Lee himself. It wasn't my place to blow the whistle. Whether or not it was true or ethical, I clung to that notion as I endured Freeman's probing.

When he was finally convinced he'd wrung all the information he could from me, he closed his pad. "I'll pass this along to the lead investigator. One last question, and I think I know the answer, but I've got to ask. Any drugs involved?" Freeman worked narcotics, so there must be some drug angle here, somewhere.

"No. Not at all."

"Lin and Chun were into drugs, and just about everything else. The people they worked for were diversified. Weapons, gambling, prostitution. Hell, I think they even owned a few Qwikie-Lube shops and a menswear store. A criminal conglomerate. I'm sure there are scores of people who aren't mourning these scumbags' deaths." He got up. "Enough chit chat. Time to go catch some bad guys."

SIXTEEN

"How was your week, Channing?" my therapist asked me, before I even got comfortable on the couch.

I was going to reply, "about the usual," when an insight hit me with amazing force. What had my life become, that interrupting a mugging, finding out the muggers got murdered, and discovering your mentor had a secret gambling problem constituted a "usual" week? Maybe it was a good thing I was in therapy.

I spewed out the details of my week and, for good measure, brought up the fact I almost considered it "usual."

"Well, it does sound like you've been busy, all right. But I wouldn't say it's become normal for you to experience so many, uh, noteworthy events in one week. I'd say that sometimes 'stuff happens.' It's how you handle the stuff that's important." A pause. "So how have you handled it?"

"Strangely, the mugging and the dead muggers haven't bothered me that much. Discovering Artie's secret was a lot more worrisome."

"Why is that?"

"I thought I knew him and, whammo, he tells me something like that." The volume of my voice had increased.

"And now you feel like you don't really know him."

"Sorta. I mean I *know* him. Hell, I often know what he's going to say before he says it. But now there's a niggling little voice in the back of my head asking me if I *really* know him. Like maybe he's going to do something so weird, so bizarre, and I'll find out he's done stuff like that before. Know what I mean? He's consistent and I like being able to count on that."

"It's always rough when something—or someone—we count on changes. But in this case, Artie's behavior hasn't actually changed, right?"

"Not yet." He'd always been gruff and moody and a little prickly. Consistently so. No, he hadn't changed.

"I think it's fair to say Artie is a product of his experiences. For instance, it's possible he's become this consistent person you describe because he's learned and grown, in part, from his experience with his bookie. I'm simplifying here, of course, but bad things that happen in a person's past often can have a positive effect, depending on how you overcome them. Haven't you ever done something you weren't proud of?"

"Sure," I said, but didn't expound. There was no need; we'd talked about many incidents in the past I wasn't proud of. Was I a stronger person now because of them? Or were they somehow dogging me, holding me back from reaching my full potential?

"Why do you think Artie told you his secret now?"

I sat back, glanced out the window. A strong breeze shook tree limbs in the distance making the leaves jitterbug. "I don't think he

162

would have, except he needed info from his bookie. About the in-cident at Lee's place."

"To help you—and Lee—isn't that right?"

"Yes."

"How do you think Artie felt revealing this obviously painful and potentially embarrassing secret?"

I hadn't thought about it in those terms. I was too wrapped up in how *I* felt about Artie's painful and embarrassing secret. "I don't know, we didn't discuss it."

"Yes, but how do you *think* he felt?"

"I guess it was hard for him."

"It was probably very difficult for him. In fact, it sounds like he risked a lot by telling you—your respect, primarily. Yet he did it. What does that tell you?"

"That he cared enough about Lee to let himself look bad."

"Yes, I suspect Artie is a very, very loyal person and that he'd do anything for a friend. Would you say that was accurate?"

"Very accurate." And heaven help those Artie *disliked*.

"Moreover, not only did he care about Lee, he cared about you, too. He wanted you to succeed in your quest to help Lee. Artie could have asked his bookie the same questions without you there, right?"

Something else that hadn't occurred to me. "Sure."

"But he took you along. He *wanted* to tell you his secret. By sharing it with you, he demonstrated how he truly feels about you. He trusts you with his innermost secrets. It's quite an honor, I'd say."

"Yeah, I guess."

"Channing, we've never explicitly touched on this before, but I think it's safe to say, from both your perspective and from Artie's, that your relationship with him is something akin to the father-son relationship you never had."

Artie as a father figure? It definitely *was a good thing I was in therapy.*

———

After my session, I called Artie and told him I might not be in tonight. He must have been preoccupied with something else—something important—because he didn't grumble in the least.

When I got to my condo, instead of going directly to my apartment, I knocked on Erin's door. A moment later, she opened up, smile already in place. She wore sweats again. Must still be working on her deadbeat dad avenger novel. Even in sweats, she outshone most other women. "Hi Channing. Come on in."

I hesitated. "Why don't you come across the hall? Change of pace."

Her brow knitted for a split-second, then her smile intensified. "Sure. Sounds great. Just let me change, okay?"

Although our two apartments were directly across the hall from each other, it felt like they were miles apart. When Lauren was alive, we'd have Erin over frequently—for meals, to watch movies, to just hang out with us. Since Lauren's death, I'd always gone to her apartment.

I wasn't sure why that was; maybe on some level I was afraid of the memories it would unleash. I guess I should bring it up at a future therapy session. Now that I thought about it, this was the first time a single woman had been in my place since Lauren's death.

What did that say about me? When would I stop thinking about everything as fodder for my therapist?

While I waited for her, I walked the two steps to my place and unlocked the door, hoping I'd remembered to clean up before leaving that morning. I flipped on the light. A few sections of newspaper graced the couch and a pair of running shoes decorated the middle of the floor. Things could have been worse; the cereal bowl from my gourmet Lucky Charms lunch had found its way to the sink.

Erin joined me before I had a chance to do any last-second tidying. "Why don't we have a seat?" I hustled over to the couch and grabbed the papers, moving them to an end table. She took the hint and settled down on one side of the couch, kicking off her shoes as she sunk into the cushions.

I lowered myself onto the other side of the couch and leaned against the arm so I could face her. "I hope I didn't interrupt any important writing."

"Not at all. I was between scenes and needed the break. So, thanks."

"My pleasure." My throat tightened. My pulse picked up. Memories of the three of us sitting around, shooting the breeze, cascaded through my mind. Maybe I wasn't quite ready to be alone with a woman in my apartment. "You know what I feel like doing? Going on a picnic. You game?" It had been a while since I'd been out in the fresh air, in daylight, aside from walking to my car in parking lots. Sleeping half the day away was an occupational hazard of being a comic.

"Sure. Sounds like fun."

After stopping at Popeyes to get some fried chicken and biscuits, Erin and I drove out to Lake Fairfax. We parked in the lot next to the main building, then walked down a rocky path to a wooden fishing pier. A few people were casting their lines into the lake, but we didn't have any problem finding an unoccupied bench where we could eat with a little privacy.

We unwrapped our food and ate in silence, content to watch the people fiddle with their fishing rods. About thirty yards away, a man and two young boys tried their luck. To me, it seemed like they spent more time putting worms on hooks and untangling their fishing lines than actually trying to catch fish, but maybe that was the allure of it all. I didn't know much about fish except they tasted good fried with tartar sauce.

Skip was the club's resident expert. He talked about coming out here on the days they restocked the lake and watching the big fish trucks roll in. They'd hook huge hoses up to the tanks and let thousands of fish loose in the lake for the sportsmen to pursue. Whenever he told us about his fishing exploits, he always choked up a little. I thought it was kind of cute, but Donna always gave him grief about his obsession.

"Hey, look," Erin said, pointing out over the lake.

"Very cool." A bird had dive-bombed the surface and snagged a good-sized fish. It rose over the lake, banking toward the far side, prey squirming in its grip. A few of the fishermen we shared the pier with also turned their attention skyward and gawked. I wondered if they felt envious or if they were as awestruck by nature as we were.

I balled up my trash and stuffed it into the Popeyes bag. Next to me, Erin tore the last hunk off her drumstick and did the same with her garbage. She finished chewing and turned toward me. "Thanks for suggesting we get a bite to eat. I would have just ended up with mac and cheese. Again."

"Thanks for coming with me." I hadn't been out on a date since Lauren died, and I wasn't sure this qualified as a "date" per se, but whatever it was, it felt a bit strange. I mean, Erin had been a good friend to both of us, and spending time with her here, outside of the context of being neighbors, felt weird. On one hand, the attraction couldn't be denied. Call it physical, or primal, or hormonal. Whatever. On the other hand, every time I was with her, I couldn't help but think of Lauren. Was I somehow betraying my dead fiancée? Or would she be happy—wherever she was—when I eventually moved on in pursuit of my own happiness?

I wondered if we were somehow taking our friendship to the next level. I wondered if she wondered about it too.

"Want to go for a walk?"

"Sounds good." We dumped our trash into a receptacle at the end of the pier and set off down a trail that circled the lake. Lauren and I had come here once, for fireworks, and all I remembered was waiting in a long line of cars to exit the park.

Dusk was approaching and the temperature had dipped along with the sun. The line of trees we paralleled cast long shadows across the trail ahead of us. "I don't get out enough," Erin said. "I mostly stay in my cave and bang on my keyboard. Oh, and I watch a lot of TV, too."

"You look like you keep in shape."

"Thanks. Good genes, I guess. I don't exercise nearly as much as I should."

"Who does, right?" I rubbed my belly. I really did need to get back to exercising.

"Tired?"

"Huh?"

"You yawned. Am I boring you?" Her tone was playful, not defensive.

"No, no. It's just…" All the turmoil of the past week rushed to my head. The incident at Lee's, his insistence that I investigate, the attack on Rojo, the death of Lin and Chun, Artie's dark secret. Everything. All bad, all out of my control. I'd been keeping it bottled up.

"Just what?" Erin stared at me, dark eyes probing.

"Got a lot going on," I said, not trying to be cryptic, but unsure if I wanted to burden her with my troubles. Hell, I wasn't sure about a lot of things lately, why should now be any different?

Erin bent over and picked up a small branch. Started pulling twigs off it as she walked. "If you feel like talking about it, I'm a good listener."

"Yeah? Well… okay." I proceeded to tell her what had happened, starting with the thugs barging in at Lee's, right up through the visit to Artie's old bookie.

"Wow. Sounds like the plot to one of my books."

"Yeah, except this is real life. And it's happening to people I know." Off the path, two squirrels chased each other up a tree, chittering and chattering. "Got any thoughts?"

"The way you described them, Edward and Patrick seem like the stereotypical ambitious politicians. Trample over others—and the truth, perhaps—to get what they want."

"Well, that's just my opinion."

"I'm sure your take is pretty accurate. You've got good intuition."

"I'd prefer to have good e.s.p." I ran a hand through my hair. "So what do you think?"

"Asking a writer to speculate—a genre fiction writer—is dangerous. We could be here all night." Something twinkled behind her smile. "I usually go with the simplest explanation. The invasion at Lee's Palace was a political threat. Rojo owed some money and got roughed up, and then the two muggers got killed in a gang war."

"What about the anonymous person who paid off Fugano?"

"Perhaps the bookie was lying. Perhaps there was no payoff." One of her eyebrows arched.

"No payoff? Why would he lie about that?"

Erin stepped over a humungous tree root that had breached the path. "Could be he wants you to think it's all over between him and Rojo so you'd butt out. Could be anything, really."

"Yeah, that's what I keep coming back to. Many questions, few answers."

"Of course…" Erin trailed off.

"What?"

"Maybe it's something else entirely. Maybe Rojo and Joy are brewing something together."

My stomach clenched for a moment, and I didn't think it was the fried chicken talking back. "Like what?"

"Maybe Joy and Rojo are involved in illicit activities. Drugs, perhaps. I know he's your friend, but he *is* gambling illegally. And you know what they say about rock 'n' rollers. Maybe they've decided to fully embrace the criminal life."

I shook my head. "I've been around plenty of comics, so I know druggies. Neither of them strikes me as the type. Nor do they seem to be criminals. They're just two twenty-something free spirits."

"Beneath still waters …"

"Oh, don't get me wrong. There's nothing still about Joy Wong or Rojo Mendes. But drugs don't sound right."

"Bank heist? Some kind of insurance scam? International jewel thieves?" She smiled again, and I almost forgot what we were talking about.

"Your crime theories make good fiction. Reality doesn't usually tie up so neatly."

"How about this for some fiction? Joy's always been in the shadow of the men in her family, right? So maybe she feels neglected, or bitter, and does something extreme, trying to get noticed, and draws Rojo into it. To upstage the stars of the family and piss off her parents." Erin tossed her branch aside. "She's already taken the first step. Living with a guy your parents hate is classic rebellion, right?"

"I guess if Rojo's band makes it big, it would be an eff-you to her parents, huh?"

Erin nodded. "You're a performer. Isn't that part of the whole thrill? Getting famous enough to prove all those doubters wrong? Throwing it back into the faces of all those people who said you couldn't make it?"

"Well … maybe a little."

Erin laughed, and it reminded me of Lauren's laugh, only because it was completely opposite. Hers was melodic while Lauren's had been more like a donkey braying. I missed my donkey. "I felt the same way. When I first got published, I sent a copy of the book to my old high school English teacher who almost flunked me. It felt kind of good. I think she started to take 'credit' for my successful writing after that." She winked at me. "I promise, I won't tell anyone your secret thoughts of 'revenge.'"

"Don't worry, it's not really a secret." Of course, I'd thought about the golden "I Told You So" often. Every comic I knew did; some would point to it as their primary motivator. I didn't know if I'd go that far, but there was a certain satisfaction knowing you scaled a peak the nattering naysayers didn't think you could.

Erin's foot caught on a rock and she stumbled a bit, losing her balance. I reached out and grabbed her arm to steady her. "Thanks. I almost did a header into the forest floor. That would have been embarrassing."

I held on to her arm a little longer than I had to before letting go. She didn't seem to mind.

"I hope this whole mess is done with. It's given me an inside view of politics—or should I say politicians—I could have done without." I stopped and corrected myself. "Actually, it reconfirmed what I'd always thought about politicians. Covering their asses is Job One."

Erin laughed. "Amazing government works at all, isn't it? If I could, I would ignore everything about it. No campaign speeches, no elections, no political scandals. Give me my laptop and a TV and I'm happy. There's something to be said for living in a cave. Or perhaps I'm just simple-minded."

"I guess being simple-minded is better than being an anarchist."

"Don't worry, I'm not hostile enough to be an anarchist. Nor do I have enough energy. I'll just be an 'ignorist.'"

"Maybe we should start our own political party. Or *non*-political party. The Apathetic Party."

We walked on, done talking about the Wongs' troubles, but I still had something eating me. *Artie.* "Have you ever learned an unpleasant secret about someone you knew—or thought you knew?"

"I had an aunt once. I adored her and she was always telling me I was her favorite niece. Found out later she'd been in prison. Some kind of mail fraud thing."

"Did it change your opinion of her?"

"Yes. I think it's only natural. Although I'm not sure she noticed—she still calls me her favorite niece. Everything we learn about someone—from observation, from experience, from some other source, whatever—helps us form our opinions. They're not static, but are constantly evolving." She paused, nodded to herself. "I think it's better that way. You wouldn't want people's opinions of you to be frozen in time. Then you're always stuck with first impressions."

I couldn't recall the first time I met Erin. Must not have been a bad first impression, although if I couldn't remember it ...

"Channing? You okay?"

"Huh? Oh, sorry. Spaced out for a second." It was getting darker and with all the potential tripping hazards in the path, we'd better get going or we were going to have to crawl out of the woods. "We should turn around now."

"Yes, sir." Erin saluted. "See? I can follow orders when I want to."

"Then march!" We made it out of the woods without incident, talking of nothing more important than our favorite bands, where we'd like to vacation if we could choose anywhere, and the fact we both didn't care for soccer—not enough scoring.

When we got back to the car, Erin touched the back of my good hand and flashed me a killer smile. "Thanks, Channing. I had a great time. It's nice once in awhile to get out of my cave with a friend and do something different, you know?"

"Yeah. Ditto." *Friends* were important.

———

When I awoke the next morning, I was alone. After our picnic, we'd come straight home and gone to our separate apartments. I hadn't put any moves on her. Part of me was bummed about it, but I was glad to note a bigger part of me was relieved. Our friendship mattered too much to screw it up for the promise of some awesome sex. Maybe I'd change my mind in the future, but that was my story and I was sticking to it.

Since my therapy session yesterday, all sorts of thoughts had been bubbling in my brain. Many of them centered on Artie, although a good deal of them had to do with Rojo, too. I didn't know much about his upbringing—only what I learned from Joy—but I wondered if his desire to become a performer grew somehow from the dysfunctional relationship with his alcoholic father. I also wondered how much of my desire to be a comic came from *not* having *any* relationship with my father—whoever he was. Probably explained a lot, for both of us. Conjecture, sure, but it was one angle to look at the situation from. Sometimes going to my therapist inspired me to do a little amateur therapy myself.

When I got to the club, Donna was busy doing a spot inventory in the storage room, and Skip was getting things ready for the evening behind the bar. Cutting lemon and lime wedges, making sure his stock of napkins and straws and whatever else was adequate. Ty wouldn't show up until closer to showtime, so I had an hour or two to kill. With my father figure, the ex-gambler.

Artie was in the office, sifting through audition packages. "Glad you could grace us with your presence. I hope working here isn't cramping your style too much."

I waved my hand. "It is, but I'll muddle through somehow. Find anybody good?"

"Nah," Artie said, as he moved his unlit cigar from one side of his mouth to the other. "The usual deluded numskulls. You gotta love 'em, though. Without the bad and mediocre comics, how would we stand above the masses?" Artie tilted the monitor so I could see—if I moved my chair into his lap. "Care to join me?"

"Sure." I moved just far enough to see the screen. No need to smell Artie's coffee breath if I didn't have to. Artie had finally become comfortable opening up YouTube videos and clips sent as e-mail attachments. Before that barrier had been crossed, I'd done all the computer work. Sometimes I thought he was sorry to see VHS—the real "audition tapes"—die. Despite their poorer quality, propensity to tangle, inability to cue up a certain scene, and bulkiness, Artie had a special affinity for them. He was not one to embrace change without a whole lot of kicking and kvetching.

"Okay," Artie said, clicking a few links. A YouTube video appeared on the screen and he started it. A shot of a guy dressed all in black against a plain white wall. He began to talk about a trip he took to New York City. The Big Apple. If he could make it there, he could make it anywhere. No ambient noise could be heard. Generally, this was bad news. Generally, this meant it was a homemade job recorded in someone's basement. "Not another one. What happened to all the decent comics?" Artie hit the pause button, even before the poor schlub had attempted to land his first punchline. "Keep going, or give him the hook?" He held his hand up with his thumb out, wavering, like the emperors of Rome at the gladiator fights.

I gave him a "thumbs down," and Artie closed the YouTube window.

"Next victim." He plucked the top buff-colored, catalog-sized envelope from the stack. Opened it and extracted a resume, head-shot, and DVD in a little sleeve. He showed me the headshot. "Nice."

A gorgeous blonde displayed a set of very, very white teeth. In comedy, two appearances worked best—attractive or funny-looking. A sad fact, but true. Artie scanned the resume and, satisfied she passed the appearance hurdle, slid the DVD into the computer. This video was shot in a comedy club outside of Pittsburgh—I recognized the name of the club on the wall behind her, *Funny Bonz*. Decent club, so it figured she'd at least be a decent comic. Artie sat up a little straighter and turned the volume up. In a dusky voice she said, "Hey everybody, I'm Shasta LeDoux."

Shasta started her routine, something about her psychotic dog-chasing cat, and I sorta tuned out. It didn't matter what I thought—I could tell by the way Artie drooled he was going to try to book her.

Although things were changing, men dominated the world of stand-up comedy. And although Artie was an archaic, antique, ancient dinosaur in many regards, his support of female comics had always been strong. He'd been a champion for my late fiancée Lauren, as well as for her sister Heather. And for countless others.

Five weeks ago, we had a full slate of female comics for our Six-Pack Wednesday. At first, Artie, in full-dinosaur mode, wanted to call it Twelve-Boob Wednesday. When Donna caught wind of his idea, it only took her *twelve seconds* to get Artie to see the error of his ways. Artie might only have suggested it to yank Donna's chain, but you couldn't always tell. No matter what he ended up calling it, he'd been on to something going all female; it was one of the biggest Wednesdays we'd had in months.

Watching Shasta dredged up bittersweet memories of Lauren. She'd died eight months ago, but I still thought about her daily. Time was supposed to heal all wounds. Maybe in a couple centuries I'd feel better.

All of a sudden, the idea of being a comic the rest of my life felt like a piano tied around my neck.

Artie stopped the DVD midstream. "She's a keeper. About time, too. I was starting to think we'd never find anybody decent again." He collected Shasta's material, stuffed it back into the envelope, and wrote "Follow Up!!!" on it with red Sharpie. Then he put it right on top of his IN box. "Shall we press our luck and try another?"

"When was the last time we found two gems back-to-back?"

"There's always a first time." He reached for the next envelope.

"Artie …"

His arm stopped moving. "Yeah?"

"Why'd you decide to become a comic?" I'd known Artie for years, and I'd worked by his side for some of that time in very close proximity. I could usually predict how he would react in certain situations, based on empirical evidence. But I never really knew the reasons behind some of the stuff he did. And the whole gambling thing had thrown me for a loop—as much as I tried, I couldn't let it go.

He looked at me a beat, trying to figure my angle. Then he leaned back in his chair and adopted that professorial pose he often did when trying to infuse me with some of his wisdom. He plucked the unlit stogie from his mouth and set it on the stack of envelopes. "Let me guess. Crisis of confidence?"

"Maybe."

"Thinking about your Richmond gig?"

"Maybe."

"Thinking about Wendell White?"

"Maybe."

"Thinking about some of those young comics you see on Comedy Central, superstars in waiting? Wondering if you'll ever recapture the flame?"

"Maybe and maybe."

"It's natural, kid. I've had spells where my confidence wanes, as has every single comic I've ever known. Even the great ones are unsure of themselves at times. Hell, that's what makes them—and us—good comics. We turn those insecurities into good bits, killer routines. We transform the daily frustrations of life into humor. The same situations every person encounters, we make funny, and laughter is cathartic. We make our audience feel better about themselves, their lives. Nothing gives me greater joy than watching people laugh. That's why I became a comic. To make people happy." He picked up his cigar and pointed it at me. "And for the chicks."

Were all old comics horny? "Did you ever *not* want to be a comic?"

Artie snorted. "Millions of times. After every joke that bombed, after every routine that went south. Every other Thursday. Nineteen-eighty-one and nineteen-ninety-four. Days ending in 'y.' I question my career choice winter, spring, summer, fall, and all the seasons in-between. If you don't, if you accept this crazy profession blindly, then you are a complete idiot." He winked at me. "And I know you're not a *complete* idiot."

"Isn't it tough, with all the rejection and failure, to keep going?"

"Sure. But, really, what else are you going to do? I'm too old to become a doctor and I'm not strong enough to move furniture. So comic it is. Why? Thinking about changing careers? Want to become a gynecologist?"

Wendell White's words echoed in my head. If I wasn't having fun, maybe I *should* change careers. "Why did you decide to open up the club?"

Artie nodded a few times, as if he were having an internal conversation. An agreeable one. "Well, being on the road got old. I missed my Sophie. Plus, I thought I'd try to help other comics, best I could. Yeah, it's a little corny, wanting to give back, but, hey, no one ever said I didn't like a little corn. Great thing is I can still get on stage anytime I want. It's my club, right?"

Mostly—I was just a minority owner. "And you do. You emcee every night."

"True." He tapped his chest. "But inside, I'm still the same old headliner I always was."

I'd been holding it in, for days now, but I couldn't contain it any longer. "Tell me about the gambling. What was that all about?"

A dark cloud settled over Artie's head; I could almost see the thunderstorms brewing. Then a brisk wind blew them away. "Tell you what. Why don't you come over for lunch tomorrow? I'll get Sophie to whip us up something edible, and we can talk about it."

"Sure."

"Okay. How about one o'clock?" Artie got up from his chair. "I'm going to go see if Donna needs any help. We have a big show tonight, in case you didn't know. Catch you later, kid." He shuffled out of the office, stogie firmly planted between his teeth.

Was it my imagination, or was Artie calling me "kid" a lot more lately?

SEVENTEEN

ARTIE WAS ALMOST FINISHED introducing our headliner, Gorilla Reece, when I slipped into an empty seat in the back. I loved watching the comics, especially the good ones, but I was often handling some snafu—with tickets, with supplies, with any of a million bits of minutiae associated with running a club that took me away from the act. Tonight, everything seemed to be humming along. Just a well-oiled comedy club machine, which was nice for a change.

Gorilla bounded onto the stage, and you could feel the energy level of the room rise, as if someone turned up the dimmer switch. It was that way with all the great ones. The electricity buzzed through the room before they were introduced, then kept rising after the comics hit the stage. Gorilla wasn't yet in the "great" category, but he was young and inventive, and he had presence with a capital P, which in my mind was the key. And with a name like his, you'd better have a presence. You could always bolster the material, but that special performer's "aura" was damn near impossible to acquire.

"How's everyone doing tonight?" Gorilla said, pointing to the crowd. They applauded louder. "You're my kind of animals!"

The crowd clapped for another few moments, then quieted. They'd come to get entertained, and you couldn't be entertained if you couldn't hear. Gorilla removed the mic from the stand and set the stand behind him. "I love coming to this place. They really know how to treat their comics right. Why, before the show, I was waiting in the green room, and I was watching reruns of *The Andy Griffith Show* on an old TV. Which is quite a coincidence, because Artie, the owner of this place, is the love child of Floyd the Barber and Aunt Bee." A few chuckles. "I know, I know, you thought Floyd had a thing for Barney, but... On second thought, it might not have been a rerun I was watching. It might have been one of Artie's home movies. I don't recall ever seeing Aunt Bee topless before. And, believe me, I don't wish to ever see that again." Gorilla made a face. "But the best part of the green room were the beverages. All the RC Cola you can drink." A few more polite chuckles.

Of course, the audience didn't know Gorilla wasn't joking. He'd described our green room perfectly. Except it wasn't *all* the RC Cola you could drink, I think we only had a couple bottles left. Those jokes weren't really for the crowd; they were for Artie. Gorilla and Artie had formed a bond, and Gorilla was always ribbing Artie about something. That was one of the coolest things about Artie. He had an amazing rapport with an unbelievable number of comics, young and old. Sometimes I had a tough time getting my head around the fact that in his heyday, Artie was an A-list comedian and not the cantankerous club owner he'd aged into.

Gorilla launched into his "real" routine, and he had the place rolling. Kind of a cross between Robin Williams and Eric Wright, he alternated between frenetic and deadpan, making lightning-quick transitions that kept the audience on their proverbial toes. More importantly, he kept them howling. Even though I'd heard much of his routine before, it kept me laughing, too. That was the ultimate compliment for a comic—if you could make other comics laugh. We're such a jaded bunch.

About fifteen minutes into Gorilla's act, I heard my name being called in a voice somewhere above a whisper and below a yell. In the aisle to my left, Ty was waving at me to come over. I knew my well-oiled club was too good to be true. I caught up with Ty and led him toward the front door where we could talk.

"Boss, we got a Pryor."

"Pryor" was our codeword for a situation out of control, something that needed my immediate attention. Anything from a passed-out patron to someone who had set themselves on fire. Artie thought it was an honor to name it after the late Richard Pryor, the mercurial comic who had been frequently messed up and occasionally on fire. "What is it?"

"It's Rojo. He's a wreck and he wants to talk to you. I told him to give you a call tomorrow, but he was going apeshit. Said he had to talk to you right this very instant. Said 'they' were going to kill him if they found him."

Christ. "He didn't happen to say who 'they' were, did he?"

Ty shook his head. "Nope. And I asked. More than once. Said he'd only talk to you. For the record, I didn't see anyone chasing him. But it looked like he'd been roughed up some."

No doubt bruises left over from earlier in the week. "Where is he?"

"I escorted him all the way around the back and stowed him in the men's room. Second stall."

"Okay, thanks." I left Ty to resume his bouncer duties and hightailed it for the men's room. We had a small facility, two urinals and two stalls. The stall closest to the far wall was closed. I glanced under the door and didn't see any feet. "Rojo?"

One foot hit the floor, followed by the other. "Channing?"

"Come out here."

Rojo fumbled with the stall's slidebolt for a few seconds, then the door opened. His face had healed some—both his eyes opened— but you could still tell he'd been in quite a fight recently. "I didn't know where else to go."

I assumed he wasn't talking about our men's room. "What the hell is going on?"

He craned his head to look over my shoulder. "Not here. They'd think to look here."

"*Who'd* think to look here?"

"Them!" He shouldered past me, and when he realized I wasn't following, he stopped. "Come on. I'll tell you all about it, but we've got to get out of here." Then he spun around again and vanished through the men's room door.

Head down, he hustled through the club, and I followed. On stage, Gorilla Reece was in the middle of some story about a fraternity prank involving a three-legged goat and the audience was lapping it up. Somehow, I got the idea that whatever was going on with Rojo wasn't nearly as funny.

At the club's entrance, Rojo stopped short. "Quiet." He cracked the door open a few inches and peered out. Nothing jumped at him. "Okay. Coast seems clear."

"What are you afraid of?" I asked.

"Not now. Not here." He opened the door a little wider and looked out. "How about that 7-Eleven?"

"Sure."

"Okay. I'll go first. See if anyone follows me. If it's clear, then you can come." He glanced back at me, terror on his face. I felt the blood drain from mine.

Without waiting for my response, Rojo burst through the door and jogged across the parking lot. I stepped out of the club and watched him. The 7-Eleven was across the street, about half a block up, and Rojo zig-zagged around a couple moving vehicles to reach his destination. From where I stood, nobody seemed to be following him. From where I stood, it seemed the only person who cared about Rojo's activities was me.

Once he'd gotten safely inside, I walked across the street and into the 7-Eleven. As far as I could tell, no one followed me either.

"Over here," Rojo whispered from the far corner of the store, next to the snack cakes, loud enough for the cashier to lift his head from a magazine he was leafing through. After he saw it was just two typical Friday night goofballs looking for their hourly fix of sugar, salt, fat, or caffeine, he resumed reading.

When I got to Rojo's corner, he had flattened himself against the glass of the cold case. "What the hell is going on?"

"Oh man. Oh shit. They're gonna kill me." His teeth were chattering, actually chattering. I figured it was fear, but I suppose it could have been because his back was up against the refrigerator doors.

"Why don't we get some coffee, sit down somewhere, and talk about it? Calmly." I spoke in an even, soothing tone. "Come on, what do you say?" I reached for his arm to guide him to the coffee urns, but he jerked it away.

"They're very powerful men. They've got people everywhere. I'm not safe."

"WHO?" I yelled.

Rojo cowered, and the guy behind the counter set his magazine down, now clearly a lot more interested in what was going on in our corner of the store.

"Sorry. Come on." I grabbed Rojo's arm and steered him to the coffee. He allowed me, thankful I'd taken charge. He probably thought I had a great plan to save him, or a secret hideaway where he could go, but I had nothing. Nada. Only an urge to get out of the 7-Eleven, get him calmed down, and find out what the hell was going on. I guess that *was* my great plan.

We got two coffees, I gave the cashier a five, and we left before he could fork over my change. I thought about suggesting we sit on the curb in front of the store, but realized that wouldn't fly. We circled the building and kept to the shadows until we came to a residential side street. We trudged on in silence for about three blocks. Rojo's head moved side-to-side like some kind of robotic scanning device, with an occasional glance over his shoulder. I walked next to him, letting him do whatever he needed to in order to feel safe. Finally, he came to a halt and drew a deep breath. "I guess we're okay here."

"Good." We sat down on a concrete sewer. I sipped my coffee, waiting for Rojo to summon the nerve to tell me what was going on. I knew he wanted to—why else seek me out at the club?—but my earlier tactic of questioning him hadn't worked. I took a tip from my therapist and waited patiently.

I didn't have to wait long.

"I owe some money."

"To who?"

"Just a guy. A pretty bad guy."

"Why? Gambling?"

He nodded.

"I thought you were all square with Fugano. Done with him."

Rojo scoffed. "Fugano's not the type to use muscle. No, it's not him."

"Then who?"

"Another guy. Bookie. And loanshark. One-stop shopping."

"Jeez, Rojo. How much do you owe?"

"A little more than I owed Fugano."

That was eighteen grand. "How much more?"

"A bit." Rojo squirmed on the sewer.

"How much are we talking about?"

"Two-hundred-twenty."

"Two-hundred-twenty what?" I held my breath, afraid of the answer.

"Large."

Holy shit, that was a helluva lot more than a *bit*. I exhaled, loudly. "Are you kidding me? You owe a bookie two-hundred-twenty thousand dollars? Where did you get that kind of scratch?"

Rojo caught my eye. The nearby street lamp threw ominous shadows across his face, the effect exacerbated by my newfound knowledge. Eighteen grand was one thing, but two-hundred-twenty grand was another thing altogether. A leg-breaking, rib-cracking, skull-denting other thing.

"Yeah, well, here's the deal," he began, then his voice caught. "See, it's not my money. I'm doing this for a, uh, a friend. I'm only the go-between." Rojo sighed, and in that instant, his entire face seemed to sag with resignation, as if he'd just signed his own death warrant.

"What friend?"

Rojo sighed again, and his voice shrank. "Patrick Wong."

EIGHTEEN

"Patrick Wong? You're telling me you placed bets for Patrick Wong? As in the Patrick Wong who's running Edward Wong's congressional campaign? Your girlfriend's brother? That Patrick Wong?"

Rojo nodded, too drained to speak. Or maybe he was afraid to verbalize aloud, for fear of a recording device hidden in the nearby bushes.

I remembered seeing Rojo and Patrick talking at Hao's cook-out. Discussing gambling problems? A million questions ran through my mind. I closed my eyes for a second and tried to pri-oritize them. "Why?"

"Why? You mean why didn't Patrick place his own bets?" Rojo held up his hands, palms up, and gave me a look that said, "duh."

Of course, he was a public figure now, involved in his brother's campaign. If word got out, it would wreck two people's careers. Two people's lives. "How long have you been doing this?"

Another sigh. In for a penny, in for two-hundred-twenty large. "About a year. Started out with Fugano, and we never had any problems—Jimmy the Raisin is small potatoes. Then a few months ago, Patrick started making bigger bets. Wanted to diversify bookies. At one point, I was laying action with half a dozen. Then we found ..." Rojo trailed off and gazed into the distance. It was dark, so I was pretty sure he wasn't looking *at* anything. Just looking *away* from me.

"Found who?"

Rojo kept staring into the distance. "Found a guy who would take all his action, no problem. Guy named Don DeManzi." He enunciated the name carefully.

"Ah." I'd heard of DeManzi. In hushed tones, mostly. Rojo was correct, he was a very bad man. The DA had been after him for years with no luck, and he had his talons into everything illegal, and a few things that were not illegal, simply immoral. A true Renaissance dirtbag. "Did Chun and Lin belong to DeManzi?"

"Yeah."

"And the guys who beat you up the other night?"

"DeManzi's."

"And you think he's out to kill you now?"

"Yep."

"Does he know Patrick is the man behind the curtain?"

"Nope."

I noticed Rojo had switched to terse, one-word answers, much different from the gregarious garage band guitarist I'd come to know. "What do you think would happen if you told him?"

Rojo laughed, and the harsh sound seemed out of place in the dark. "He'd kill me first, nice and slowly. Then he'd kill Patrick.

DeManzi doesn't like to be fucked with. He's got an image to uphold, you know. Plus he likes his money."

Loansharks and bookies and nine-tenths of the population liked their money. Some more than others, to be sure. "I've known you for a few years now. A little scattered, maybe, but you were never doing anything illegal. How did you get hooked up with Patrick? And why?"

"He pulled me aside at some family get-together and asked if I wanted to do him a favor. Said he'd 'make it worth my while.' The way he said it, though, didn't give me much of a choice. And ..."

"What?"

"I wanted to please him. You know, being Joy's brother. Some of the Wongs aren't too into me, and I was trying to smooth things over. Be agreeable and flexible and, well, helpful. Didn't want Joy to be ashamed of having me for a boyfriend. You know how it is."

I recalled the relationship I had with Lauren's family. Her father and brother didn't much like me either, and I tried to please them as best I could, for Lauren's sake. I knew *exactly* what prompted Rojo to agree. "How much did Patrick pay you?"

"It was never about the money. I only took it so he wouldn't feel like he had to *owe* me, you know? Jeez, all I've ever wanted was for the Wongs to accept me, to like me. Things with Patrick were going fine until they got out of control."

Famous last words. "What did Joy think about all this?"

Even in the dim light, I could see Rojo's eyes grow larger. "She didn't know. *Doesn't* know. Please don't tell her. She'd kick me out, she'd be so pissed. And I don't want her hating Patrick, either. She looks up to her brothers, big time, despite how she busts on them."

"I heard you and Joy arguing that night after the concert, and Fugano's name came up. You need to be straight with me, Rojo."

"I am being straight. Joy just thinks I made a few bets now and then, on my own. That night, I told her I had one last payoff, then I was through." He paused. "Actually, I was thinking about telling Patrick the same thing. That I'd had enough of this."

"But you didn't?"

"Didn't have the chance. Don't think Patrick would have been happy about it, if I did. He likes the action."

"He could've gotten someone else to do his dirty work, don't you think?"

"Dunno. Patrick was pretty scared someone was going to find out. Always gave me cash, always had some complicated scheme for the money exchanges, drop-off points, stuff like that. Paranoid, if you ask me. I wasn't going to rat him out. He's Joy's brother, for Pete's sake."

Sometimes, family members were the worst rats of all. "So what happened? Why didn't Patrick pay his debts?"

"Good fucking question. I think he made a boatload of money at his law firm, but he said he's a little short at the moment. Wanted me to tell these guys to be patient, and he'd come up with the dough."

"And?"

"I tried that." He clutched at his ribs. "They weren't the patient type."

"No offense, but surely this bookie can't think you've got that kind of cash. He must know you're placing action for someone else."

"You're probably right. That's why they haven't killed me yet. They need me to lead them to the cash cow."

"Why don't you take a little vacation?"

"Don't think it hasn't crossed my mind. But I want to stay close for when Patrick comes up with the money. I'm also worried about Joy. What if they go after her?" He grabbed my arm. "Channing, you've got to help me."

I didn't happen to have two-hundred-twenty thousand bucks lying around. "How?"

"I don't know. For starters, let me crash at your pad. Please, dude."

"Hmm." On the one hand, I didn't want to invite trouble into my home. On the other, I'd offered my couch to lots of wayward comics over the years, and I'd always felt better having done so. *Decisions, decisions.*

"Please. They're gonna torture me if they find me." He grabbed his side again and winced.

"Why don't we march down to the police station and tell them what's going on? I've got a friend there who can help us out."

"No, no, no, no. If we do that, I'm a dead man—really a dead man. Nothing will happen to DeManzi, he's insulated from the street action. Patrick will be exposed. And Edward will lose the election. Their careers will be ruined. And Joy ... she'll hate me for keeping secrets and she'll hate Patrick for dragging me into this. No. No cops."

Rojo did have a few points.

Shit.

———

I dumped a pile of sheets, blankets, and towels on the couch. "Here you go."

"Thanks, man." Rojo had already taken off his shoes and plopped into the recliner—*my* recliner—as he waited for me to fetch his linens.

"No problem. You can stay here until this gets straightened out. Help yourself to whatever you want to eat and drink. I'm not fully stocked or anything, but what's mine is yours." My mother hadn't taught me how to be a good host; I think I must have picked up the basics from Lauren, the most generous person I've ever known.

"Thanks." Rojo smiled. "You saved me here, you know. I owe you."

Lot of people owing people lately. "Forget it. Lee's pretty fond of you and I'd hate to see him bummed out if something bad happened."

Rojo's grin deepened. "Yeah. I hear you."

I stood for a moment, and when I realized Rojo wasn't budging from my recliner, I sat on the edge of the couch. "So what's your plan?"

"Try not to get killed," he said, running a hand through his long hair. "That's all I've got."

"Good plan, but you might want to figure out some intermediate steps. Why don't you go talk to Patrick? This is all his mess."

Rojo eyed me.

"What?"

"Patrick's a little hinky about me talking to him. Or contacting him at all, really. He's afraid of any kind of trail leading back to him or Edward. Electronic, paper, smoke signal. Told you, he's paranoid. I kinda see his point. If word gets out, a lot of people get screwed."

"You live with his sister. It would be normal for you to talk to him. If you don't, you might be the one getting screwed. More than you are now."

"Yeah, I know. It's just…" Rojo sighed. "Okay, I'll call him tomorrow."

"That's a good start. And while you're talking to him, tell him to stop gambling."

"He'd better, or bad things will certainly happen. Whatever, I'm retiring from this life of crime. I've got a music career to think about."

I glanced at my watch. Past two o'clock. "It's late. See you in the morning. Be sure to let Joy know where you are." I rose from the couch.

"Goodnight, Channing," Rojo said. "And thanks again. You're a life saver." He picked up the remote control and clicked on the TV, then pulled the lever on the side of the chair and leaned way back. Just like I always did.

I went to my room to get ready for bed. Just inside the door, a snowdrift of dirty clothes rose up to meet me. As usual, I was a tad behind on my laundry. I tried to imagine a pile of dirty underwear stinking up any of the bedrooms in Hao's mansion. Unconscionable. Were people neat or messy because of who they were, or how they were raised? Nature or nurture? Was there a cleanliness gene?

Growing up, my mother never paid much attention to housekeeping. Our apartment was always overgrown with clutter. Stuff was everywhere. Stuff grew on top of other stuff. The clutter was cluttered. Once in a while—every few months or so—my mother would get the cleaning bug and pull out a dust rag and fire up the vacuum. That would last about forty-five minutes. Then we'd be back to moving stacks of magazines out of our way whenever we wanted to eat at the kitchen table.

I suppose if there had been more people in my family, we might have been forced to be neater. If I had been part of a bigger family...

As a kid, I'd wanted two things in the way of a family: siblings and a father. I envied my friends who had brothers and sisters to play with, people to stick up for them when the bullies came calling, shoulders to cry on when things got tough. I could tell Edward and Patrick were tight. I bet they'd covered each other's backs more times than they could remember. Who was watching my back on a daily basis? Artie?

Not quite. According to my therapist, Artie was a father figure to me, not a sibling.

Hao was an actual father to Edward and Patrick and he was on top of them like crust on bread. Did fathers ever stop meddling in the lives of their kids? It seemed to me, though, Hao went way beyond meddling. One thing I knew for sure—I wouldn't want to go against him with something serious on the line.

Would I have wanted a father like Hao? Authoritative and demanding? Harsh? Cold? Hell yeah, I would have settled for that. Beggars can't be choosers. At the time, I enjoyed my mother's laissez-faire attitude, but in retrospect, I might have done better with a little more discipline. In *retrospect*, I think some of my mother's leniency shaded toward neglect, or at best, indifference. She just couldn't be bothered.

Whenever Artie didn't want to rehash something out of his control, he'd trot out one of his favorite sayings, "Things without remedy should be without regard." Then he'd grunt a couple times and move on to something else.

I grunted a couple times as I waded through the mess on my way to the bathroom.

NINETEEN

"Everything is delicious. Heck, it's better than delicious," I said, finishing up my third helping of green beans. Sophie was an excellent cook so I didn't have to pretend the food was good like I'd done at countless meals in the past.

"It's a pleasure cooking for someone who appreciates food," Sophie said, somehow managing to be gracious toward me while sniping at Artie. "You're welcome here any day of the week, Channing. You know we love you."

Artie grunted.

"Thanks, I may have to come over more often." I leaned in and said sotto voce, "I'll *definitely* come over more often, if you lose the old geezer."

Sophie's face flushed, and Artie grunted again.

"How are you doing?" Sophie said, voice gentle, and I knew she was asking about how I was coping without Lauren.

"Good days and bad days. More and more good days now, so I can't complain, I guess."

"Hang in there. It'll keep getting better. You won't ever forget completely—and that's good—but the memories will start being more pleasant than depressing, and your heart will open itself up to new potentials as you heal."

This time, Artie cleared his throat instead of grunting, but I wasn't sure what he meant. Sometimes it was like trying to decipher a two-year-old's comments. An immature two-year-old.

"You're probably right. Things'll get better with time," I said, smiling, having heard Sophie's New Age philosophies before. Her heart was in the right place, as was Artie's. They just had different ways of showing it.

"You're a good person, Channing Hayes, and good things happen to good people. Make that *great* things."

Where was that logic eight months ago when Lauren was killed?

"Everybody finished?" she asked.

"Yes, and I think I'm about to explode."

Sophie looked crushed. "What about dessert? I made pie."

"Now we're talking," Artie said. Interesting that when talk turned to pie, he stopped grunting.

"Channing? Home-baked apple pie," Sophie said. "À la mode."

I patted my belly with both hands, like some clichéd character from a fifties sitcom. "Sure, I'd love some." If I was going to explode, at least I'd go out happy.

"Soph," Artie said, "Channing and I are going to talk a little business. Could you bring our pie out to the sunroom?" Artie's chair screeched as he slid it out from the table.

I followed him through the kitchen into a cheery room in the back. Windows on three sides let the sun pour in, and a variety of potted plants covered a low wrought-iron bench against one wall. Obviously, this room belonged to Sophie. Artie eased himself down into a wicker chair with a bright yellow cushion, and I sat next to him in a matching chair.

Artie pulled a cigar stub from his pocket—who keeps stuff like that in their pockets?—and stuffed it into his mouth. If I knew Sophie, Artie hadn't actually lighted up a cigar in the past ten years, at least not in this house.

"So," he said. "How's your 'investigation' going?"

I filled him in, leaving out the stuff he wouldn't care about. Artie was a "highlights only" kind of guy. When I told him about Patrick's huge gambling debt, Artie's eyes dilated for a moment, but he kept his trap shut. I ended my story with Rojo moving in to my place.

"I always thought your place would make a nice bed and breakfast. Hope you're charging him enough. Don't make Rojo too comfortable, though. He may never want to leave."

That exact thought had crossed my mind as I tiptoed out of the apartment around eleven this morning. Rojo had still been asleep on the couch, a small smile on his face and an empty package of Oreos on the floor. He'd looked *quite* comfortable.

Sophie bustled in carrying a silver tray. I wasn't sure how I rated the good stuff, but I wasn't complaining. So what if no one ever served me on a silver tray before? There was a first time for everything. "Here's your dessert, gentlemen." She handed me a plate with a gargantuan wedge of pie and a huge scoop of ice cream. Then she handed Artie his plate, which held a tiny scoop atop a barely visible sliver of pie. He started to fuss, but Sophie cut him off with a flip of her wrist. "I don't want to hear it. Enjoy your dessert. I'll be back with some coffee." She scowled at Artie, then smiled at me as she glided from the room.

Before I could take a bite, Artie grabbed my plate and handed me his, in one smooth, swift motion. "Thanks."

"But—"

"Stow it. Can't you let an old man enjoy some pie?" Artie forked a bite into his mouth. He had no problem playing the "old man" card whenever it suited him, but he'd be the first to start bitching if someone else tried to play it for him. "Ahh. Wonderful. Relax, you can always ask for more, and Sophie will love you for it. She's always saying you could use a little more meat on your bones."

I shook my head and sampled the pie. Delicious. Now that Artie mentioned it, I *could* use a little more meat on my bones. "I noticed you didn't make any comment about Patrick's gambling problem."

"What do you want me to say? That gamblers are stupid, foolish schmucks?"

I took another bite of my pie and waited.

"Well, gamblers are stupid, foolish schmucks. Some of them, anyway. And I should know, I was one for a while." Artie leaned forward and placed his plate on the table in front of us. Half of his pie sat there, blob of ice cream on board, melting. "Gambling's an addiction. A sickness. A disease. Of course, not everyone who gambles has it. But . . ." He shook his head. "For those of us who do, the feelings never go away. You're always craving the next score. The rush of adrenaline is very hard to describe."

I gambled occasionally, but frankly, I could take it or leave it. Kinda like a turkey sandwich. "I'm listening." I set my empty plate down on the table next to his.

200

"When you win, you're on top of the world. You feel invincible. No obstacle too great—I mean, you picked a winner—a winner! Many people think it's all about the money. That's bullshit. It's all about the winning."

"Then why not bet ten bucks, instead of hundreds? Or thousands?"

A knowing look grew on Artie's face. "Channing. Be glad you don't know the answer to that question. It's the thrill. You can't taste the thrill, unless you've got something at stake. Something big to lose. Take skydiving. The thrill of cheating death is part of the attraction."

"So the thrill of cheating bankruptcy is part of the attraction of gambling?"

"Yeah, something like that." He snorted. "I know. It seems screwed-up. And it is. But … it is what it is." He strangled the arms of his chair with his grip.

"Was it hard?"

"What? Gambling? Hell, no. Easiest thing in the world. Reach into your wallet, take out a fifty, slap it on the table. Red or black. Lucky seven. Twenty-one. Lakers minus four." Artie flashed me a tight smile. "The hard part was quitting."

"How did you finally kick the habit?"

"Oh, if only it were truly kicked. Let's just say I've subdued the monkey. I give credit for that to Sophie. Without her to set me straight, I'd be in a gutter somewhere. No career, no friends, no money, no nice house, no great wife." He tipped his head at the plates on the table. "No pie."

"How come you never told me this before?"

"It's in the past. Didn't tell you I've got high blood pressure either."

"Yes you did. In fact, you tell me that all the time."

He waved his hand. "You know what I mean. It's personal, and it doesn't affect my day-to-day life. If I ever get the urge to place a bet, I simply think of my Sophie and the feeling disappears."

A vision of Lauren shimmered before my eyes.

"It's a dark chapter in my past, and I'd like to keep it in my past. *Capisce*?"

Thoughts of Lauren dissipated. "Sure, Artie. I won't tell a soul."

We sat in silence. A few moments later, Sophie returned with coffee. "Two coffees, black." She set the mugs down on the table. "I'll let you get back to whatever it is you were talking about." Her eyes twinkled. Once again, she glided from the room, and Artie's gaze followed her out. Artie was a lucky man, and I suspected he knew it.

"What's your take on Patrick's gambling?"

"Sounds like he's got a gambling problem. Sneaking around, short on funds yet he keeps going. Figures one big score and he's back in the black. Classic symptoms. Secrecy is a big red flag. On some level, gamblers are ashamed of themselves. He's got some added pressure. He knows if he's discovered, he's not only fucking up his life, he's fucking up other people's lives. All the more reason to keep things under wraps. Hell, he'd probably do just about anything to keep his secret from being discovered."

How desperate was Patrick? Desperate enough to murder those who might give him away? Un-Lucky Lin and Mohawk were already dead. Did Patrick have something to do with that? Was Rojo next on the hit parade?

"Channing? You feel okay? You look like you might hurl," Artie said, staring straight into my eyes.

"Huh? Yeah, I'm okay. How far do you think Patrick would go to keep his gambling secret?"

"Hmm. Obviously, he didn't want anyone to know what he was up to. He used Rojo as his drop-man, and I'm sure Jimmy the Raisin didn't have a clue where Rojo's money came from. Then, evidently, Patrick paid Jimmy off anonymously so he wouldn't have to come out in the open. I'd say Patrick was being pretty damn careful."

"You think Patrick paid off Fugano?" Something didn't quite add up. "Why would he do that, and tell Fugano not to take any more of 'Rojo's' action, but keep doing business with DeManzi's crew?"

"Who the hell knows? Something you have to remember about gamblers. Their logic doesn't always make sense. You're always stealing from Peter to pay Paul while you're lying to your mother. Feeding a gambling jones tends to skew one's priorities."

So did many things. I knew a lot of comics and a disproportionate number seemed to have addictive personalities. Mostly I'd seen alcohol and drug abuse, but how many of them had hidden gambling problems? Probably more than I cared to guess. "Hypothetically, if you were in Patrick's shoes and owed a ton of money, and if you were terrified of your secret getting out, what would you do about it?"

"Hypothetically? Why don't you just go ask Patrick?"

———

After I finished my coffee—I passed on another piece of pie despite intense lobbying from Sophie—I said my goodbyes. From the car, I called my apartment. It rang six times before my voice greeted me. I didn't leave a message. Then I tried Rojo on his cell. No luck. He was probably still racked out on the couch—staying up until four a.m. watching infomercials took its toll.

My imagination stirred. I'd practically insisted that Rojo call Patrick this morning. What if he had, and Patrick had lured Rojo to some out-of-the-way rendezvous location to "discuss" the situation. Then Patrick could run a dagger straight through Rojo's heart. Problem solved. No fuss, no muss. The gambling could never be traced back to Patrick.

I tried Rojo's cell again. This time, I left a message for him to call me ASAP.

My next call was to Patrick at campaign headquarters. The staffer who answered the phone said he wasn't there. I asked for Patrick's cell number, and after some hemming and hawing—on the staffer's part—I managed to persuade him to divulge the information I needed. I guess telling him I was on Hao Wong's bowling team carried some weight.

Patrick answered on the second ring. "Hello."

I exhaled, relieved that Patrick wasn't down some dark alley torturing Rojo. "Patrick, this is Channing Hayes."

"Oh, yes. How are you? Decide to join our cause?"

"Not exactly. Can we talk?" I started up Rex as I spoke. "Where can I meet you?"

"Now? I'm ... what's this about?"

"Something I'm sure you want to hear. Something I'm also sure you want to keep private."

"Is that right?" A bit of defiance.

"Joy has a very nice boyfriend, doesn't she? He's a pal of yours, right? Does favors for you every so often?"

A few beats of silence. "I'm at my home. Please, come by. I'd love to talk with you." His clipped words belied his statement. He gave me directions and clicked off with a terse goodbye.

Patrick lived in a condo in Rosslyn, about twenty minutes from Artie's house near Tysons. I hopped on the Beltway and got off on I-66 East toward D.C. It was a pretty straight shot, mostly highways, and with Saturday traffic, I managed the trip without having to hit my brakes too often.

The most difficult part was finding a parking spot.

I did, and got buzzed into the building with another terse, "Come up," from Patrick. He was Mr. Charming when trolling for votes, Mr. Sourpuss when his keister was on the line. So typical.

Patrick answered the door in jeans and a long-sleeve polo shirt with some tiny animal embroidered on the chest. He had a can of Coke in his hand. "Come in, Channing."

I followed him into the main living space. A large plasma TV was on, sound muted, and a laptop laid open on the coffee table. Next to the laptop, an assortment of electronic toys: BlackBerry, iPod, Bluetooth earpiece, and a calculator. A green-tinged banana—the sole representative from the organic world—looked out of place on the table.

"Have a seat," Patrick said, pointing to a Queen Anne chair upholstered in a gold-flecked fabric. It looked uncomfortable, and it was even more uncomfortable than it looked. I squirmed a bit, trying to feel at ease.

He descended onto the couch, in front of all his stuff, and I was reminded of Jimmy the Raisin sitting amidst all his electronic toys. Was that another symptom of an addictive personality? Acquiring toys?

"So," Patrick began, setting his Coke on the table with a thud. "You had something important to tell me?"

"Have you spoken to Rojo today?"

"Rojo? No. Why?"

He was probably still asleep. "I know about your gambling problems."

"What gambling problems?"

"Rojo told me what's going on."

A look of surprise leaped onto Patrick's face.

"Rojo said he'd been placing bets for you with a series of book-ies. That you'd built up quite a debt and people were clamoring to be repaid. Loudly and forcefully."

Patrick rose. "Why would he say something like that? Is he in trouble? Is Joy okay?" Surprise had morphed into concern.

"He's been roughed up. Twice. By enforcers looking for their money. Money *you* owe them."

Patrick shook his head as he paced the floor in front of me. "I don't know what you're talking about. If Rojo's in trouble ... I guess getting the police involved might not be the best for him, huh? Maybe I can help. How much money does he owe?"

I'd come around to Artie's way of thinking; politicians chapped my tuchas, too. I didn't trust them farther than I could throw their horse manure. But Patrick was putting on a pretty good show. Of course, I'd tipped him off on the phone, so he'd had a little time to work on his act while I drove over. "He owes enough money to really piss off his bookies. And he doesn't have it."

Patrick kept pacing, faster. "Why would he say I was involved? He must know I'd find out and refute him."

Someone was lying. A carefree, go-with-the-flow rock-n-roller, or a buttoned-down, lawyer/politician. A tossup. "I just want to be clear. You're saying you don't gamble, and you've never placed a bet with any bookie using Rojo as a go-between?"

He stopped moving and faced me. Pasted a most-sincere look on his chameleon face. "Yes. That's exactly what I'm saying. I don't gamble, certainly not with illegal bookies. Do you have any idea what that would do to Edward's campaign if someone found out? To my career? Ludicrous."

Which is exactly why he'd lie. "Rojo's bruises aren't ludicrous."

"Oh, I have no doubt he was beaten up. It's the accusation I'm somehow involved that's flat-out crazy." Patrick resumed pacing and started mumbling to himself. "This is bullshit. What is he after? Is this some kind of shakedown?"

Patrick's concern had transformed into anger.

In my mind's eye, I saw Rojo tilted back in my recliner, drinking my beer, watching my TiVo. Was he working some kind of scam? Doubtful. There had to be easier ways of being a freeloader that didn't involve getting yourself pummeled every couple days. "That's not how it came across to me."

Patrick stopped creating a rut in the carpet and returned to the couch. "I don't get it. If he needed money or something, he should have come to me and asked. I would have loaned him some, for Joy's sake. But I still don't see how fabricating this story benefits him." He nodded at me. "Got any ideas?"

"He also seems to think you're having money, uh, issues."

"What? No, I'm doing fine." He spread his arms out. "Haven't had to hock anything. The campaign pays me okay. I managed to save up a nice little nest egg from the firm. Like I said, Rojo is shoveling it. Why, I don't know. But I think I'm going to find out." He reached for his iPhone.

"Hold on. He's feeling pretty scared right now. Says whoever is after him is going to torture him if they find him. He's actually waiting for you to come up with the money so he can pay them off."

"How much?"

I wasn't sure why I hadn't told Patrick the amount yet. Maybe I wanted to see if he'd bring it up, or maybe I just wanted to tease him a little before lowering the boom. Mostly though, I think I wanted to see his face when I told him that somehow Rojo had gotten himself on the hook for two-hundred-twenty thousand bucks. Hoping Patrick's face would give away who was telling the truth.

"Channing? How much does Rojo say he owes?"

"For the record, he says *you* owe the money."

"*For the record*, no one's busting up my kneecaps." Patrick's left eyebrow flinched. "How much money does he owe?"

I stared at him, ready to spot any telltale signs of deception, obfuscation, or chicanery. "Two-hundred-twenty thousand dollars."

His pupils dilated and the corners of his mouth inched upward. A flash of something hot. Could be genuine surprise. Or more great acting. "Holy shit. How did Rojo run up that kind of tab?"

"Seems unlikely, doesn't it?"

"The money didn't come from me. And it didn't come from Joy. Hard to believe it came from playing in his band. I'm beginning to think that Rojo's one big fat liar."

As little Seanie might say, *it takes one to know one.*

TWENTY

I DROVE HOME, TRYING to make sense of everything. Rojo had been roughed up, twice, and there was no doubt the injuries were real. Nobody gives themselves cracked ribs as part of some ruse. And the terror I saw in Rojo's face was real, too. So it seemed obvious someone was after him for something. According to Rojo, it was because he lost lots of money gambling, money Patrick had wagered on credit. But if the bookie didn't know anything about Patrick's supposed involvement, why would he front Rojo that much money to play with?

It didn't make any sense.

Now if Rojo were lying as Patrick asserted, he'd still have the same problem. Why would a bookie extend credit to a guy with a very slim bank account?

Could the gambling angle be a smokescreen? I'd met Fugano and he was definitely real—a loser, to be sure, but real. And he'd admitted Rojo had been a client, right up until a mysterious payoff. Was Fugano lying for some reason? Was the mysterious payoff simply a convenient lie to throw me and Artie off track?

But what could Rojo have gotten himself into? Drugs? Maybe he was a dealer who'd pissed off his supplier. Maybe he was a pimp and had gotten into a turf war with another pimp.

Maybe Erin was right, and he'd just knocked off a bank and was quarreling with other members of his crew.

Yeah, and maybe I was going to win an Emmy starring in an ABC sitcom.

Enough maybes. I returned to Earth, and my mind returned to the original scenario, Rojo's story. What if DeManzi and his lackeys knew Patrick was the money behind Rojo, the one placing the action? Then he'd be more apt to extend credit, and he'd have some extra leverage to collect. He could threaten to go public with the information about Patrick's gambling and potentially wreck Edward's campaign. But assuming this was true, why go after Rojo to collect the debt? Why not go straight to the man holding the purse strings, Patrick?

Somebody was lying, but damned if I knew whom. Throughout my life, I'd always had a pretty finely tuned bullshit detector. In fifth grade, Liam Carnahan pegged me with a rock while I wasn't looking on the playground, then pointed his finger at Danny Horton. Danny denied it, and they ended up elbows and knees on the blacktop, trying to "work things out." When the dust settled—literally—I marched up to Liam, looked through his eyes into his soul and knew he was the perpetrator. The best part was his unspoken acknowledgment—the guilty flicker in his eyes—that told me he knew that I knew what he'd done.

Of course, back then, the task had been a little easier; Liam hadn't been a politician or a rock 'n' roll performer. On the other hand, maybe my powers of detection had weakened.

My head hurt. All I wanted was to go back home, pull out a composition book, and work on my routine. Escape back into the world of stand-up comedy. Face my current struggles and really—*really*—buckle down and hammer out twenty primo minutes. Then take the routine out for a spin at some small clubs and see how it played. It's what I do. Stand-up is more than a job, it's my life. I needed to get back to it. People getting beaten up and lying and gambling and thugs getting murdered didn't belong in my world.

Laughter belonged in my world, and there hadn't been nearly enough of it lately.

I changed lanes to pass a slow-moving minivan, then turned on the radio. Cranked up the volume. Hit the gas. Just me and Rex cruising along, leaving our problems in the dust.

Oh, if it were only that simple.

I found a good spot in the condo lot and locked Rex. Listening to the music had elevated my spirits a tad, and at this point, I'd latch onto any morsel of good cheer I could find. I was reaching for the outer door of the building when I heard someone call my name from the bushes flanking the entryway on my right.

I whirled and put my dukes up, like a seven-fingered Rocky Balboa. Weight on the balls of my feet, ready to explode into action. I could almost feel the adrenaline pumping through me.

"Pssst." To my ears, it sounded a lot like "pissed."

I kept my guard up as an arm gestured to me from the greenery.

A head followed the arm. Why was I not surprised the head belonged to Rojo? "What's going on now?" I relaxed and took a step in his direction, but not close enough for him to grab me. I didn't want to get dragged into the bushes for a conversation

"Are you alone?" he asked.

I made a show of glancing around. "Yeah. I gave my groupies the day off."

"Is anyone around?"

"Damnit, Rojo. Get your ass out here. We've got a few things to talk about. But I'm going upstairs. I'm hungry." And fed up with all this nonsense, for sure. My racing heart had returned to normal.

Rojo extricated himself from the bushes and darted inside. I followed him in and watched him hop from foot to foot as we waited for the elevator. The entire time, he stared at the numbers above the elevator, tracking its progress. We didn't speak.

Once we entered my apartment, I heard Rojo exhale. "Jesus. This is getting to me. I think there are goons around every corner, waiting to grab me." He crossed the room and flopped into my recliner, as if it were his. I'd have to speak to him about that at some point, but for now, I settled onto the couch.

"Why did you leave the condo?"

Rojo offered me a shaky smile. "Got antsy. Kept imagining them tracking me here and cornering me. No way out. You can understand, right?"

"Yeah, I guess."

The smile fell off his face. "So, I was getting ready to call Patrick, like you said, when he called me."

"He did? When?"

"About twenty minutes ago."

After I'd left his condo. Made sense. "And?"

"Said he wanted to meet so we could talk about things. I asked if he had the money to pay off DeManzi, but he didn't answer." Rojo swallowed and his face looked a little paler. "He sounded real strange. Anxious, you know? Something's fishy, real fishy."

Fishy, indeed. "Why do you say that?"

"I've been thinking. Lin didn't know where the money's from, right? All along, he thinks it's just me making these bets. And even if he believes there's someone else involved, he doesn't know who it is. His bosses don't know either. So if I'm gone, there's no way for them to track it back to Patrick." His voice wavered. "See?"

I saw perfectly. The thing I was having trouble with was why it had taken Rojo so long to see it himself. "You think Patrick is out to get you?"

"I didn't. Until that phone call. Now I'm not so sure."

"You're his sister's boyfriend. Do you think he'd get rid of you? Wouldn't that devastate Joy?"

"Yeah, yeah. That's what I thought all along. But I'm telling you, he sounded cold on the phone. And evasive." Rojo blew a big breath out. "I don't fucking know. I see bogeymen everywhere. DeManzi is after me on one side, and Patrick is after me on the other. You're the only one I can trust, Channing."

"What have you told Joy?"

"She thinks I'm sitting in on a friend's recording session in Philly. I told her I was out of it, the gambling thing, and the last beating was some leftover stuff from my involvement with Lin. I think she bought it."

Time to spill. "There's something you ought to know."

"What?" His eyes went wide.

"I just came from Patrick's. He denies your entire story. Says he doesn't gamble, never had you place bets for him. Says you're a complete liar."

Rojo's nostril's flared and he bared his teeth slightly. "He's lying. I swear, Channing, I'm telling the truth."

"But you have no evidence, nobody to corroborate your story, do you?" I said softly.

He shook his head, slowly, somberly. "No, I guess I don't." He took a few measured breaths and stared at a spot in space, evidently mulling the ramifications.

I sat there, too, thinking. What if Rojo was right? What if Patrick felt the only way out of his jam involved silencing Rojo? Seemed improbable, but not impossible.

Rojo cocked his head at me. "Channing? What am I going to do?" He seemed on the verge of tears.

"Hang in there. We'll figure something out." Comforting words. If only I felt confident that I could back them up.

———

"He asked me a few questions. I answered them. He thanked me and took off," Ty said, telling me again—for the third time—about Freeman's visit to discuss the mugging.

"Anything else?"

"Nope. Just said he was crossing his t's and dotting his i's. They're pretty sure it's a gang war. I'm just glad we didn't get caught in the crossfire." Ty smoothed out his sportcoat. We still had about an hour before the customers started arriving for tonight's first show.

"Good. Hopefully all that's behind us."

"Amen to that," Ty said.

My phone rang, and I left Ty, looking imposing, at the front door while I ducked outside to answer my call. I didn't recognize the number. "Hello?"

"Channing? This is Hao Wong. How are you this evening?"

"Fine."

"I know this is very short notice, but I'd like to meet with you to discuss something that's very important."

"When?"

"Is now good?"

Not really. "Well, Saturday night is our biggest night, and the first show will be starting soon. How about tomorrow?" *Or better yet, how about never?*

"Please. It's important. I won't take much of your time—I wish to thank you. I happen to be very close to your club right now."

"Okay, then. I guess I can spare a few minutes. I'll meet you out front."

"Actually, I would prefer if we met nearby. How about if we go for a little stroll on the W&OD trail. I can meet you behind the Whole Foods in five minutes."

"Okay, see you in five." I hung up on Hao and called Artie. He was in our office working on the introduction for tonight's comics, but I thought it would be better if I called him on the phone rather than walk thirty yards and face him in person.

"What?" Artie couldn't be bothered with manners, especially when he was busy.

I told him I might miss the beginning of the first show, then held the phone eight inches from my ear while he yelled at me for upsetting the rhythm on a Saturday night. When the verbal storm slowed to a drizzle, I brought the phone back to my ear. "Artie, trust me, it's important. I'll be back when I can."

Artie grunted and told me not to worry about it. Then he clicked off without waiting for me to say thanks.

The trail was only a short walk away. I crossed the shopping center parking lot, dodging people heading for the Sofa Showroom or looking to score bargains at Dave's Dollar Store. Then I hung a right on the sidewalk along Maple Avenue and humped it through the heart of Vienna.

Vienna, Virginia, is a suburb of D.C. with a hometown feel. Small independent stores and restaurants vied with national chains for business. The bank tellers knew every customer's first names, and the Little League All-Star teams always made a deep run in the World Series tournaments.

A great place to live or work, except for the traffic.

I arrived at the spot where Maple Avenue intersects with the trail, behind the grocery store, and looked around. The Washington & Old Dominion trail cut through Vienna, on its way from Alexandria to Purcellville. Although it was late evening, the trail was still crowded with folks getting exercise; runners, bikers, and rollerbladers all shared the narrow paved path. Lauren and I had biked portions of it from time to time, but we'd never covered the entire forty-plus miles. A few moments after I got there, I picked Hao out from the crowd, coming toward me. He wasn't hard to spot; he was the only one wearing a business suit.

Three feet away, he thrust his hand out. Now I knew where Edward and Patrick got their affinity for shaking hands. "Thank you for coming," Hao said. "And thank you for all your efforts with regard to our problems. Shall we go for a walk?"

"Sure."

"This way." He touched my elbow to get me started, then proceeded along the path, away from Maple Avenue, with short, precise steps. I followed. We drifted to the right side of the path, with me on the inside. He was older and smaller than I was, so I ambled while he walked at his normal—slow—pace.

"Channing. Again, let me thank you for your efforts. Patrick called and filled me in on the troubles. With regard to gambling. You've brought a very serious—and potentially disastrous—situation to our attention, and we are indebted to you." He spoke without looking at me. Instead, he seemed to be concentrating very hard on the path before him. "Without your intervention, we may never have known what was happening until it was too late." He glanced over his shoulder, and I followed his gaze.

Brad Ames trailed us, thirty yards behind.

"What's he doing here?"

"He's my driver today."

"I thought he worked for Edward. On the campaign."

"Yes, he is on loan to my son. His main job is the Chief of Security for my company."

"And he watches your back."

"Yes. He is a valuable person to have." Hao glanced behind him again, just to make sure Ames hadn't gotten lost, then resumed walking. "Patrick is worried that if news of this gets out, it will be devastating for the campaign. And I agree with him."

"So Patrick owned up to his gambling?"

Hao stopped cold and faced me. I was a few inches taller so he tilted his head up. "No. No such admission was made. You see, it does not really matter who incurred these debts. Rojo, Patrick, whomever. As long as they are owed by someone connected to us, Edward's campaign is in jeopardy. Xun and I have arrived at a decision. We will pay off these gambling debts and put this issue behind us." He said it as if he were telling me he would go get his car washed because it was dirty.

"What do you mean it doesn't matter? Of course it matters. Anybody who runs up those kinds of debts gambling has a problem. A big one. And Patrick's problems have become other people's problems."

"I'm sure whoever ran up this debt—Patrick or Rojo—has seen the error of his ways and will not be taking those kinds of risks ever again."

"Rojo isn't the one with the gambling addiction."

A bicycle bell dinged behind us, followed by a man's voice. "On your left." A moment later, a little girl in a pink helmet passed us riding a two-wheeler with training wheels. A man—her father, presumably—jogged next to her. Somehow, I had a tough time picturing Hao running beside a young Joy as she learned to ride. My previous notion, that having a father like Hao just to have *any* father, had soured.

Hao waited until the man and his daughter were ten yards ahead of us before continuing. "As I have said, laying blame does not solve the problem. It is counterproductive. We have all agreed to settle the debt and move on."

"Rojo has agreed to this?"

"Edward and Patrick will speak to him. They can be quite persuasive."

My right fist flexed at my side. Another snow job from a family of politicians. What did I expect? That they'd be different because they were related to a friend of mine?

"As I'm sure you understand, you must not speak of this. Ever. To anyone. This is a family matter. I cannot stress that enough. We will not shirk our obligations, of course, but there is no reason to make this public. Agreed?"

I took a few quick breaths. Making this public wouldn't do anyone any good, but it sure felt dirty somehow, sweeping this under the rug, no matter how fancy and expensive and hand-woven that rug might be. "With all due respect, I think this stinks. And no, I can't promise to bury this. It isn't right."

Hao stopped walking and faced me. He clenched his teeth so tightly you'd need the Jaws of Life to feed him dinner. Then he relaxed just enough to squeeze out his words. "If this gets out, it will destroy Edward's campaign. His career. All the good he will do for society will be flushed down the drain. Because of something he did not do. That *isn't right*. Surely you can see that."

I saw his point, at least how it related to Edward. He shouldn't have to suffer because of Patrick's self-destructive choices. Unfortunately, I didn't have a compromise solution.

"Time to head back now." Hao turned around. "Channing. I know how this seems to you. Dirty. Underhanded. But it really is none of your business. You must respect that."

There was nothing about this situation I respected, but I kept quiet. Up ahead, Ames stood by the side of the path, in the weeds, waiting for us to pass so he could trail Hao again, like a good lackey.

Hao and I continued in silence. The breeze that had been at our backs had stiffened, and now that we walked into it, dirt and grit from the path peppered our faces. Hao ducked his head slightly and kept on trucking. When we reached Ames, we stopped, and Hao signaled to Ames, who removed an envelope from his pocket and handed it to Hao. The beefy security man glared at me the entire time. If that was his best fright-inducing look, he needed a few lessons from Ty.

Hao waved for Ames to move behind us, and Ames took about ten steps backward.

"I want you to know that I do not forget those who help me. And you helped me—and Edward—by bringing this whole gambling thing to our attention. This is for you. Your services are no longer needed." Hao handed me the envelope.

I dug a fingernail under the flap and ripped it open. Counted what was inside. Fifteen Benjamins stared at me. All of a sudden, I got a familiar copper taste in my mouth. "Why don't you just admit it? Patrick got in over his head. He used Rojo to do his dirty work, and then when things fell apart, he let him take the fall. You *all* let him take the fall. Poor Rojo was the one getting beaten up while you stayed nice and cozy in your sheltered world. I can't believe you won't even own up to what you did." I'd raised my voice and moved closer to him, invading his space.

Hao's nostrils flared, but he kept his lips pressed together like a toddler who didn't want to eat his strained peas.

First, Patrick tried to hire me to work for the campaign. Then Hao and Xun tried to scare me off. Now Hao was going with the tried-and-true to get me out of the picture—cold cash. I was getting the message loud and clear. The Wongs didn't want me mucking about in their lives. I pointed my finger right in Hao's face. "This isn't over."

A beefy hand clamped down on my shoulder. "Actually, it is," Ames said. "Run along now, Channing. You've said what's on your mind."

I squirmed out of Ames's grip, and he tried to regain his hold, but I dodged him—he was well beyond his playing weight and his bulk slowed him down. He lunged at me again, and I had no trouble sidestepping him. Hao shook his head at Ames, clearly disgusted. "Let him be."

Ames backed off, face red. From exertion or embarrassment, I couldn't tell.

Hao addressed me. "You must not discuss what we've talked about with anybody. And Channing, just so you know, there will be no more potential embarrassments. I'll see to that. Edward is going to the Capitol and, believe me, that's simply his first stop on the way to the White House."

I made sure I had Hao's complete attention before speaking my well-chosen words. "You can kiss my ass." Then I tossed the wad of hundred-dollar-bills into the air, where the wind grabbed them and sent them fluttering down the path. Ames squawked and ran after the money. As I stalked off, I noticed a few joggers stop to watch Ames leaping and grabbing after the swiftly disappearing payola.

I also noticed the expression on Hao's face.

Priceless.

TWENTY-ONE

AFTER THE FIRST SHOW, Artie and I retreated to our office and let Donna and Skip supervise the clean-up before the late show. Artie was on the phone "discussing" a future date with some comic's manager. And by discussing, I meant he was outlining exactly what we expected from the comic. I'd heard it a million times, and no matter how often Artie told these guys' managers, the comics still came in clueless. They'd arrive late or they would try to smoke cigarettes on stage, or they would expect a vat of blue M&Ms. We'd spelled out most of the important stuff in the contracts—at least all we could anticipate—but inevitably there'd be some things that fell through the cracks. Most of the comics were decent; after we pointed something out, they'd comply. But every once in awhile, we'd get some jerkoff and he or she would put up a giant stink and someone's nose would get out of joint. Often, it was mine.

And speaking of getting my nose out of joint, I was still royally pissed at Hao for thinking he could pay me off. I felt sorry once again, not just for Joy, but for Edward and Patrick, too. Being raised by a prick like that had to be unpleasant.

Artie said goodbye and set the phone on the desk with a thud. "Okay. We are now booked out for the next six weekends. Finally." He exhaled and I could smell the remnants of his dinner from where I sat.

"Good work, sir. Business has been booming lately, and you deserve a lot of the credit." Always felt good to pump Artie up.

"We are on a roll, aren't we?" He picked up his cigar stub and wedged it between his teeth. "So where did you disappear to earlier this evening? What was so important?" He tipped back in his chair and put his feet up on his desk. Settled in for a nice story. If only I had one for him.

"Hao Wong wanted to talk to me."

"Oh?"

"He and his brother are going to pay off Patrick's gambling debt. Keep everything quiet so they don't mess up Edward's campaign."

"Figures. Politicians would sweep the gold medals in the Covering Shit Up Olympics."

"And the kicker? Hao wouldn't even admit it was Patrick who was making the bets. Implied the whole thing was Rojo's problem."

Artie snorted. "Effers. I feel bad for Lee. And for his sister, of course. Stuck in a family of wolves."

"Yeah." Maybe being in a big family wasn't always such a good thing.

"So now what?" Artie asked.

"I was thanked for my help. And told to butt out, everything is taken care of. Hao said, in no uncertain terms, the *matter was closed.*" I didn't mention the envelope of cash. Didn't want to send Artie into apoplectic seizures.

"So are you?"

"Are I what?"

"Going to butt out?"

"Hell, no."

He pointed his cigar stub at me and was about to give me his unsolicited opinion, when Dan O'Rourke, Korbell's Jack-of-All-Trades, stuck his head into the office. "Hello Channing. You got a minute?"

"Sure," I said.

"Just on my way out," Artie said, getting up. "Here, you can have my seat."

Artie left and O'Rourke took his chair. Glanced around the office as if he were planning to redecorate. "Good show. Funny."

"Thanks. We are a comedy club, after all." I wish I'd known O'Rourke had been in the audience; I would have loved to see him crack a smile, or—heaven forbid—laugh out loud.

"Right. It's a nice club. Cozy, but not too small. I guess you'd call it intimate."

"We like it."

"And it's not too fancy and modern."

Code for plain and old? "Thanks."

O'Rourke picked a pencil off Artie's desk and tapped the eraser against his chin a couple times. "Have you given any more thought to hosting a fundraising event here? I think we could make it very successful. People always seem to donate more money when they're having a good time."

"Still considering it." I guess you needed to be persistent to be an effective fundraiser.

"Good, good. Nicole will be pleased." O'Rourke twirled the pencil in his hand. "I'm not sure you understand my role in Sanford's campaign."

"Why do I have the feeling you're about to tell me?"

"My official title is 'Campaign Researcher.' But I do a lot of other things for the campaign. For instance, I'm in charge of vetting potential donors and backers, so if you decide to host an event, I'll be looking into your background."

I tried to keep an even keel. "Sure. No sweat."

"You know what else I do for Sanford?"

"What?"

"I make sure nothing pops out of the woodwork and bites him on the ass. In fact, I guess you could say that's my most important function."

"I suppose it's important that someone does that. Hate to have your ass bitten." I checked my watch. Fifteen minutes before the next show got under way. "Does that happen often?"

"Not since I've been in the job. I'm very good at what I do." The Wong's muscle—Ames—was a brute, but didn't frighten me. O'Rourke came across like an actuary and scared the living crap out of me.

"That's good." I made a show of checking my watch again. "Listen, I'm glad you stopped by, but I've got—"

He held his hand up. "On my way in tonight, I couldn't help but notice that Lee's Palace is next door to your club. I'm sure you're aware that Sanford's opponent is Edward Wong, Lee's nephew."

"Yes." I held my breath.

"I've been meaning to try that place. Good?"

I exhaled. "The duck really is fabulous."

O'Rourke rose. "Goodbye, Channing. I'm sure we'll be in touch."

"Glad you enjoyed the show," I said to his back as he walked out the door.

————

I slept in the next morning, but still woke up exhausted. I gobbled two toaster waffles for lunch and tried to put the whole Wong thing out of my head, at least for a little while. Maybe I should butt out. If Hao and Xun were going to pay off Patrick's debt, and if Patrick was going to stay out of trouble from now on, maybe Hao was right—the matter was as good as settled. Maybe this really wasn't any of my business.

But I'd be damned if I was going to let my buddy Rojo swing in the wind.

My dirty laundry was calling to me, but I could hardly hear it over the racket the food-encrusted dishes were making in the sink. The carpet hadn't been vacuumed in who-knew-how-long and the dirty blankets on the couch—souvenirs from Rojo's visit—were still in a jumble.

Too much crapola to do, too little motivation. I mean, who cared if my condo was clean? I didn't. Time to go to work.

In the elevator, my cell rang. I answered and thought it was Freeman. I wasn't certain because the reception kept cutting in and out. "Freeman? What's up?"

Something about murder, keep my head up, and wire hangers. Or maybe he said something about dire dangers, hard to tell.

Then the line went dead. I called him back to see what was going on; the call didn't connect. I was a little worried, but I figured if it were something really important, he'd get back to me quickly. There wasn't much I could do about it. After all, as Artie would say, things without remedy should be without regard.

I drove to The Last Laff with my cell phone resting quietly on the passenger seat.

At the club, Donna started in on me three seconds after I walked through the door. "Artie's jabbering on about changing the menu again. Can you please talk to him, tell him it creates a lot more fuss than it's worth?"

"Sure. I've got nothing better to do, you know." He was always fiddling with something. If not the menu, then the format of the shows or the brands of top-shelf liquor we bought. I often wanted to pull out one of my pet sayings about idle hands being the Devil's something or other, but I never quite remembered it. Plus Artie rarely listened to me when I tried to get philosophical on him. "Anything else?"

"Nope. Just the weekly get-Artie-off-my-back plea. Otherwise, things are great." She started off, then turned back. "Hey, don't forget about Career Day. At Sean's school?"

"Looking forward to it."

Something about my tone caused her to give me a double-take. "What?"

"Channinggggg." She dragged out the *g*. "Don't go over the top. That would only embarrass Sean. Tell them what you do and be done with it."

"Why would you think otherwise?" I pretended to be hurt.

"Because I've heard Skip mumbling stupid jokes to himself for the past week. When I asked him what he was doing, he told me he was still trying to help you with your kiddie routine."

I tried not to blush. "You know how Skip is. I promise I'll behave."

"Promise?"

"Absolutely. I remember what it was like being in second grade. Nothing embarrassing. Really." I crossed my heart with my fingers.

Donna rolled her eyes as she walked away.

I spent the next two hours catching up on paperwork, reviewing audition packages, and reading the latest *Sports Illustrated*— just about anything other than working on my routine. When my phone rang, I was thankful for yet another distraction, even if it was Freeman on the line.

"Got some good news, Channing. We found Don DeManzi's body in a Dumpster with three bullet holes in the back of his skull."

"That's *good* news?"

"Well, not for DeManzi, but for you. Your *friend* can rest easy. We can now say, beyond a shadow of a doubt, that Lin, Chun, and DeManzi all got killed in a gang war."

"You sure it was a gangland hit?" I asked.

"Part of a territorial squabble." Sarcasm dripped off the word *squabble.*

"Oh?"

"Yeah, there's been a turf battle going on, and Lin, Chun, and DeManzi were all executed in the same fashion. Three in the skull. I guess you could say the situation finally came to a head."

Another example of why Freeman should stick to law enforcement, not comedy. "So you're positive?"

"Absolutely. Here's the capper: a rival gang took credit for the three murders. And they've laid claim to all of DeManzi's business ventures. Gonna keep us busy for a while, I'd say. I gotta run, man. Talk to you later." Freeman clicked off.

Although Freeman was positive the murders were gang related, I wasn't so sure—the coincidence in timing was hard to accept. With DeManzi out of the way, Patrick was off the hook for his debt, and Hao had just saved himself a load of cash.

All in all, a pretty solid motive for murder.

———

I sat in the office mulling the latest news, trying to noodle through all the possibilities. Artie came in a few minutes later.

"Do me a favor, will you?" he said. "Donna's being a stick-in-the-mud about the menu. Doesn't want to make any changes. Of course, I could force her to accept them—I'm the boss around here, you know—but that's not how I like to handle things."

"So you want *me* to force her to accept the changes?"

"You've got a better bedside manner than I do."

Don Rickles had a better bedside manner than Artie. "I'll talk to her."

"That's my boy." Artie stared at me. "What's wrong?"

"Huh?"

"I can always tell when something's wrong with you. What is it?" Artie put his feet up on his desk.

"You know how Hao said that Patrick's gambling *matter* was closed? Well, the matter is now very much open again. At least it is for me."

"I still think you should butt out."

Mental images played back in my head. The masked thugs threatening us at Lee's. A bag of frozen peas on Rojo's swollen eye. Patrick playing fast and loose with the truth. Hao slipping me an envelope of cash to get lost. Ames, O'Rourke, Xun, Joy. Something very wrong was going on, and no one wanted me involved. I felt an obligation to see this thing through until I was satisfied with the explanation of events. I owed it to Rojo and I owed it to Lee and I owed it to myself. "I'm not butting out of anything," I said. "Not even close."

Artie looked at me funny.

I rose and grabbed my keys. "Artie?"

"Yeah, kid?"

"I'm taking the rest of the night off. I've got some things to think about."

For once, he didn't razz me about leaving early, just told me to have a good night and he'd see me tomorrow. When I got home, the first thing I saw was Rojo lounging in his customary place—my recliner.

"Hey, man. I thought you were working tonight," he said, looking like I'd caught him with his hands in the till.

"And I thought you were going home to Joy."

"Yeah, well ... I was."

"And?"

"And I'm not sure this thing is really over, you know?"

I did know. "Here's a news bulletin. DeManzi bought it last night. Police say it was a gangland killing. An assassination."

"DeManzi's dead?" Rojo snapped the chair into its upright position with a clang. "That means ... that means Patrick and I don't ... We're ..." A wide grin grew on his face. "Thank God."

I stared at Rojo without speaking.

He stared back. Then he spoke. "Kind of a coincidence, huh?"

"Kind of a big one."

"What does it mean?" Rojo's grin was long gone. "Did Patrick kill DeManzi?"

"Patrick doesn't strike me as the kind of guy who could take down a crime boss. Does he?"

Rojo shook his head.

"Hao, on the other hand..."

"No way. He wouldn't. Would he?" Rojo wanted me to say *no way, no how, not in a million years, bucko.*

I didn't oblige, shrugging instead. "I'm going to get some dinner. Want me to bring something back?"

"Sure."

"Pizza okay?"

"Great," Rojo said. He swallowed. "Uh, Channing?"

"Yeah?"

"Mind if I stay here a little longer?"

"Be my guest. And lock the door when I leave, okay?"

TWENTY-TWO

No GOONS CAME CRASHING through my door, but that was about the only encouraging thing that transpired during the night. I tossed and turned and tossed some more, too many bizarre thoughts racing through my mind to get any sleep. Finally, at about six a.m., I nodded off for a few restless hours. Evidently, Rojo had no such problems, judging by the thin stream of drool hanging out of his mouth when I went to get the newspaper. I left him in my apartment—snoring—as I headed out for the day.

When I got to the club later, Artie and Skip were sitting on stools at the bar, facing each other at point blank range, engaged in some sort of animated discussion. Of course, almost every discussion involving Artie was animated.

"No way, no honking way," Artie said, pointing a crooked finger at Skip. "We are not serving sushi. This is a comedy club, for Chrissakes!"

"You don't think raw fish is funny?" Skip asked. Then he saw me over Artie's shoulder and winked, and I knew he was only trying to get Artie revved up—a favorite pastime. It meant things around the club were dull, boring, and routine. Exactly how a business was supposed to run. "Hey, Channing. Artie was just saying how much he loves raw fish."

Artie flat-out ignored him and spoke to me. "Listen, Lee wanted me to tell you he wants you to stop by to see him as soon as you get in. I think it's about you-know-who doing you-know-what."

I tried to parse Artie's request. Sometimes he went pronoun-crazy. "Lee wants to talk to me?"

"What I said, isn't it?" Artie jerked his thumb over his shoulder. "He's waiting." Then he went back to his conversation with Skip. "We need sliders on the menu. The meat of land animals. You know, things that go moo in the night. And more fried things. That's what people want."

"Nothing funny about onion rings. Now squid, squid is funny," Skip was saying as I left those two to entertain themselves while I went next door to see what Lee wanted.

Lee's Palace was quiet; the lunch crowd had dispersed and the dinner crowd hadn't yet arrived clamoring for World Famous Peking Duck. No hostess met me at the entrance so I wandered back into the restaurant proper. Edward Wong sat all alone in the last booth on the right, poring over some papers with his suit jacket off. His sleeves were rolled up, he wore a blue and red striped tie, and if you didn't look too closely, you could definitely see a resemblance to JFK. At least in youthful, earnest appearance.

I approached and Edward rose when he spotted me. Offered his hand like he did a thousand times a day on the campaign trail. "Good to see you, Channing. Thanks for stopping by." He pointed at his stack of papers. "Getting ready for the rally tomorrow. You coming?"

"Planning to," I said. "Where's Lee?"

Edward gestured toward the seat opposite him in the booth. "Please, join me. Uncle Thomas stepped out for a bit."

I plopped down. "Do you know what he wanted?"

"Actually, I'm the one who wants to talk to you." He smiled. Perfect, white congressional teeth.

"Oh?"

"I heard about your conversation with my father." He loosened his tie barely enough to undo the top button of his shirt. To most people, it might have looked natural. To me, it looked rehearsed. *Just one of the regular hard-working common folk.*

"What about it?"

"I apologize for his behavior. His way of dealing with things is a touch old-fashioned. And authoritative. And insulting. And I could go on. Now you see how I was raised."

"I guess you heard that DeManzi got murdered."

Edward nodded. "I heard. And I know what you're thinking. That we had something to do with it. Well, that's why I'm here. To tell you we didn't. The cops got it right—it was a gang thing. I even talked to some of my P.D. contacts to make sure I got the straight scoop. All signs point to a power play amongst the criminal element."

"You've got to admit it's a convenient coincidence for you and Patrick."

"True. That's why I want to set the record straight with you. We were fully prepared to pay off DeManzi. Pay our obligation and move on. We know how this looks." He swallowed. Hard. "That's why it's so important you believe us and don't jump to any conclusions. Patrick may have some issues, but we didn't kill anyone."

I stared at him. I'd spent too much time lately listening to politicians spin and counterspin and superspin everything that happened, and everything *about* to happen. Listening to Edward, I realized I wouldn't recognize the truth if it came along and sat down next to me in the booth with a nametag that read "Mr. Truth." Regardless of what I believed, there wasn't much I could do about the chain of events. "I hear you. You say you weren't involved in DeManzi's death. Okay."

"Do you believe me?"

"What difference does it make? The police are convinced it's gang violence. Nobody would even listen to me if I wanted to say otherwise."

Edward gave me a barely perceptible nod.

"Okay, then. We done here?" I'd had enough of the Wongs' problems. I was ready to get back to my own problems.

"Not quite." Edward reached into his bundle of papers and withdrew a catalog-sized white envelope with slightly shaking fingers. He bit his lip, then slid it across the table at me. "You know anything about these?"

I undid the clasp and withdrew the papers within. A stack of photographs. The one on top showed a man and a woman, both naked, engaged in sexual activity. It was kind of hard to discern any details given the graininess of the print. I couldn't be sure, but the man looked a lot like Patrick Wong. "Nice composition, but the subjects are a bit shadowy. I'd try using more light next time."

"There's nothing funny about this situation. As you can see, that's my brother. Of course, this picture proves nothing. You can barely tell it's him."

"So? Patrick's an adult."

"Look at the next one."

I examined the next photo. It showed the woman's face, very close to Patrick's private parts. Again, I couldn't be sure, but the woman looked a lot like KayKay Korbell. She was indeed very photogenic.

"Now do you see the problem?"

"I'd be a fool not to." Patrick was a loose cannon, all right, and there was no telling where or when he'd go off next.

"Even if these pictures have been Photoshopped, they could still do some irreversible damage. To Patrick. To me."

"And to Korbell, too."

"Yes. The voters don't want to vote for someone who screws his opponent's wife, and they don't want to vote for a candidate whose wife screws around on him. Especially not one espousing 'family values.'"

"Technically, *you're* not screwing KayKay Korbell."

"I'm not sure the public cares so much for technicalities." Edward's face had turned ashen.

Suddenly, my mouth got dry. "Where did you get these?"

"The envelope showed up on my doorstep. Sometime early this morning. Eight pictures. The ones before you are the tamest. There's even a couple pictures of them snorting..." He trailed off.

I'd seen enough. I slid the photos back into the envelope. Secured the clasp. Pushed it across the table to Edward, who took it and inserted it halfway into his mound of papers. "Blackmail?"

"Yes."

"And you got them today?"

"Yes."

"So I guess that means they didn't come from DeManzi?" I said.

"From beyond the grave? Doubtful."

"Sounds like your problems are getting worse."

"Yes. They are." Edward steepled his hands in front of him on the table.

"Do you think Korbell got the same photos?" Maybe this was what O'Rourke feared would pop up and bite his candidate in the ass.

"I don't know. I sure hope not. He'd probably think we did this to ruin him," Edward said. "And I assure you we did not."

"You sure?" I asked.

"I'm sure," he said, tilting his head a fraction. "Do *you* know who sent them?"

"Me? How the hell would I know?"

Edward didn't take his eyes off me. "You've been doing a lot of digging around in our lives. You knew about the gambling problem. Maybe you stumbled upon the person responsible for this."

"Don't you think I would have told you if I knew?"

He shrugged. "Maybe. Maybe not."

I'd spent a lot of time and energy trying to help Lee with this mess. Now Edward was casting aspersions? No good deed goes unpunished. "What are you implying?"

"What are you inferring?"

I must have missed the first act. "You think I'm involved in this? You're crazy." I tried to keep my voice down, although we were still the only customers in the place. I wonder what Lee would have thought if he heard the bullshit spouting from his nephew's mouth.

"You've been following various members of my family around, and you've been delving into our lives. Then, when DeManzi gets offed and the money my father had pledged to pay him just happens to 'be available,' I get this blackmail attempt. I was never very good in math, but I can add two plus two."

"You think I took these pictures of Patrick and waited for the perfect moment to spring them on you? You've got quite an imagination. Not everyone is an underhanded, scheming, ambitious politician. You should start hanging out with a better crowd."

Edward didn't flinch. "You knew exactly how much Patrick owed, right?"

"Yeah. Two-hundred-twenty thousand dollars. So?"

"The blackmailer asked for two-hundred-twenty-one thousand dollars."

"What? Two-hundred-twenty-*one* thousand dollars?"

"Interesting, don't you think?" Edward's eyes burned dark. Now he didn't resemble a Kennedy at all.

"Sounds like someone has a sick sense of humor. Who else knew the exact amount of his debt?"

"Well, that's the question, of course. DeManzi knew, probably some flunkies who worked for him. My father. Patrick. Ames. And whoever they might have told."

I exhaled. "In other words, it could be anybody. Why do you think I'm involved?"

"You had the opportunity. You had the inside knowledge. You probably could use the money." He gave me a smile, the oily, glad-handing kind. "I'm not saying I think you *are* involved. I'm just asking."

"I'm not. And if I were, I wouldn't have asked for two-hundred-twenty-one thousand dollars. I'm not stupid."

"No, I didn't think you were. Did you tell anyone about this?"

I thought back. I'd kept my mouth shut, hadn't even mentioned the details to Artie. I had told Erin, but, aside from the fact she was no more a blackmailer than me, I was sure she hadn't been following Patrick around with a camera. She was an "ignorist," after all. "Nobody capable of this."

Edward tried to stare a hole in my head.

"Maybe we should go to the police. Maybe they have some ideas about this." I knew it would put a speed bump in Edward's political career to have your brother the campaign manager caught sleeping with the enemy, gambling, and doing drugs. Not to mention what it would do to Patrick's *life*.

Edward unclasped his hands, leaned back, smug look on his face. "The police, huh? Might be a good idea. I've got your fingerprints on the photo. They might be interested in them."

I opened my mouth to scream at him but closed it without uttering a peep. I felt like reaching across the table, grabbing his tie, and yanking on it until his face turned the color of an eggplant. A very ripe one. Instead, I gathered myself, tucked my anger neatly into my pocket, and got up slowly from the booth. Took a deep cleansing breath. And another. "Good luck, Edward. Good luck with everything."

TWENTY-THREE

I stormed out of Lee's Palace, not even stopping to grab a fortune cookie from the big basket on the hostess stand like I usually did. I didn't go back to the club, didn't feel I could listen to Artie and Skip discuss appetizers without my head exploding. I needed some time by myself to digest things. Equally important, I was afraid I'd bump into Lee, and I didn't have a clue what I would tell him. I had to figure out what needed to be done before announcing my intentions to others. Once the words came out of your mouth, it was tough to stuff them back in.

Inside the car, I pulled my phone out and called Rojo at my condo. He picked up on the second ring. "Hey, Channing. What's up?"

What did people do before Caller ID? "Got a question for you."

"Shoot, man."

"Do you know anything about any pictures?" I didn't want to be more explicit and tip my hand, not yet, not if I didn't have to.

"Pictures? What pictures?"

"Pictures that would be memorable."

"You talking porn here?"

Probably exactly what Mrs. Family Values would call porn. Ironic she had a starring role. "The pictures I'm concerned about could wreck people's lives."

Silence on Rojo's end. I should have waited until I could see his expression. "Rojo?"

"Yeah, man. Sorry. Nope. Nothing's ringing a bell. Who's in these pictures? Whose lives could get wrecked?"

"Don't worry, not yours. Never mind. We'll talk later. I gotta go."

"Sure man. Later." He clicked off.

I jammed the key into the ignition and aimed Rex for the nearest highway, I-66. Rush hour in the D.C. area was a downright ugly affair, too many cars ferrying too many short-fused drivers. But rush hour had been increasingly losing its definition—traffic was thick no matter what time you were on the road. I took the entrance ramp to the highway, going west, and after a few miles I was in the left-hand lane, going as fast as the other cars would allow. And my mind was trying to keep pace with my wheels.

Someone was using Patrick's illicit activities to blackmail Edward. Was it for the money, or was it for some kind of political advantage? Two-hundred-twenty-*one* thousand dollars didn't seem like an exorbitant amount, at least not by blackmail standards. Not that I was an expert or anything. Of course, once you've insinuated your hooks into somebody, you could keep milking him forever. Could be this was just a down payment.

If this was simply another example of dirty-pool politics, then why blackmail? Why not simply release the photos and let Edward's campaign implode on its own? Maybe there was a certain protocol you had to follow when taking down your opponent with incriminating photos.

Had Edward seriously thought I was involved, or was he trying to get a rise out of me, hoping I'd leak some bit of information he wanted? I suppose I could have been following Patrick around— hell, I followed Rojo around—and set up a hidden camera someplace, but even if I had taken the photos, how could he possibly think I'd use them against him? Trying to be as objective as possible, I could—on the most forgiving of days—see his point. After all, he didn't really know me. Still, my blood boiled at being accused of something so distasteful. Did he think all comics were sleazeballs? Did he have the same regard for comics I had for politicians?

I fell in behind a black Beamer, and we cruised along, barely at the speed limit. As the western suburbs had exploded over the years, so had the traffic. Would the sprawl continue to creep, all the way to West Virginia, or would the souring economy put a halt to it? I feared whatever slowdown would be temporary. Eventually, the suburbs would begat suburbs would begat more suburbs. Can't squelch progress.

I considered telling Lee about the photos. They would shame him, for sure. No one wants to think his nephew is out of control. Lee would take on a mountain of worry. About how his sister would take the news, about Edward's campaign, and of course, about Patrick. It would crush him if he found out. Did I have a moral obligation to tell him, or did I have a moral obligation, to Patrick and Edward, *not* to tell him? Or was I up shit's creek without a paddle? And what about all those people who supported Edward and his political ambitions? Did they have the right to know about Patrick's self-destructive ways? After all, if Edward won, Patrick would have his ear as Edward strode the halls of Congress.

What if I went straight to the police? I didn't actually have the pictures; Edward did. I doubted he'd give them up. Blackmail was a crime, but without any evidence, the case wouldn't even get opened and I'd be dismissed as a vengeful crackpot. Of course, if Patrick wasn't guilty of anything, if it had all been some kind of Photoshop wizardry, then Edward's career—and Patrick's reputation—would be ruined for no valid reason.

The black Beamer, tired of poking along, suddenly switched lanes, darting right in front of a minivan in the middle lane. Then the driver hit the gas, and zig-zagged past a few other vehicles as if he were jockeying for position on a NASCAR oval. No one blew their horns in protest, everybody so accustomed to the aggressive driving brought on by the familiar rush hour frustrations. Luckily, I wasn't going anywhere I could be late for.

Who could be behind the blackmail? Most likely, it was someone who worked for DeManzi—from what I knew of the guy, it would be right up his alley to take incriminating photos. Another thought occurred to me. Maybe that's why DeManzi let Rojo run up such a huge debt with no collateral. He'd discovered Patrick was the real money behind things and he set up the whole blackmail scheme from the get-go. Seems like he'd be able to make a lot more money from extortion than from gambling. How did people end up in these messy situations? Too bad Patrick didn't have a Sophie to get him on the straight and narrow.

I changed lanes, and then again, until I was in the exit lane. I took Route 28 north toward Sterling. Traffic was heavy here, too, and it was going even slower. Good thing I didn't have to mess with it on a daily basis—make that a *twice*-daily basis. Another advantage of working the two p.m to two a.m. shift.

My phone rang. Rojo was calling back. "Hello."

"Hey, man. Listen, I just got a call from a buddy of mine. In Dover. Needs me to fill in for his guitar player who broke his wrist. So I'm heading out. Be gone for a few days. Or longer."

"Okay. Might be good for you to get out of the area for a while." I wasn't quite sure what was going on, but having Rojo out of my hair would be one less thing to worry about.

"Yeah, what I thought, too. I'll check in when I get back. Uh, thanks for everything." He hung up before I could wish him good luck with his gig.

I tossed the phone onto the passenger seat and thought about DeManzi getting killed immediately *before* Hao paid him off. One fortuitous coincidence, at least for Hao. Had he known photos of Patrick existed? Had Hao received blackmail threats in the past? Maybe that was why he was so willing to pay off Patrick's gambling debt. Of course, if he'd planned to kill DeManzi all along, that whole walk-and-talk on the trail, including the phony pledge to pay off Patrick's debt, was all bogus.

If Hao knew about the photos, the gambling debt was just a minor distraction—the pictures were the weapons of mass destruction. In his mind, the only solution might very well have been murder. Erase DeManzi and eliminate the blackmail. The only problem? He hadn't murdered enough people; someone alive still had the photos. I wonder if Edward had shared that tidbit with his father.

When I came to Route 7, I took the exit east, toward McLean, the town where Lauren grew up. I'd spent some time there visiting her parents, in their big white house and three-car garage. Her mother loved me; her father's attitude toward me deteriorated from "barely tolerated" to "wanted dead." To say the last time I'd been there hadn't turned out well would be the understatement of my life. I usually avoided this area whenever I could, afraid the memories would rip open old scars.

I drove on, trying to concentrate on my current problems rather than dredge up my old ones.

I'd come up with a lot of questions but no sensible answers. Nor had I come up with a good plan of action. Hell, I'd settle for a "non-catastrophic" plan of action. Unless someone did *something*, Patrick was going to take a tumble for sure, and Edward was probably right behind him down the chute. Rojo would undoubtedly take a hit, too, for his involvement.

I came to the place I was looking for and turned onto the long narrow drive. Two hundred yards inside the entrance, and I'd entered a different world. No bumper-to-bumper lines of cars. No exhaust fumes. No hip-hop blaring from the hot rod idling next to me at the stoplight, waiting to beat me off the mark. Only trees and the great green expanse of the undulating lawn, broken up by dusty white granite headstones.

It had been awhile since I'd talked to Lauren, and I had a few things to share with her.

———

I slept fourteen hours, and would have made it to eighteen, if not for some guy calling with a surefire way to double my investment in only four short months. I yelled at him to take me off his stupid list and felt a little better. Maybe I shouldn't ask to be removed from the telemarketers' lists—it gave me a perfect opportunity to vent at someone who probably deserved it.

I needed to hurry. Edward's rally started in about an hour.

I'd been too tired last night to notice, but on my way out the door, I saw that Rojo had been kind enough to fold up his blanket and sheets, and he'd stacked them on my recliner. A Post-it note stuck to the pillow. *Thanks, man! I owe you.* Too late to rehabilitate his reputation as a houseguest, but a nice gesture nonetheless.

I arrived at Edward's campaign headquarters with about ten minutes to spare. They'd set up a podium outside the front door and a few TV cameras had their sights set on it. A cluster of microphones sprouted from the top of the podium, like some kind of bizarre, futuristic weed. In front of the lectern, forty or fifty people waited. All stared straight ahead; most of them belonged to the under-forty demographic. That probably pleased Edward; he'd always strived to appeal to the younger set, but it struck me as being a little short-sighted. I mean, there were an awful lot of people over forty who voted, and many of them occupied positions of power and sway within the community. And some just had big mouths, like Artie.

Artie. When I asked if he wanted to come along to the rally, he repeated his line about politicians chapping his tuchas, and not-so-politely declined. Artie voted the party line—he was a Democrat—unless he happened to come up with an excuse on Election Day for not voting at all. Which, now that I think about it, was just about every November. I guess it was his right as a citizen *not* to vote, if he so chose.

I scanned the crowd, looking for Lee or anyone else from the Wong family, but came up empty. Maybe politicians had taken a lesson from entertainers and adopted a "green" room for getting themselves psyched up. Or calmed down. Or into whatever state was best for conducting a successful campaign rally.

I noticed a couple of Edward's security staff, clad in their khaki-and-blue blazer uniform, patrolling the crowd. To me, they looked bored. Large, but bored.

Off to my right, a school bus disgorged its occupants. A high school marching band, dressed in white and green uniforms with lots of ruffles, stomped this way. They formed lines off to the side, facing the podium. Three tuba players brought up the rear, giant brass flowers glistening in the sun. The Wongs were determined to throw a good party.

At the back of the throng, I spotted a familiar face. Dan O'Rourke, clad in jeans and a sportshirt, leaned against a signpost, waiting for the action to begin. I guess it made sense that he'd be there, scouting the opposition's rally, but didn't he have better things to do with his time? The campaign could have sent an intern or lower-level grunt instead. I edged to my left, hoping that O'Rourke wouldn't spot me. I wasn't sure if he already knew about my little ruse—not that it would take much digging to find out I was tight with Lee—but I had no desire to be confronted today.

As the crowd waited for the star of the show to appear, a few young campaign workers circulated through the crowd passing out literature. With a sincere smile, one young woman thrust a pamphlet at me and I took it, smiling in return, although not as widely. Taking up the entire front panel, a picture of Edward in shirtsleeves rolled up—natch—gazed at me in earnest, seeming to say, "Vote for me, and I'll work my ass off for you." For all I knew, that might even be his official campaign slogan.

I felt a presence next to me, followed by a deep voice. "What are you doing here, Hayes?" The baritone belonged to Brad Ames. Last time I saw him, he was chasing money blowing in the wind. I hoped he was in a better mood today.

"Supporting Edward. What else?"

He eyed me, probably trying to decide if I were toying with him. "Uh huh. Just don't create a scene." From his relatively calm voice, I got the feeling that after what had happened between us, Hao had instructed Ames to show some restraint and not create any more scenes himself. Especially not at a campaign rally.

The crowd had swelled to perhaps a hundred people. Now the campaign workers were passing out blue and white helium balloons. In the background, disjointed sounds bleated from a few instruments while the band teacher tried to get everyone coordinated.

Ames didn't say anything, just stood next to me, soaking in the festivities. Or fuming. Hard to read his doughy face.

A few more press types with video cameras showed up and elbowed their way toward the front. Must either be a slow news day or they were expecting Edward to say something controversial. From what I'd seen of Edward's campaign, I'd bet on the former. Of course, I knew what the press would think if they found out about Patrick's wild ride. *Ka-ching*, ratings bonanza.

"See anybody or anything that looks suspicious?" Ames asked. "Crowd this big poses more of a security challenge than most of our other events. Being out in the open doesn't help." He glanced around, head on a swivel, searching for bad guys.

"Nothing seems off to me. Why, you got a specific reason to be concerned?"

"No. Not at all. But you can't be too careful now, can you?" He glared at me.

"No, you can't."

Ames checked his watch. "I need to get up there. They'll be out in a minute." He started to leave, then changed course and got so close I could count his nose hairs. Grabbed my upper arm and put his mouth an inch from my ear. "Listen up, Hayes. If you cause any more trouble for Edward, Patrick, or any of the other Wongs, or for this campaign, you're gonna find out about a few of my personal eccentricities. Some of my *hobbies*. And while I'd certainly enjoy that, you most certainly wouldn't." He squeezed my arm until the blood stopped flowing. "Understood?"

"In case it hasn't registered, *I'm* not the one causing trouble for this family. Now, buzz off, Bigfoot." I felt his hot breath in my ear, and for a moment, I thought he'd rip my arm off and club me with it. Instead, he gave a final squeeze and let go.

"You're a smart guy. I think you understand." He stepped on my toes as he headed for the podium.

So much for Ames showing restraint. I moved him higher on my mental shit list.

The doors to campaign headquarters opened, and a cheer erupted from the crowd. The band launched into a song with lots of brass and a pounding drumbeat. Edward Wong strode to the podium, arms raised, expression of fierce determination on his face. Directly behind him came Patrick, followed by a few other campaign workers. Lee, Margaret, Hao, Joy, and Xun brought up the rear of the little parade. *The family that campaigns together, stays together.*

Edward and Patrick stood side-by-side at the podium, while the others took seats in a row of chairs near the band. As they took their places, the crowd continued its thunderous applause. Every time it sounded like the ovation was subsiding, I noticed the campaign workers revving things up again. Appearances were everything when it came to political rallies, I guess.

After about three solid minutes of noisy adulation—it reminded me of a Presidential State-of-the-Union address—Patrick stepped forward and gestured to the crowd to quiet down. I half-expected him to use one hand to quell the noise while he used the other hand to encourage the crowd to keep clapping, à la Johnny Carson. But he played it straight, and after a minute or so, it was relatively quiet. Even the band had stopped *oompa-loompahing.*

Patrick adjusted the microphone bouquet and a loud screech assaulted us from the speakers. "Sorry about that," he said, fiddling around some more. Then he tried again. "How's that?" No screeching. "Good. Welcome everyone, we're so glad you could come out today and give us your support. We're heading into crunch time, and it's great to see so many of you joining us on our journey. That's right, I'm talking about you!" He pointed at the crowd with both hands, and the people ignited in spontaneous applause, if having a dozen campaign volunteers wave at you like cheerleaders could be called spontaneous.

As if to punctuate Patrick's message, the drummer in the band pounded his bass drum a few times under the approving eye of the band director, who punched the air with each drum beat. Would it have mattered who the candidate was, or did the band boogie for any old politico, one field trip as good as the next?

Patrick waited for things to die down again. "See, you guys are the greatest!" Another spate of applause. At this rate, it would be nightfall before anything meaningful got said. *If* anything meaningful would be said. "Okay, okay. Enough celebration. It's my distinct honor to introduce to you someone I've known for a long time. All my life, in fact." He paused for some laughter, not nearly as raucous as the cheering. "With your help and hard work, with your confidence and commitment, with your perspiration and inspiration, we can make it happen. It gives me great pleasure to introduce my brother, the future Congressman, Edward Wong."

Edward stepped forward and grasped Patrick's hand, gathering him up in a great big bear hug. Then they broke apart and clapped each other on the back a couple times. Finally, they both faced the crowd and held up their arms together, like a referee crowning the heavyweight champ. Pure theatrics, and the crowd ate it up. I had to admit, the entertainer in me ate it up too. Maybe politics *was* mostly appearance. If so, Edward had a bright future. The people still loved the Kennedy mystique.

The crowd kept cheering; there'd be a lot of hoarse throats this evening. Patrick took a seat next to Hao, while Edward waved and looked stately—and made sure to smile boldly for the TV cameras. A few helium balloons drifted skyward and the band played on. If I closed my eyes a little, and let myself get caught up in the moment, I could almost forget the nasty things I knew about Patrick, the secrets that could cause this campaign to crash and burn. But not quite.

Edward motioned the crowd to quiet. "Thank you. Thank you very much. It's my honor to be here today. Without your belief in me, and in our mission, I wouldn't have even entertained thoughts of running for Congress. But it's the things I've seen living here, in this wonderful, yet flawed, state that have spurred me to action. There are too many of us who need help and aren't getting it. I'm not talking about welfare or government handouts here. No, I'm talking about the kind of help that levels playing fields for people at all socio-economic levels. I'm talking about the kind of help that holds corrupt big businesses accountable for their egregious policies. I'm talking about the kind of help that makes sure we don't have families out on the streets wondering where their next meals are coming from. And I'm talking about the kind of help that will employ all those people who want good jobs so they can work to help themselves. That's the kind of help I'm talking about!" He stabbed his index finger into the air to emphasize his point. Once again, the crowd voiced their approval, and the band joined in, full of brass and bass drums.

I glanced around the crowd. Men, women, even a few children, of all colors, united around a common mission: to make their lives better. The hope was evident on their faces, in their movements, in their shouts of solidarity. In that moment, goosebumps popped up along my forearms. I'd felt the rush of an adoring crowd onstage countless times, and this had to be a similar experience for Edward, probably more so, since the stakes were so much higher. I mean, we were talking about bettering these peoples' lives, not giving them an hour of laughs.

If I blew the whistle on Patrick publicly, I'd potentially be dashing these peoples' dreams right along with Edward's career—and Edward really had nothing to do with Patrick's problems.

Edward waited for the crowd noise to subside. Then he leaned into the mics. "Before we go any further, I'd like to recognize my family. My parents and my sister, and my two uncles. Thanks for all your support." He waved his hand at the group. I noticed he didn't name names, probably hoping for a modicum of anonymity. "I'd also like to thank all those people who have worked incredibly hard on my campaign so far, and I don't mean to discourage anyone, but we've got a hell of a lot more work to do. And finally, I'd like to thank the West Oaks High School band for coming out today. Let's hear it for all these great folks!"

The band started up, and the crowd applauded and hollered and cheered. All the noise and commotion would sound and look good on the evening newscasts.

A sharp sound rang out, barely distinguishable above the beats of the drum. Then a few people near me scattered, and I saw someone pointing and shouting. "Shooter! Shooter! He's got a gun!" Two more shots cut through the yelling. The band, oblivious, kept playing. More people, frenzy on their faces, started running and screaming. I tried to spot the shooter in the bedlam, but it was impossible, there were so many people stampeding in all directions.

I didn't know what to do, so I ran for my life too.

TWENTY-FOUR

AFTER ABOUT FIFTY YARDS, I stopped. Glanced back at the scene behind me. No more shots had been fired—that I'd heard, anyway—and the plaza was empty, save for a scattering of musical instruments the band had dropped as they ran for cover. In the sky, a couple dozen helium balloons floated lazily, unperturbed by the chaos below. All around, I saw heads poking out from behind parked cars, trashcans, and other hiding places. Two Fairfax County police officers crouched behind a bush, weapons drawn. Next to them, also in a crouch, was Ames. His hands were empty.

O'Rourke was nowhere to be seen.

I didn't see any bodies lying on the ground. I hadn't heard any shouts for medical assistance. One could pray no one got hurt.

I pulled out my phone and punched a few buttons. My call got answered on the first ring. "Lee, you okay?"

"Yeah, we're all fine. Edward, Patrick, everyone. How about you?"

"Fine. Where are you?"

"Back inside. We've got the doors locked. I ... Margaret's pretty shook up. What's it like outside?"

"Calm now."

"Anybody hurt?"

"I don't see anyone who's been shot."

"Thank God. I gotta go. Stay safe." I clicked off. Still quiet. A few sirens sounded in the distance, coming closer.

The cops would take an hour to secure the scene. Maybe cordon off the area. Try to round up witnesses. Transcribe statements. *Get to the bottom of this.* But I knew in my heart that whoever had been shooting was long gone, and in all the pandemonium, odds were nobody got a good look at the perpetrator.

I dusted myself off and walked to my car. No sense sticking around, I had nothing to report to the police.

———

At The Last Laff, Artie found me in the office. "How was the pep rally?" he asked.

"Lots of fireworks."

"That's nice," he said, plopping into his chair. "Swipe any good jokes lately?"

Obviously, he hadn't heard the news, so I filled him in. When I finished, he shook his head. "Jesus, Channing, you're becoming a magnet for violence. Remind me not to go out with you anywhere. And try not to bring any of your 'friends' in here, okay? I got my health and well-being to consider, not to mention Donna's and Skip's and everyone else's."

I knew Artie was plenty worried about me. His cavalier nonchalance was simply a cover. A transparent one. "Thanks for your sympathy."

"Sympathy, schmympathy." He grunted, picked up a newspaper, and started reading, done with me. I tried calling Lee. No answer. I waited a few minutes, then tried again. And again. And again. Left messages each time. Getting more agitated with each roll into voice mail, I left Artie with his nose in the paper and went next door to see if Lee was there.

The assistant manager, Kyle, met me at the door. "Did you hear what happened? Someone tried to assassinate Edward Wong," he said, with uncontained excitement. "Just like Ronald Reagan."

"I heard." I didn't point out Hinckley's bullets actually found their mark. "Is Lee around?"

"No. He called, said he was going to be late, that he wasn't feeling well." Kyle leaned toward me, eyes bright. "Can you blame him? I mean, wow!"

I snatched a fortune cookie from the bowl and returned to the club. Went straight to the green room, turned on the old TV and waited for it to warm up. A news anchor's coiffed head came into focus. "…and police are still investigating. A spokesperson for the Wong campaign thanks all their supporters for their bravery in the face of danger, and they've announced the reassignment of campaign manager Patrick Wong. He will step aside from his campaign duties and lead an internal probe of the incident." The anchor stared into the camera, which had panned back into a two-shot. "Scary situation."

The other anchor said, "Yes indeed, Rog. Now, let's go to the storm center and see what's on tap for the rest of the week."

I changed the channel on the converter box—Artie was too cheap to get satellite for the club—but all I found was another weather forecast and commercials for antacids and prescription medicine. I hit the power button and the TV sputtered off with a click and an asthmatic whirr.

I called Freeman. He worked in narcotics, but I knew he'd have the latest facts on the shooting, especially since Edward Wong was involved. He answered, and I let out a breath I didn't realize I was holding.

"Hey, Channing. What took you so long to call? I was feeling a little forgotten. You know how I get when I don't hear from you in awhile."

"You have any info for me about the shooting at Edward's rally?" I said, cutting through the introductory banter. Usually it was Freeman cutting through *my* bullshit.

"No need to get touchy. Here's what I know. We can't corroborate the existence of a shooter. We've got one witness who says he saw a guy with a gun. We've got two witnesses who think they *may* have seen a guy with a gun. And we've got about a dozen witnesses who *might have maybe possibly perhaps* seen someone who may or may not have had a gun. In other words, we've got squat. No bullet holes, no shell casings, no physical evidence of any kind. In fact, the noises everyone seems to have heard may have just been firecrackers. Or the drum from the marching band. Or even the popping of helium balloons. We do know someone started shouting the word 'shooter,' and that sent everyone else into a tizzy. Or more accurately, a gigantic fuster cluck."

"Hmm."

"What?"

"Nothing." If the incident wasn't an actual shooting, had it simply been a "panic," brought about by a car backfiring and some nervous Nellie's active imagination? Or could it have been a dirty trick from Korbell's camp to disrupt the rally? Why *had* O'Rourke been there?

No, it didn't seem like his—or Korbell's—style.

Something in my gut had started kicking.

Patrick, the guy who was going to be at Edward's side all the way to Washington, had been "reassigned." Patrick, the guy who gave up his lucrative position at the law firm to be part of history, will no longer run interference for his brother. Patrick, the campaign's spinmeister, will no longer be spinning garbage into gold.

Patrick had been distanced from Edward and was being eliminated from public view.

Very interesting. Very convenient. Very *strategic*.

Had the Wongs staged the whole thing as a way to remove Patrick from Edward's campaign before news of his transgressions got out, while still allowing him to save face? *Internal probe, my ass*.

"Channing, you still there?" Freeman's voice cut through my mental hypothesizing.

"Huh. Yeah, sorry."

"If you know something, now's the time to pass it along," Freeman said. "You were there, right? At the rally?"

"Yeah."

"Did you see something that would contradict what I just told you?"

"Nope. Not at all."

"Anything Lee might have said to contradict it?"

"Haven't spoken to him yet."

"Uh huh. Well, if you suddenly think of something, let me know, okay?"

"Sure, man. Of course."

A slight pause. "You know I got your back, right?" Freeman said.

"That your job?"

"Sure. To protect and serve. Everyone, including you. Hell, *especially* you."

"That's what I like about you. Your sense of humor."

"Goodbye, Channing."

"Goodbye, Freeman. Love you, too," I said, but he'd already hung up.

———

I spent about thirty minutes shooting the bull with Skip while he got the bar ready for the night, then I helped Donna balance the club's checkbook. Actually, she balanced the checkbook while I showered her with questions about what Artie was like a dozen years ago. She mostly nodded absently, muttering something about "needing to concentrate." After awhile, I got bored talking to myself and retreated to my office. Artie wasn't around; he was probably out front, trying to lure people in, like a carnival barker. I took a seat at his desk, propped my feet up like he always did, and opened up the *Sports* page.

A faint knock on the open door interrupted my perusal of the box scores. Lee stood at the threshold. "Channing. You busy?"

I popped out of Artie's chair. "Where have you been? I've tried calling you. Repeatedly. Everybody okay?"

"Yes. Physically, we are fine. But ..."

"What?"

"Are you busy?"

"No. Not at all. What's up?"

Lee seemed nervous, not his usual jocular self. With what had happened, it was understandable. "Someone would like to speak with you."

"Who?"

"If you've got a few minutes, come with me."

I didn't press the issue. "Sure, hang on." I scribbled a note to Artie, telling him I'd be stepping out for a few, and asking him if he'd take care of scheduling the open mic comics. Then I followed Lee. Instead of turning right, toward the front door, Lee turned left, deeper into the club. He passed the kitchen and storage room, and walked right out the rear door. Artie had given Lee the run of the place many years ago; funny what privileges one could receive by providing us with free chow.

Once in the alley, we took a few steps toward the back of Lee's restaurant. A small figure stepped out of the shadows. Margaret, Lee's sister, pulled a sweater around her shoulders, although the temperature must have been near eighty. The pungent smell of garlic fought with the foul odor of festering garbage in a nearby Dumpster, and a breeze stirred up a few pieces of trash around our ankles. A lovely place for a conversation.

"Hello, Channing. Thanks for meeting me." Her words were precise, but I could hardly hear them over the ambient noise of the air handlers on the roof and the ever-present hum of the traffic. Even though we were behind the shopping center, you could hear the cars whiz by on the main drag.

"My pleasure. You okay after what happened this afternoon?"

She turned to Lee. "Thomas, would you mind? I'd like to talk to Channing alone."

Lee glanced at me, then at her, then back at me. He nodded, but his feet remained rooted. "Uh, okay, if you're sure about that. I don't mind sticking around, though."

Margaret patted Lee's arm. "You have always looked out for me, and I have always appreciated that. I will be fine. I'll come in when we're done, and we can have something to eat. Some hot and sour soup sounds delicious." Once again, she pulled her sweater tight. Lee remained, until his sister shooed him away with her hand. Unfortunately, the flies buzzing around the Dumpster didn't take the same hint.

The door to the back of Lee's Palace closed, with Lee on the inside. Margaret turned to me and spoke. Her voice was louder now. "Do not worry about what happened this afternoon. I do not think it was a real shooting, after all."

"What makes you say that?"

"Later, after the boys had gone, I heard Hao, Xun, and their unpleasant security chief talking. I did not hear their words, but from their tone, whatever happened wasn't serious. More like a prank of some sort. Please, do not concern yourself with that." She motioned me closer. "I am sorry you are involved in my family's mess. Thomas asked you to help, and you've gotten dragged into it."

I opened my mouth to protest, but she held her hand up. "Thomas told me he asked you to check into things. Although he promised he wouldn't get involved, I knew he would. In fact, I think some part of me would have been upset if he had not."

"He's a great guy," I said, as if she didn't know her own brother and his virtues.

"Yes. He is." A wan smile. "What Patrick has done is unforgivable. The shame he has delivered to his family." Her eyes closed for a second. "I have remained in the shadows too long. They think I do not know what is going on, because they regard me as furniture, or as a servant. Yet I am there, on the periphery, listening and observing what is happening all around me. And it is time for it to stop. For them to stop. To act like men. What Patrick is doing is wrong and it is hurting others, especially his family. He must stop. Do you agree, Channing?"

I wasn't sure exactly how much Margaret knew about Patrick's activities, but somehow I got the sense she knew everything I did, and then some. Of course, getting someone like Patrick to recognize he has a problem is step one, followed by step two—getting him to stop. Neither of which is easy. "Yes, I do. What are you going to do about it?"

"That is the question, isn't it? If I expose Patrick's actions publicly, then Edward's political career is ruined. And he has not done anything to warrant that. He should have dealt with Patrick when he found out, but I do not blame him. They are brothers, after all, and Wong brothers are very loyal." She paused and regarded me. "What do you think I should do?"

"Have you spoken to Patrick yet? About his problems?" I didn't get anywhere when I tried, but then again, I wasn't his mother. Just a potential monkey wrench in his plans.

"Of course, that is what I must do. I have known that now for a while. But … it is a conversation I am not looking forward to." She nodded, to herself, it seemed. "I think my conversation might go better if I had some photographs. Do you know what photographs I'm referring to, Channing?"

I blinked a few times, unsure how to answer. She rescued me from my quandary.

"There are pictures of Patrick that would ruin his career, and the careers of those around him. And another man's family and career, as well. I have not seen them, but I overheard Hao talking about them. If I had these pictures, then I am sure I could persuade Patrick to change his ways and apologize to those he's harmed."

By blackmailing your own son? "Has Patrick seen these pictures?"

"It seems he has not. I don't even believe he knows they exist. Hao and the others do not want to frighten him. They are worried what he might do if he knew about them. He is not always so ... predictable. But he must be confronted. He must know the extent of the consequences of his actions."

"Do you know where the pictures are now?" I asked, wondering if Edward still had them in a manila envelope, stuffed in a pile of paperwork, hidden in plain sight.

Margaret reached into her sweater pocket and withdrew something. Held it out to me. I opened my hand and she dropped it into my palm. A key ring with three keys on it. "Hao keeps all his important *business* files at his office. Do you know where that is?"

"Yeah, I've been there. But is it possible someone else has them? Edward for instance?" I offered, not wanting to come out and say I'd seen them in his possession.

"It would not surprise me if he has a set. But my husband controls things in the Wong family. He keeps extensive records. If there are pictures, you can be sure he has a set as well. And his set would not be a copy. The powerful Hao Wong has the originals." The way she said it made me wonder if there was some stress in the marriage. That and the comment about being treated like furniture. "There are also files ... files that contain much information."

I stared at the keys in my hand. "What do these go to?"

"Hao's office. Outer door, inner office, that gargantuan desk he loves so much. Do not worry about him missing them, these keys are copies. You would be amazed what one can learn when you are invisible. A part of your surroundings. Not an equal." With every sentence, her bitterness became more apparent.

"And why are you giving these keys to me?"

A knowing smile from her split me open. "Lee speaks the world of you. How dependable you are. How trustworthy you are. There is no one else I can ask. So I ask you now, Channing Hayes. Will you help me get these photographs—and the files—so this madness can stop? Hopefully, I can use the pictures to force Patrick to end his downward spiral before he destroys himself and those he loves. And the other files will prove to be useful, too, I'm sure. Before you answer, you must know you are my only chance. My only chance."

Well, when you put it that way ... "I'll see what I can find."

TWENTY-FIVE

IT WAS FOUR MINUTES to one on Thursday.

I'd had my chat with Margaret Wong on Tuesday night, and ever since I'd said I would do my best to retrieve the incriminating photos, I'd been trying to come up with an excuse not to. I didn't relish the thought of breaking into Hao's place of business. Even though she'd given me the keys, I had the feeling my entering in the dead of night and pillaging the place in search of something that didn't belong to me wouldn't be looked upon kindly through the eyes of the law.

It wasn't exactly a guilt trip Margaret Wong had laid on me, but it was effective. I wasn't a stranger to guilt; my mother had dropped a nuclear bomb of guilt on me. She'd killed herself with a Valium and gin highball, and I'd been the one to find the body. I felt guilty about causing the unhappiness that led her to her final deed, and it was something I still struggled with—despite some intense sessions with my therapist. Would helping Margaret reach out to her son Patrick assuage some of that guilt?

Most of yesterday had been spent wandering around in a daze, the key ring burning like a white-hot ingot in my pocket. I'm sure Artie and Donna wondered what the heck was going on in my head. Hopefully, they assumed I was just lost in some new routine I was working on—I got that way sometimes when the creative juices were flowing well. I guess it really didn't matter what they thought. They didn't ask me about it and I didn't offer up any details.

But the entire day went by and I remembered very little of it, except for two things. I didn't make any midnight trip in search of the blackmail photos, and I didn't see anybody from the Wong family on the evening news.

The door to the waiting room opened and my therapist smiled at me. Time to get busy.

Thirty minutes later, we'd covered the week's events. I saw no reason to dredge up the guilty feelings I'd just had about my mother—we'd be getting back to that another time, I was sure. Besides, I had something else I wanted to explore.

"So why do you think I often bring home strays to stay with me? Comics that need a place to crash, or—" I trailed off.

"Or Rojo?"

I nodded. "Could it be that I'm just a nice guy?"

"That's part of it, of course. But I think it goes deeper than that."

In these sessions, I was discovering that everything went deeper. "Maybe I'm somehow trying to compensate for the lack of care my mother gave me. Maybe I'm trying to be the mother to some of these wayward friends of mine." I was also discovering it was difficult to keep my mother *out* of these sessions.

"That's entirely possible. These folks you've invited into your home remind you of yourself, and you're treating them in ways you wish your mother had treated you. That's why you find it difficult to say no to them. Because your mother—explicitly or implicitly—said no to you frequently."

Yeah, she sure did.

"It seems to me that inviting Rojo to sleep at your condo puts you in some danger. Would you say that's accurate?"

"I suppose. He's mixed up with some violent characters. But..."

"But what?"

"It just seemed like the right thing to do."

"And sometimes things worth doing involve some risk? Especially when they're the 'right things' to do?"

I nodded.

"Let's change topics. Last session, we talked a bit about your relationship with Artie. Close, loyal, with aspects of a father-son dynamic. A relationship you never had as a child. Have you thought any more about that?"

"Some." Every time I saw Artie this past week, I imagined him twenty years ago, telling me to take out the trash. Which, I guess, wasn't so different from the present day.

"And?"

"I don't know. I guess he is a father figure." What difference did it make? I needed a father when I was a kid, not now.

"How do you think your feelings for Artie are affecting your quest to help Lee?"

My face scrunched up. "You think they're related?"

"As I understand it, Lee was Artie's friend before you knew him, and they are very close. So it seems to make sense that you'd want to succeed in helping Lee to please Artie. You seek his approval, as we all seek our parents' approval. What better way than to help your father figure's best friend?"

I stared out the window while I considered this. Lee was my friend, too. Was I helping him because of our friendship, or was my need for Artie's approval the driving force? "Suppose you're right. Suppose I'm doing this all for Artie. What difference does it make?"

"I doubt you're doing it 'all for Artie.' Few things in life are so clear-cut. There can be multiple reasons for doing anything. But let me address your question, 'Why does it matter if you're trying to gain Artie's approval?' I believe it's very worthwhile to know one's motivations. It can help guide you in making difficult decisions, it can help you avoid no-win situations, it can help you in your search for happiness. Learning about yourself is perhaps the biggest goal of our therapy sessions, don't you think, Channing?"

Yeah, yeah, yeah. If only learning about yourself wasn't such a drag.

———

On my way through the parking lot to my car, I turned my phone back on and it beeped, telling me I had a message. Seth Phillips, Dark Danger's drummer, wanted me to call right away—Rojo was freaking out and Phillips didn't want to involve Joy. Evidently, she and Rojo had one whopper of an argument. I called him back. "Hey, this is Channing Hayes. What's up with Rojo?"

"Oh yeah, man. Thanks for getting back to me. I didn't know who else to call, you know? We can't do shit for him. He said he'd been staying with you a few nights, and he's totally in the toilet with Joy, so … maybe you could lend him your sofa again? My old lady's kinda strict about her 'no musician sleepovers' rule." In the background, I heard voices and an occasional guitar chord.

"When did Rojo get back from Delaware?" I was under the impression he'd be gone for longer.

"Delaware? Rojo's been practicing with us for the past week."

"He told me his buddy broke his … Never mind. What's going on?"

"He's flipping out about something, won't tell us what exactly. One minute he's bouncing off the walls, the next minute he's curled into a ball. Can you talk some sense into him? And, you know, let him crash at your place."

I sighed. "Sure. Why not?" Phillips gave me directions to his house, where they were practicing, and asked me to hurry.

When I got there, I let myself in through the side door of the garage. Three musicians practiced while Rojo gave a rocking chair in the corner a workout. Dark Danger took the "garage band" moniker literally.

Rojo saw me, and his muscles tensed for a moment, then he relaxed, almost in an "ah, fuck it" way. The drums stopped first, followed by the guitar and bass petering out. "Hey man, thanks for coming," Phillips said. Then, to his bandmates, "Take five everyone." They fled from the garage, with nary a glance over their shoulders at me or Rojo.

"What's going on?" I asked. Rojo drew his knees up against his chest and covered them with his arms, a protective barrier. From what, I didn't know. The chair stopped moving.

"Shit, Channing. I sure stepped in it this time."

"Care to tell me?" I felt weird, standing over him as he sat in a ball, but unless I wanted to sit on the garage floor, I didn't have much of a choice.

"Well…" He stared into the far corner of the garage, eyes moist.

"Rojo, you know you're going to tell me, right? So just get to it. Save us both some time. You want me to help you, don't you?"

A barely perceptible nod.

"Then spill."

He took a deep breath. "Those pictures you asked about the other day. The ones of Patrick? I know about them."

"How did you find out?"

"I took them."

My head snapped back as if he'd just smacked me in the face. "You're blackmailing Edward?"

"What? No. Of course not. I'd never do that. What kind of guy do you think I am?" He looked away, clearly hurt.

"Why'd you take the pictures then?" I tried to keep my voice calm, afraid he'd clam up if I seemed too angry.

He shifted positions but didn't face me.

"Rojo. I'm on your side. You know that. But I need to know the truth here." And everywhere else, too, would be nice.

A glance, followed by a longer look. Then he let go of his knees and unfurled himself. "Patrick had me placing his bets for him, right? But if something went wrong, I knew he could deny everything and I'd be holding the bag." He swallowed. "I didn't mind helping him out, you know? I just wanted a little insurance, in case he decided to screw me."

"So you followed him and took the pictures?"

"Yeah. I know, not the brightest idea."

Actually, given the circumstances, I could think of many worse ideas. "How'd you know you'd find him in a compromising position?"

He shrugged. "I didn't know for sure, but I figured if he had a gambling problem, he might have some other kind of problem. He has that kind of personality."

The sleazy kind? "Did he know you took these pictures?"

"No, I followed him a few times, and he and his lady friend always ended up at his place. One night when he wasn't around, I let myself in and set up a hidden camera, one of those super mini spy-cams. He never spotted it. He had his mind on other things, as you can tell if you've seen the pictures. *Have* you seen them?"

"Yeah, I saw them." I continued my interrogation. "How'd you get in?"

"Joy had a key to his condo that I, uh, borrowed."

"Shit." Things just kept getting more complicated. "And you never told him about the pictures?"

"Nope. I almost did a couple times, especially when the heat came down on me. But he never cut me loose, kept telling me that he'd figure something out, so I didn't want to get him riled unnecessarily. Plus I didn't want him to think badly of me."

"No, of course not." I held Rojo's gaze, trying to tell if he was stringing me along, but he simply stared back, dark eyes sincere. "Do you think Patrick murdered DeManzi to get him off his back?"

"Like I told you before, no way. Patrick wouldn't hurt a fly."

"So if you're not blackmailing him, who is?"

"I have no freaking idea." His nose twitched.

"Help me out here, Rojo. You took the pictures, you didn't tell anyone about them. How did someone else get their hands on them?"

"Best I can figure, someone took the memory card from the camera, downloaded the pictures, then returned it."

"Where did you have the camera?"

"In my backpack. Still there, if it matters."

I thought a moment. "Who had access?"

"Anybody. I usually keep my backpack with me, but it's not always *with me*, you know? Like when I'm doing a show, I'll keep it backstage or someplace."

"Any of your band members into blackmail?"

He shook his head. "Naw. I would have known. None of them can keep a secret."

"So it could be anybody."

"'Fraid so," Rojo said. "Sorry. I fucked up. My bad."

Lot of people fucking up lately. "What's going on between you and Joy?"

Rojo squirmed in the rocking chair. He glanced at the open garage door, at daylight, as if he were planning on making a run for it. "Nothin'."

"Nothing? According to Phillips, she tossed you out."

His face seemed to shrink, and I saw a sullen, rebuffed teenager. "I told her about the pictures. She got royally pissed at me for following her brother around, taking photos that could ruin him. She actually thought I was going to blackmail him. For money. I denied it, she called me a liar and a bunch of other names she never called me before. She'll cool down in a few days. Don't worry."

Rojo sounded just like a teenager, too. "Why'd you tell me you were going to Delaware?"

"I...I...When you mentioned the pictures, I got nervous. Thought someone would figure out I took them and come looking for me. Told you I was going to Delaware so you wouldn't have to lie about where I was, if people came asking."

"Well, why didn't you actually go to Delaware? Let things settle down some."

He shot me a hurt look. "I've got to practice, man. We've got a gig this weekend. Can't let my buddies down, you know."

"No. Can't let your friends down."

Rojo stared off into space and I paced a bit in the small garage. Outside, I heard the banter of the bandmates. Casual, sarcastic, light. Rojo was probably right—they didn't seem like the blackmailing type, assuming there was a blackmailing type. I always pictured some strung-out dude, squirrelly and desperate, chainsmoking while he cut letters from a magazine to paste on the ransom note. Probably not how it was in real life, but who knew?

I thought about what Rojo had just told me, weighed it to see if it made sense. I didn't fully understand Rojo's priorities, but I was at least heartened he had some sense of loyalty guiding his actions, no matter how potentially self-destructive. Right now, though, I think we had the same top priority. Find out who swiped the pictures and we'd find out who was trying to blackmail the Wongs. I didn't really know where to start, but I did have three keys in my pocket. Perhaps there was a ransom note with the photos that might shed some light on the situation.

I turned back to Rojo. "Whatever plans you've got for tonight, cancel them. You and I have some stuff to do."

I was taking Rojo with me to Hao's to snoop around and retrieve the photos. I could use his help sure, but the real reason I was taking him along was so he wouldn't disappear again. I had the distinct feeling I wasn't getting the truth, the whole truth, and nothing but the truth.

So help me, God.

TWENTY-SIX

IT WOULD HELP ME figure out what was going on—or at least who might be involved—if I knew whether Korbell was being black-mailed too. But I needed to tread carefully. My goal was to wreck as few lives as possible. Unfortunately, that was proving harder than it sounded.

I called the Congressman's campaign office and asked to speak to Nicole. A chipper intern put me right through. "Hi Nicole, this is Channing Hayes."

"Hey there. I was hoping I'd hear from you. Decide to host an event? Or invite me to your club?"

"Uh, not exactly."

"Oh?"

"I need a favor. A big one."

"What can I do for you, Channing?" Her tone had cooled a hair. Less flirtatious.

"I need to speak with Katy Korbell. ASAP. It's about the campaign."

A moment of silence. "Really? Why?" Flirtatious had given way completely to *defensive*.

"It's a personal matter."

"A personal matter with Mrs. Korbell that could affect Sanford's campaign? You're being pretty cryptic here."

"I wish I could say more, but…" I paused. "I know it's a lot to ask, but you'll have to trust me. It's important. To her. To your boss, too. How about if I come over and we can discuss it in person?"

"Maybe you should just tell me. I mean, if it's—"

"Nicole. Please."

"Give me a minute."

"Sure." I could have just given up and walked away from the whole mess, letting events play out as they may. I didn't agree with many of Korbell's positions—anti-abortion, anti-gay rights, anti-welfare, the whole "family values" euphemism for conservative conformity. But I had to admit, he'd devoted his public service career to helping the citizens of Fairfax County, and he'd done a pretty good job. Bottom line: I wouldn't ever vote for Korbell, but I didn't want the man's career to be ruined by photos of his wife's peccadilloes.

"Okay, I'm back. Meet me in front of the building in twenty minutes."

"Thanks, Nicole."

I drove to Korbell's campaign office in Fairfax and circled the parking lot until I found a spot. After slipping Rex in between a black Lexus and a blue Lexus, I locked the car and took up position on a bench outside the office building's front door. And waited.

After a while, I checked my cell phone for the time. The twenty minutes had elapsed fifteen minutes ago.

I was about to call Nicole again, when the door opened and O'Rourke walked through it. I turned away and ducked my head down, pretending I was making a call. I felt someone sit next to me but didn't flinch. Just kept fake-talking into my cell phone.

A tap on my shoulder. I said goodbye at my phone and closed it. Turned around into O'Rourke's steely gaze.

"Hello Dan." I tried to smile, but it came out wobbly.

"Why do you need to talk to Mrs. Korbell?"

So much for pleasantries. "It's a personal matter. Where's Nicole?"

"I handle these types of things."

"What types of things?"

"Secretive types of things. Threatening types of things. Ass-biting types of things."

"I think you've got the wrong idea here." I held up my left hand and feigned indignation.

O'Rourke didn't even glance at my incomplete hand, just kept staring into my eyes. "Then set me straight. Why do you wish to talk to Mrs. Korbell?"

I put my hand down and modulated my voice. "Listen. It's very important that I talk with her, but it's for her own good. It has nothing to do with me."

O'Rourke pressed his lips together. Considering. "Come on. Let's go." He got up and started walking toward the parking lot.

I stayed on the bench.

When he realized I wasn't following, he retraced his steps. Stood over me. "If you have something you need to tell Mrs. Korbell, come with me. Otherwise…"

I'd expected more of an interrogation, but I wasn't complaining. "Where to?"

"For a drive."

We left the parking lot in O'Rourke's nondescript Camry, and in a few minutes we were heading east on I-66. "I understand you don't want to disclose any details, but maybe you could tell me—in vague terms—what's so important," O'Rourke said, expression neutral and attention on the road. He kept the Camry in the right lane, at the speed limit. Not that we could go any faster, not in late rush hour traffic.

"I think it's best if I just talk with Mrs. Korbell. She'd probably prefer that, too."

"I'm sure she appreciates your discretion, but it's my job to screen things for her and for the campaign. You don't want to make me look bad, do you?"

"No, I don't. But this really can't be helped."

He found an opening in the left lane and accelerated into it. "Channing, I have a feeling our time together will be limited, so why don't we cut to the chase?"

"I'm not sure I know what you mean."

"I told you before, I dig into people's lives. And I'm very good."

"You checked up on me?"

"Of course."

Unfortunately, Lee and I hadn't come up with any Plan B, should my little ruse be discovered. Time to call on my improv skills. "Okay, then. I don't think we'll be able to hold a fundraising event at the club. We're very busy, you know."

"You can save the comedian b.s. for those who give a crap. What's your angle here? Or are you only trying to get into Nicole's pants?"

"No angle." Better to deny everything, than give O'Rourke information that might come around and bite *me* in the ass.

"What's your connection to the Wongs?"

"Thomas Lee is a friend of mine. Edward and Patrick are his nephews. That's it."

"You can't bullshit a bullshitter." O'Rourke didn't take his eyes off the road, making the conversation seem a little creepy to me. "You tell Edward Wong that we don't appreciate his dirty tricks. We don't want to run a negative campaign, that's not who Sanford Korbell is. But we will expose him if we have to. You'd think he would have found someone a little more, uh, experienced than you to be his mole. Someone a little more effective."

I wanted to spring to my own defense, but O'Rourke had a point. If I were a political operative, I'd be a lousy one. Of course, I was just looking for the elusive truth. "I'm not really working for Edward."

"Goddamn it, Channing, tell me what's going on."

I could see how O'Rourke might be confused by it all. Hell, I knew all about the affair between Patrick and KayKay and I *still* was confused by it all. "Sorry. It's personal."

"It's your funeral. Sometimes the answers come quickly, other times they may take a little longer and require a little more effort. But I always get the answers I'm looking for. I don't expect this time will be any different."

We left I-66 and headed north on the Beltway. *A bullshitter.* My mind kicked into gear. What if O'Rourke already knew about the affair? And about the pictures? If he'd been sniffing around my life, he'd know about Rojo staying with me. What if he somehow found out Rojo had *taken* the photos? What would he do? Was this some kind of trap? "Where did you say we were going again?"

O'Rourke didn't answer, and I thought I detected the first trace of a smile.

Flop sweat darkened the armpits of my shirt. A more sinister train of thought rumbled in my mind. What if Lin and Chun hadn't been after Rojo to repay a gambling debt? What if they knew about the pictures and were involved in the blackmail scheme? And what if O'Rourke was aware of that? I tried to picture O'Rourke putting three bullets into the backs of their skulls. Unfortunately, it wasn't too hard to imagine.

I glanced out the window. We were taking the exit for Tysons Corner. "Are we getting close?"

This time, O'Rourke glanced at me while he spoke, "Yes. Not much longer now."

My heart started to beat double-time, and I tried not to let panic overtake me. Could O'Rourke really have killed those thugs, and DeManzi, too, just to keep the affair between KayKay and Patrick secret? Was he that much of a company man? And more importantly, was he still trying to tie up loose ends? Were Rojo and I to be silenced next?

O'Rourke turned right, down a side street. We'd left the retail malls and car dealerships behind and entered a world of empty lots and warehouses, with the occasional computer repair storefront. If you looked between the buildings, you could still catch a glimpse of the burgeoning Tysons skyline where construction cranes forever loomed.

"Where did you say we were going again?"

"I didn't." O'Rourke slowed and maneuvered the Camry down a narrow alley that wound around the back of a long, two-story brick building. No lights were on inside, no cars in the parking lot. When we were completely hidden from the street, O'Rourke stopped and put the car in Park, but left the motor running. Across the back lot, a solitary dark sedan was parked in the building's shadow.

"This is where we're going to meet Mrs. Korbell?" I asked, trying to ignore the alarm bells going off in my head.

O'Rourke turned to face me. "Last chance, Channing."

"I'll be glad to talk." I tried to slow my racing heart. "But only to Mrs. Korbell."

"I guess we'll see about that." He flashed his hi-beams twice.

The other car answered with two flashes of its headlights.

Shit!

"Maybe my associates will have more luck getting answers than I did."

Double shit! "Look, I know you think I'm up to some kind of partisan political prank, but I assure you I'm not. Can you really take the chance that I'm not lying? I mean, what would Mrs. Korbell do if she found out I had this vital, life-changing information but was prevented from giving it to her?" The words spilled out. I had the feeling I was negotiating for my life. "If Mrs. Korbell—and Sanford's campaign—go down the tubes because of this, heads will roll. Yours first."

O'Rourke remained silent for a full minute. Then he reached out and flicked the lights again, once. A couple seconds later, he got a single flash in response. "Wait here." He got out and walked ten paces away. Put his phone to his ear.

I waited in the car, nerves jangling. If I tried to make a run for it, O'Rourke's friends would chase me down in sixty seconds. And if I somehow managed to escape, they'd still be able to hunt me down, no problem. I didn't have any experience as a fugitive. If only I had Ty in the back seat to protect me.

O'Rourke returned a few long moments later. He slid into his seat and buckled up. "Well, well, well. We're off to see the queen."

———

"This is the place," O'Rourke said, turning into the entranceway for the Tysons Hilton. "Mrs. Korbell is giving a speech here. She can spare exactly five minutes for you."

We parked, but before we got out, O'Rourke grabbed my forearm. "Listen up. I know a lot more than you can possibly imagine. As you might have guessed, I don't think this is a good idea, but I was overruled by Mrs. Korbell. Don't think I won't find out what's going on here. When I do, you'd better hope I don't come after you." He let go of my arm. "One more thing: stay away from Nicole."

Inside the hotel, we walked without talking, past the banquet ballroom, which seemed to be overflowing with middle-aged women, then stopped at a room down the hall. A young, well-dressed man stood outside the door clutching a can of Sprite.

"Hello, Ray," O'Rourke said.

"Evening, Mr. O'Rourke. Always nice to see you. Is this Mrs. Korbell's appointment?"

"Yes, this is Channing Hayes. He only needs a few minutes of her time."

"Sure thing," Ray said. He handed his soda to O'Rourke, then reached down into a little attaché case and pulled out a wand like they used at airport security. "Hope you don't mind."

Next to me, O'Rourke observed, stone-faced.

"Whatever you have to do, go ahead." I held my arms out and Ray passed the wand over my body. Evidently I was clean, because Ray stowed it away quickly. "Can't take chances, right?"

"Right."

O'Rourke handed the Sprite back to Ray and spoke to me. "I guess you're all set, then. Remember, I'll be out here. Just in case."

Ray knocked three times on the door. He waited a moment, then opened it and spoke to me. "Go ahead in. Sorry, but you've only got five minutes. She's on a schedule."

It was an ordinary room—a few chairs, a counter, a small, round table. A mirror on one wall, a few stock pictures of a landscape on another. But an effervescent glow emanated from the center of the room where KayKay stood. She faced me, neither relaxed nor tense, wary perhaps, but not nervous. She was already made up for her speech and not a single strand of blonde hair strayed from its appointed place. This was the first time I'd ever seen her in person, and I have to admit I wasn't prepared for her *presence*. Everything in the room seemed to pale against her aura.

She also seemed much younger and, if it were possible, better looking in person.

"Hello, I'm Katy Korbell," she said, taking a step toward me.

"I'm Channing Hayes."

"A pleasure to meet you. May I call you Channing?"

"Please."

"Okay, Channing, what is it you wish to speak to me about?"

Her tone and manner were pleasant, but there was an underlying bit of tension. Understandable, I suppose, if a stranger says it's crucial he speak to her, ASAP. I'd rehearsed what I was going to say on the ride to the campaign office, something clever and subtle, but I threw it all out the window. "It's about Patrick Wong."

Two quick blinks, then it was back to implacable KayKay. "What about him?"

"Do you know him?"

"Certainly. He's managing his brother's campaign against Sanford. Seems like a good enough guy. If you like liberals, that is." She smiled at her attempt at humor.

"Have you spent much time with him?"

"We've met on several occasions. The local political scene is tighter than you might expect. As I said, he seems nice enough."

Not a crack in her veneer. "It's come to my, uh, attention that you may know Patrick a little better than 'casually.'"

"Really?"

"Yes. And there's some photographic evidence to support that."

"Interesting," she said. "Maybe we should sit." We sat in two chairs facing each other. She still hadn't broken down in tears or anything. "You say there are some photographs? In your possession?"

"No, they're not mine."

"And how do you know about them?"

"I've seen them."

"What kind of photos are these?"

I didn't answer right away, trying to think of a tactful way to describe them. I came up empty. The silence stretched on.

"I see." She sat back and licked her red lips. "Well, I hope I look good in them."

Not the response I was expecting. I refrained from telling her she looked quite good. "So you do know Patrick?"

"Why are you here, Channing? Is it money you're after? Curiosity? Or is it simply sport?" Amazingly, she remained as poised as when I walked in.

"Actually, I'm just here for some information."

"Oh? What kind of information?"

"Is this the first you've heard of these photos? Or has someone already approached you about them?"

KayKay stared straight at me, crystal-blue eyes piercing. "Who sent you?"

"Nobody sent me. I learned of these photos, and I came to give you a heads-up. And to see if you already knew they existed."

"So you're a do-gooder?" she asked, with the slightest trace of sarcasm. Had her marble veneer developed a hairline crack?

"As hard as that might be to fathom, yes, I guess you could say I am."

"Did you vote for my husband?"

"No, I didn't."

KayKay tilted her head slightly. "Interesting. Have you spoken with him yet?"

"Not about this. And I really don't have anything to say to him about it, either. I just wanted to know if you were aware these pictures existed."

"Thanks," she said, and I heard the note of sarcasm again, basso profundo. "Is there anything else you wanted to know? Our favorite position, perhaps? The dirty words we hissed at each other while we fucked?" Although the tone was even and civil, the words came from that raw place, far beneath the candy coating. From the heart. On one level, I felt like crap. On another level, I admired her. No denial, no excuses, no lame justifications.

"Please. I'm not trying to ruin anybody. If you could answer my question, I won't bother you any more. Have you been contacted by anyone about these pictures?"

"Go to hell," she said, her photogenic ex-Miss Virginia face now showing no trace of a smile.

This wasn't going well, but it was going better than I expected. She hadn't slapped me yet. "Mrs. Korbell. I plan to do whatever I can to prevent those pictures from becoming public. What you do in your personal life is your business. Other people are involved here, and I'm trying to help them, too. As hard as it may be to believe, I really am trying to do the right thing here."

"Your five minutes are up," she said, rising. "Thanks again for coming."

TWENTY-SEVEN

I SAT THROUGH THE first show that night patiently, only checking my watch sixty times. The comic, Benjy Skaar, was a funny guy, but he had the annoying habit of laughing at too many of his jokes. A shame, because it made him seem like he was trying too hard. Luckily it didn't bother the audience, because they ate it up, and he performed well enough that we'd probably invite him back. Maybe not for a weekend show, but he proved he could handle a Thursday night.

Between shows, I located Artie in the office doing a crossword puzzle. He sat there, subconsciously trying out different facial expressions as he chewed on the pencil eraser while noodling through the clues. Sort of like watching comics on Comedy Central with the sound muted—a stupid idea on the surface but more entertaining than you'd guess. "Hey."

He glanced up from his puzzle, saw me, then jotted a word down. "Persistent."

"Huh?"

"Ten-letter word for 'relentless.'" He pointed the pencil at me.

"Okay. Listen, I've got to cut out early. Probably before Skaar wraps up. I trust that's okay?"

Artie set the folded newspaper down on his desk. Took the unlit stogie out of his mouth and licked his lips, the precursors to one of his pep talks. I stifled a sigh. "You've been pretty distracted around here lately, what with all Lee's family stuff going on. You doing okay?"

"Sure. I'm fine."

"You don't seem fine. Okay if I give you a little friendly advice?"

My ears heard Artie say "friendly" but my brain translated it to "fatherly." Of course, I didn't have a choice; I'd be getting his advice regardless. "Lay it on me."

"You've spent a lot of time and energy on this favor for Lee. It's gotten to the point where it's affecting you too much. Tell him you've done all you can do. Tell him you're finished. He'll understand. I know Lee, and he wouldn't want his problems to eat at you like this."

I pictured Margaret's face, saw her huddling in her sweater, warding off evil to no avail. "I'm almost done. Just a few more things to take care of, and it will be over." One way or the other.

Artie squinted at me, as if that would help him get a better read on my emotional stability. "I can tell you won't be dissuaded, at least by me. If that's the case, please be careful. I spoke to Lee earlier, and he was awful worried. About what, he wouldn't say. You know what might have him spooked?"

Hell, what *didn't* have him spooked? "I need to get going. Don't worry, I'll be careful." And if I couldn't be careful, I'd settle for lucky.

He aimed his pencil at me again. "You better be careful, and I'm not kidding, kiddo."

———

I met Rojo in my car. He wore a black t-shirt and black jeans, like I'd told him. I'd also changed into a dark shirt and black jeans. I knew we both had black baseball caps, too, because I'd stowed them in the car earlier.

"How was the show?"

"Good. How was the wait?" I asked as I put the keys in the ignition and started Rex.

"Fine. Gave me some time to clear my head." Rojo originally thought he'd put on shades and a cap and sit in the back of the club, but he chickened out at the last minute and decided to wait for me in the car. Three hours in an RX-7 seemed a bit claustrophobic to me, but Rojo didn't seem any worse for the experience.

"Okay. Let's go. With any luck, we'll be home and in bed—or on the sofa—in an hour."

"Roger that," Rojo said. He popped the radio on and punched the pre-sets until he found a song he liked. Then he leaned back and closed his eyes. I guess his head wasn't totally clear yet.

I didn't mind, thankful for a chance to clear mine.

At that time of night, it didn't take long to get to Elm Industrial Park, world headquarters of Wong Enterprises. I drove past the entrance slowly, looking for any indication of activity. A single light struggled to illuminate the parking lot in front of Hao's building, and it failed, resulting in mostly shadows. I thought I made out the shape of a few cars, but they could have been some of the decaying hulks I'd seen before.

Wanting to escape notice, we'd decided to enter the industrial park on foot, so we left Rex in an empty parking lot about half a mile away under a Wells Fargo Bank sign. I had Margaret's key ring in one pocket, cell phone and a penlight in another. "Ready?"

"Let's do it," Rojo said.

We walked along the shoulder, backtracking to the industrial park. Every time a car drove by, we averted our heads, careful not to get our faces caught in some driver's headlight beam. Just two stealth ninjas on a routine mission.

We paused at the mouth of the access road. "Remember, we're going to go in quickly and calmly. We're going to find what we're looking for, then we're going to leave. No drama, no extra snooping around, no graffiti scrawled on the bathroom walls. No bullshit. If someone catches us, we'll tell them we're doing a favor for Mrs. Wong. They won't believe us of course, but hopefully she'll back us up when they call her. Got it?"

"Hopefully no one shoots us before we can tell them that," Rojo said.

"Hopefully."

We walked along the side of the access road, not too fast to catch someone's eye, but not dawdling either. Although there was no time constraint, we wanted this adventure to be over.

At night, in the dark, the place didn't seem quite as seedy. The fleet of vans occupied the same spot as before; chirping crickets and the occasional passing car were the only sounds cutting through the silence. As we rounded the corner of the building next to Hao's, we noticed a car and a van parked near the entrance.

"What does Hao drive?" I asked Rojo.

"Something new. Something expensive."

We couldn't quite determine the make of car from our distance, but Hao didn't seem like a guy to work long hours at the office. To be totally safe, I thought about calling Margaret to confirm Hao's current whereabouts, but decided she probably didn't want to know any more about this little operation than she had to. Plausible deniability, or some such nonsense. I couldn't say I blamed her.

"Maybe we should come back another time," Rojo said. "Like never."

"I thought you wanted your pictures back."

"I do, but I value my freedom more. The idea of spending time in jail doesn't excite me."

"Come on, we haven't done anything," I said, crouching low and setting off across the parking lot. "Yet."

We duckwalked across forty yards of asphalt until we got to the corner of Hao's building. We could see the vehicles in front now, a Ford Econoline van and an old Subaru. Although neither was Hao's, it didn't matter. Whoever owned the cars was supposed to be there; we were not. I thought about taking Rojo's advice and coming back another time, but I wasn't too afraid of getting caught. Embarrassing perhaps, but we did have Margaret's "permission," and we were Lee's friends, after all. What could Hao do to us, except slap us on the wrist? They wouldn't prosecute; it would bring too much bad press to the situation.

"So what's our plan now?" Rojo asked.

"Same as before, except we need to be stealthier. We sneak in, see what's going on. If the coast is clear, we go to Hao's office. I'll snoop around, you stand watch. If someone's here, we wait, and then we go in." Sounded easy as I said it. Also sounded like I'd been watching too many reruns of Magnum, P.I.

"Okay."

Keeping close to the wall, we made our way to the outer door. We were directly below the second-story windows, so no one in Hao's office could see us, and the windows on the ground floor had the shades drawn.

I tried the door. Locked, as expected. I pulled out the keys and the second one I tried did the trick. We slipped inside. Only one of the six overhead lights was on, probably an after-hours, energy-saving strategy.

We avoided the elevator and took the stairs. At the second-floor landing, we paused at the fire door. I held one finger up to my mouth until Rojo nodded.

Cracking the door open an inch, I peered down the hallway. Empty. I could see the glass door with *Wong Enterprises* etched on it.

All the lights were on inside the office. I watched for a few moments, and a guy wearing jeans and a t-shirt passed by the door pushing a vacuum cleaner.

The cleaning crew was hard at work.

I pulled the door closed, making sure it latched silently. "The cleaning crew is here. I guess we wait."

Rojo shrugged and leaned against the cinder block wall. Closed his eyes.

Every few minutes, I'd open the door a crack and scope things out. As long as the lights were on in the office, I figured they were still doing their thing. About thirty minutes after we'd arrived, I heard voices in the hallway. In Spanish.

I gently tapped Rojo on the leg. "I think they're leaving now."

I gave them another five minutes, then gazed through the crack in the fire door. The main lights in Wong Enterprises were dark. Some light seeped out from within, but it might have been emergency lighting or more fluorescents set to energy-saving mode. I waited another couple minutes to make sure the cleaners hadn't forgotten anything, then I swung the door open and tiptoed down the hall, Rojo on my heels.

This time, I didn't pause at the door. I had my key out and ready, and we were inside in seconds. We ducked behind the receptionist's desk to gather ourselves. I was breathing so hard it sounded as if there were a rhino hunkered down with us. Next to me, Rojo's eyes were dinner plates. The smell of lemons and astringent chemicals hung in the air.

What the hell were we doing?

I took a deep breath and whispered to Rojo, "Okay. We're halfway there. You know the rest." I'd gone over the plan three times during the drive over and once again as we walked from the car. I wasn't positive Rojo had been listening during any recitation.

I found the key to Hao's office—the middle-sized key on the ring—and gripped it in my good hand. Then I counted. "One. Two. Three." I got up and hustled down the hallway, past the photos of plastic utensils and mugs, to Hao's office. Rojo's footsteps echoed mine. Key in the lock, turn the knob, and we were in. Guess we had a knack for burglary.

We didn't turn the lights on, but we could see well enough from the emergency lighting coming through the glass windows. Rojo crouched and kept watch, while I crossed the office to the ginormous desk. It was as clean as it was the other day, spotless.

I removed the penlight from my pocket and switched it on, then I moved it to my left hand, where I held it steady with my thumb and forefinger. The two drawers on the right side of the desk had keyholes. I unlocked the top one first, but it only contained paper clips and pencils. I slid it closed and re-locked it. Opened the bottom drawer. This was a file drawer, and it was jam-packed. Each tabbed file was labeled in a very neat hand. People's names, mostly. As I riffed through them, a knot formed in my gut. Many of the names I didn't recognize, but there were plenty I did: Chun, DeManzi, Lin, Patrick, Brad Ames, Rojo, Lee. I even spotted the names of a couple members of Rojo's band. A fat one had Korbell's name across the top.

As I flipped through them, the knot in my stomach tightened. I came across a folder on Ty. One on Skip. One on Artie. *One on me.*

"Holy shit," I said, aloud.

"What'd you find?" Rojo whispered, without turning his head. Nice to know he was taking his lookout duty seriously.

"Hao's got files on everybody."

"Huh?"

"You, me, everybody."

"What the fuck are you talking about?" Rojo left his post and joined me at Hao's desk.

I showed him the *Rojo* file. He snatched it. Opened it. I shined the light down so he could read. I felt his anger grow. "He's been checking up on me. Seeing if I'm good enough for his daughter. Jesus, did he hire a PI or something?"

I felt violated, too.

"He sees I'm a decent guy, I treat Joy well. Then why does he hate me?"

"You're not Chinese, are you? Could be that simple."

"Maybe. But in this day and age, you'd think…" He trailed off. Would there ever be a day and age without small-minded bigots?

I plucked the file labeled *Lin* from the drawer. It held a copy of a police report and a page of notes written in longhand. A few words were underlined, but it would take more time than I had right now to decipher them. I replaced the file and took out De-Manzi's. More police reports, more notes, more information. Next to me, Rojo read over my shoulder in silence.

Bigotry was the least of Hao's sins. I had the sinking feeling he was behind the trail of death that followed Patrick. Chun and Lin, then DeManzi. There was no gangland war. It was Hao eliminating those who could bring down his two precious boys on their way to Washington.

I closed the folder and picked up the one marked *Artie*. In it were a few pages of Google effluent—some listings, some newspaper clippings mentioning him, the articles of incorporation of The Last Laff. For the life of me, I had no idea why Hao needed to know about Artie. Or Ty. Or Skip. I knew why he might want to know about me after my intrusion into his life, but not my *friends*.

Rojo said what I'd been thinking ten seconds ago. "A lot of these people are dead. We don't want to be next. Let's go."

Good idea. "Hang on. We need to find the pictures." I went straight for Patrick's folder. Inside, there was a white envelope, identical to the one Edward had shown me. I opened it. Bingo. A dozen incriminating photos of Patrick. Some with KayKay, some solo. Some with drugs and one with two other women I didn't recognize. Luckily, there wasn't one with a farm animal. I stuffed them all back into the envelope. Then I grabbed the folders of any-body I recognized and pushed the file drawer shut.

I switched off the penlight. "All right. Mission accomplished."

"Now we can get the hell out of here."

"Just a second." I switched the penlight on again. Opened the drawer and grabbed the rest of the folders.

"What are you doing?"

"Evidence. With all this stuff, the police can nail Hao for ev-erything bad that's gone down in the D.C. area in the last twenty years."

"I don't know, man. He's Joy's father."

"What were you just saying about him? Jesus. If he had those guys killed …"

"Yeah. You're right, of course, but …" Rojo sounded like a kid who'd lost his puppy.

"Come on." I shut the desk drawer and relocked it, although I didn't think it would take long for Hao to realize his files were missing.

Rojo glanced out into the hallway. "Nobody's around."

We left Hao's office and walked—fast—toward the exit. I won-dered if this was how the jokers at Enron felt hauling out incrimi-nating evidence. Would Wong Enterprises fold with Hao in jail? What about all the workers' jobs? No time to worry about that now, as we headed for the doors and the night beyond.

We didn't get to the night beyond.

Hao and Ames stood by the glass doors. And Ames had a gun in his hands.

TWENTY-EIGHT

"OH SHIT," ROJO MUTTERED under his breath.

"Let me do the talking," I whispered back.

Hao stepped forward and pointed to the stack of folders in my arms. "What are you doing with those?"

"I think the bigger question is why are you investigating all these people? And why are you investigating *me*?" I tried to maintain some level of calmness. After all, Rojo and I were the ones who snuck in here and swiped Hao's files.

Ames reached for the files, but Hao held out an arm, preventing his ape from getting too close. "It is a time-honored tradition in your country, is it not, to investigate those who you do business with? As well as those who may oppose you, in politics, in business, in life? Richard Nixon, Oliver North, Jimmy Hoffa, Joseph McCarthy. Didn't they all research their opponents?"

"Not exactly sterling role models." I wanted to scream "murderer" to his face, but didn't think that was a wise strategy, at least not at this particular moment.

"I might have known you were behind this," Hao said, glaring at Rojo. "What Joy sees in you is beyond me. After she finds out what you have done, she will change her tune."

Rojo's hands curled into fists. I could almost feel his core temperature rise, and I was standing two feet away from him.

"Who sent you to steal my files?" Hao asked.

"Nobody sent us," I said.

"Where did you get the keys to the office?"

"What keys?"

"Don't play coy with me. Ames saw you enter on the security cameras. They are fed to his home via the Internet. That is how we knew to 'meet' you here," Hao said.

Shit! I'd forgotten about the security camera in the entrance lobby. I could cross "burglar" off my list of potential careers after I flamed out doing the comedy thing.

Hao's tone turned nastier. "Tell me who gave you the keys. I shall have him or her fired."

"You're going to fire your wife? She doesn't share your hatred of me, you know. She knows I'm good for Joy," Rojo said, still hot. I glared at him. Now wasn't a good time to delve into the reasons why Hao hated him, not after he'd been caught red-handed breaking into his office.

"Margaret gave you the keys?" An expression halfway between disbelief and cold anger grew on his face. Next to him, Ames had the look of a hungry jungle cat.

I held my hand up and tried to defuse the situation. "Look. She was worried about Patrick. She asked me to get something to help her convince him he needs help. That's all. We meant no harm to anyone involved." All true, except we'd like to see Hao punished for murder, too.

Hao pursed his lips, considering what I'd said. Ames stood by his side, knees flexed, anxious to jump into the fray. I had the feeling he'd enjoy wrestling me for the files. "So Margaret is concerned about Patrick. That's nice. So am I. That's why I can't let you take those files. If some of that information gets out, much harm will come to him."

I remained there, frozen. In my hands, I held the evidence Hao had been amassing. But would it incriminate him in murder? In any crimes? In one sense, Hao was correct—spying on your enemies was a time-honored tradition. What would I do with all the files? I could pass them along to Freeman, tell him I was pretty sure Hao murdered Chun, Lin, and DeManzi. But without proof, real proof, it was all supposition. What about the lives that would be ruined if the information in those files became public knowledge? I got dizzy just thinking about the potential fallout from Hao's dirt-digging operation.

"Hayes?" Hao had raised his voice. "Hayes? Please give Mr. Ames the files."

I didn't see any viable options. Hao had won this round. Ames moved closer, sticking his gun back into a holster on his hip. He beamed as if he'd just won the Super Bowl.

With a sigh, I handed him the files I'd taken. Rojo mumbled something, but I didn't make it out. Ames set the whole stack of folders on the receptionist's desk. Then he turned back toward us and crossed his arms and stuck out his chest. *Beast.*

"What about the pictures?" I asked.

"What pictures?" Hao smiled, and I could tell he knew exactly which pictures I was talking about. "There are lots of pictures in those files. And none of them concern you. Now, it's getting late." He held out his arm toward the door.

"You're not going to get away with this," Rojo said.

"I have done nothing against the law. In fact, you are the ones who have broken in and tried to steal my possessions. I should call the police. But because you are Thomas's friends, and because I don't want my daughter hating me," he said, as he glared at Rojo for an extra beat, "I will let you go. This time. Should you be so foolish to try this again, you can be sure I will call the police and have you arrested. Do you understand?"

"Why don't I take over from here?" Ames said, stepping forward and rolling his massive shoulders. "Teach them a little lesson?"

Hao paused, seeming to consider Ames's generous offer. "No. Not this time."

"But Mr. Wong, I think that—"

"Thank you, but that won't be necessary. I think Hayes and Rojo have already learned their lesson. Isn't that right?" Without waiting for an answer, Hao started for the door. "We will escort you out now."

Ames took that as his signal to get involved, so he shoved me and Rojo toward the door. Rojo turned around and glared at the big oaf, but didn't try anything.

Rojo and I followed Hao, mutely. I wouldn't even know what to say. Hao had a point. He'd caught us red-handed with his stuff, and we were on the security camera's video to boot. Any objective person—like a judge—looking at the situation would conclude

Rojo and I were the ones in the wrong, and it wasn't even a close call.

The four of us took the elevator in silence. Rojo seemed pissed, and scared, and frustrated, and completely unlike the happy-go-lucky laid-back musician I knew. I half-expected him to grab Hao by the neck and squeeze. Maybe if Ames hadn't been there.

We exited the elevator into the tiny lobby on the ground floor. Someone had turned on more lights, and Hao's demeanor seemed to brighten, too. He smiled and shook our hands and even patted Rojo on the back.

"We're just going to let them go, just like that?" Ames asked, practically foaming at the mouth.

"Yes, we are," Hao said. "Goodbye, gentlemen."

Rojo and I pushed through the outer door into the night.

A bad feeling grew in my gut, like mold on week-old Wonder bread. Why was Hao so friendly? Why was he letting us go so easily, without more threats about what would happen if we tried to blow the whistle on him? Then I remembered the security camera in the lobby. "Rojo, I think something very strange is going on here."

"If that asshole wasn't Joy's father, I think I'd rip him a new one. Two new ones. In fact, I think we—"

I grabbed Rojo's arm. "Did you notice how friendly Hao got, right when we entered the lobby."

"Huh?"

"As soon as we were in view of the security camera, Hao turned friendly."

"So? He's a fickle SOB."

"No, it's more than that. We're being set up."

"Like how?"

"Like now there's photographic evidence of Hao being nice to us as we left his place. In one piece."

Rojo's brow furrowed.

"Come on, let's get out of here."

We'd taken about four steps when we heard someone's voice calling after us.

"Wait up," Xun Wong said, as he stepped from the shadows. He must have been waiting against the side of the building.

"Yes?" I asked, skin starting to vibrate. Next to me, Rojo's eyes grew wide as he finally realized what was happening.

"Where is your car?" Xun said, stopping about ten feet in front of us. He wore a light windbreaker, both hands in the pockets.

"We parked it down the road a bit," I said.

"Excellent. I'll walk you there."

"Thanks, but we parked kinda far."

"No problem. It's a pleasant evening."

"Look, I've got a two-seater, so I can't drive you back here. We'll be able to manage. Trust me. Have a good night." I started to walk away.

Xun removed one hand from his jacket and brandished a pistol. I stopped walking. "This is a bad neighborhood. I'd feel guilty if something happened to you. Plus, I don't mind the exercise. So, let's go." With the gun, he gestured for us to start moving.

No rise out of Rojo. He walked as if he were a brain-dead zombie. I wondered if he'd shut down, knowing what we were in for. We headed down the access road, past the rotting vehicles and abandoned buildings of the office park. Xun kept about five paces behind us. Every time we'd slow down, he'd slow down, too.

Our odd parade made it to the main road, then we turned toward where I'd parked Rex. We walked on the gravel shoulder; streetlamps every forty yards or so illuminated our path with cones of harsh white light. Chirping night insects provided the soundtrack.

No one spoke. Right now, Xun had the gun and we were following his agenda. At some point, though, I had the very strong feeling Rojo and I would need to do something in an effort to escape.

We trudged along the gravel shoulder. With each step, I became a little more encouraged. Xun had to be getting more tired, and Rojo seemed to have a little more pep in his step. Maybe he'd snapped out of his trance. No cars passed us as we walked and I wondered if this was how old-time death row prisoners felt as they were marched toward the gallows.

"Stop," Xun said.

Rex wasn't yet in sight; if I remembered correctly, it was parked about two hundred yards farther down the road, around a sharp curve. A copse of trees was on our left; on the right, across the road, sat a squat, white-brick building with its windows painted over and two empty garage bays. Looked like an abandoned service station or something.

"Cross here."

I glanced back at Xun and he waved the gun in the direction of the building.

"The car isn't here. We've still got a ways to go," I said.

"We're taking a shortcut."

Rojo snorted. I considered making a dash for it, but Xun wouldn't have much trouble putting one in my back from ten yards, even in the dim light. Then he'd put a slug in Rojo and call it a night. If we had any chance of succeeding, this was going to have to be a joint effort.

We crossed the road, still five paces in front of Xun. "In there."

"Huh?" Rojo asked.

"In the garage. Come on, hurry up," Xun said. He marched us into the garage bay on the right. "You can turn around now."

We did, and I examined the spot where I'd be taking my last breath.

A floodlight hung on a wire above where the gas pumps once stood. It shined into the front part of the bay, leaving half the garage in shadows. Broken beer bottles and fast food wrappers littered the concrete garage floor. A jumble of broken pallets occupied one corner, a stack of old tires balanced precariously in the other. A swirl of dead leaves, from autumns past, covered more of the floor. Although the place had been abandoned for some time, the smell of motor oil was strong, invasive.

Xun turned toward Rojo. "You thought you could get away with blackmail? We all have been correct about you. You *are* a loser. Joy deserves much better."

"I wasn't trying to blackmail anyone." A tendon in Rojo's neck stood out.

"We know you took the photos of Patrick. It's your style, isn't it? You were enabling Patrick by placing his bets for him, and you met with him secretly. How easy it would be to follow him. You knew exactly how much he owed DeManzi. And now you deny it all? How stupid do you think we are?"

Rojo didn't say anything, but he didn't have to—the answer was clearly heard in his silence.

Xun raised his weapon, pointed it at Rojo. "Blackmailers are scum. They should be punished, don't you think?"

I kept my eyes glued to his trigger finger, bracing for an explosion. Waiting for my chance.

"I . . . I didn't send Hao those pictures."

"Who did?" He lowered his weapon, just a hair. "Mr. Hayes here? You two in this together?"

"I don't know, it could have been anyone." Rojo's voice cracked. Again, you didn't have to be a genius to realize he knew who sent the pictures. Now we were exploring some new ground, at least for me.

"Yes, but it wasn't. You know who sent them. And you will tell me." He aimed the gun directly at Rojo's forehead again.

"Don't shoot! Don't shoot! Joy didn't mean anything. It was a joke, really. She only wanted to make a point about Edward and Patrick being the favored children and all. She would never have exposed them. Never. She's got a little . . . mean streak."

"Joy sent them?" Xun asked. Then the expression on his face changed, and despite the shadows, I thought I detected a gleam in his eyes.

Rojo nodded like a bobblehead doll in an earthquake. "Yes, yes, yes. She sent them. Just a stupid prank. Let's all forget about this, okay? No harm, no foul."

Xun looked from Rojo, to me, back to Rojo again, but he didn't lower his weapon. "Joy sent them," he repeated, to himself.

So, Rojo had been lying to me. Again. I wondered what else he'd been deceiving me about. "Okay, Xun. You've got the pictures. You know who sent them. I assume you can get this all settled, since it's a family matter. Patrick's secrets are safe and you can get on with whatever underhanded political dirty dealing you want to."

"Yes, I can get this settled," he said, and I realized if we somehow escaped unharmed, warning Joy was our first order of business.

"Well, if it's all settled, I guess we can go now." I took a step toward freedom. A tentative step.

"Please do not move," Xun said.

I stopped moving.

"Look," Rojo said, "we've got no gripe with you. We know Hao killed ..."

I shot Rojo a nasty look, but the horse had already left the barn, at a full gallop.

"Who do you think Hao killed?" Xun asked.

Was it possible Xun didn't know what his brother had done? Rojo started to answer, but I talked right over him. "It's a pretty big coincidence, don't you think, that DeManzi got knocked off, right before Hao said he was going to pay off Patrick's gambling debt to him? Not so much a coincidence as a smart business decision. Saved him what, over two hundred thousand bucks? Who else is he planning to bump off to make his life easier? Maybe Sanford Korbell?"

A creepy grin grew on Xun's face. "And you were going to turn him in, yes? With all the files to corroborate your theory? Your friend Freeman Easter would have been so grateful."

Did the Wongs have a file on Freeman, too? I'd had enough of the Wong family's shenanigans. Investigating their business competition was one thing, investigating their political opponents was another thing, but investigating me and my friends? That was complete and utter harassment. If I was going to die tonight, I had a few things to say first. "Fuck you, Xun. You won't get away with this. My *friend* Freeman Easter will figure this out and pin it on you and your brother. I'm only sorry how this will affect Lee and Margaret. They're the innocents in this mess."

Xun's nostril's flared, the only visible sign of emotion I'd seen. I always thought of him as the even-keeled, elder Wong brother, but I guess he could be riled, too. Everyone could be, just a matter of where the line was drawn. "*You* certainly are not innocent. Patrick harmed no one. His gambling was extreme, yes, but he was the victim. And his dalliance? Foolish, of course, but consensual. Yet his actions could serve to be his downfall. And more insidious, his brother's. I do not think that is fair. Because of your actions, because you have stirred all this up and refused to let it drop, you have given me no choice. You must be eliminated."

"What about the people Hao killed? DeManzi and his flunkies? You say Patrick harmed no one, but they're dead because they got involved with him."

"Scum. Criminals. Those drug dealers and sex merchants have killed many people, destroyed many lives. They deserved to die for their past sins and for what they were planning to do to Patrick. And what they did at Thomas's restaurant. The city is better off with them dead. Surely you can't argue that." Xun stood straighter. "Let me set the record straight. *Hao* did not kill them. He believes what the police believe. Gang violence."

A chill skittered down my spine. So, Xun was Hao's fixer. Not that it mattered at this exact moment in time.

"Rojo is not the blackmailer. You've got the files back. We really can't harm you, right? It would be our word against yours.

No proof. You should just let us go so we can get on with our lives."
I shrugged. "Come on. We should be going. It's getting late." I tried
to inject a casual air into my words and failed miserably.

"Yes, it is getting late," Xun said, and I had the feeling he wasn't
talking about the time. "I hate loose ends. Hao hates them, too,
and he knows he can count on me to tie them up. Always has, ever
since we were boys. I'd do anything for my younger brother. And
I have."

"I don't think we need to hear the details right now," I said.
"Maybe some other time."

Xun waved the gun in the air. "Ames called Hao. He'd been checking the security video feeds—he often does when the cleaning crew
is working—and he noticed two intruders. He called Hao, who met
him at the office. Who did they find? You two, nosing around. They
corrected your misunderstanding and sent you on your way, no hard
feelings. Unfortunately, you were attacked on your way to the car.
Like I said, this is a very dangerous neighborhood. Do not worry.
Hao and I will make a generous contribution in your names to your
favorite charities." The evil grin spread on his face like it had before,
only this time it seemed more ominous. Way more ominous. "And
you know what? The ballistics will match the bullets taken from the
bodies of DeManzi and his crew. It's a pity you walked into gang ter-
ritory. You really should have been more careful."

The chill skittered double-time back up my spine.

"Margaret knows we're here. She sent us."

"Yes. I'm counting on her to corroborate that." He shrugged,
smirk still evident.

Cold bastard. "You and Hao won't get away with this. Freeman knows. Joy knows. The truth will come out. Killing us will only complicate matters."

Out of the corner of my eye, I caught sight of Rojo nodding vigorously.

Xun kept waving the gun around. I couldn't tell if he was losing touch with reality or had already thought this whole thing through from every angle and toying with us was part of the fun. "As I said before, Hao knows nothing of my deeds. And I will tie up as many loose ends as I need to. After the first, the rest are much easier."

Being thought of as a loose end didn't sit well with me. I don't think it sat well with Rojo, either, because I could sense him tensing beside me.

"Do you know the fool with that haircut cried when I told him to turn around and get on his knees? I hope you both are man enough not to cry."

"This is a big mistake, Xun."

"Enough talk. Get down on your knees." He pointed the barrel of the gun toward the filthy concrete floor.

"You can't shoot both of us," I said, moving to my left. Rojo got the hint and moved to his right. Xun's eyes narrowed as he took a step backward. "Give it up. You won't get away with this. You're too smart to think you can. I bet that you—"

Before I could finish my sentence, Rojo sprang forward. Xun wheeled in his direction and fired. Rojo went down, screaming and grabbing at his side. Xun spun back toward me, but I dove to my left, deeper into the shadows of the garage. I kept rolling, through dirt and trash and discarded shop rags. Xun fired twice, then stopped. "You're trapped, Hayes. Don't make me hunt you down like a rat. Come out here and I promise I'll make it quick and painless."

I didn't answer. In the background, Rojo's anguished cries had diminished to intermittent howls.

I found myself behind the stack of tires. I felt around on the floor, searching for some kind of weapon. All I came up with were machine screws, some miscellaneous bits of plastic, and a handful of dead leaves. I tried to quietly move farther into the shadows, but my knees scraped on the floor. I steeled myself for a bullet in the skull. I wondered if I'd feel it.

"You can't escape. If I have to come find you, it won't be pretty," Xun said. Unfortunately, I didn't think he'd get bored of this game and go away.

I stayed hidden behind the stack of tires, and reached as far as I could, hoping I'd find something to use against Xun. I thought I heard movement, a slight scuffling, so I froze. The sound stopped. I slowly got into a crouch, keeping my left hand on the tires, figuring if Xun came at me, I could topple them into his way to buy a few precious seconds while I ran for safety. But I was hoping it wouldn't come to that—tires were heavy and the odds of that plan working were slim, at best.

Rojo's screaming had abated altogether, and the silence worried me more than his wailing.

I took another little hop to my left and extended my right hand, searching. Would it be asking too much for some gangbanger to have left his switchblade behind? My heart skipped as my knuckles grazed something hard. Metal. My fingers closed around a heavy metal rod of some sort. Rebar, perhaps. I hefted it in both hands.

About three feet long, not quite an inch in diameter. A formidable weapon. Now all I needed was a little room to swing it.

I picked up a couple screws and tossed them into the rear corner of the garage, deep in the shadows. Waited, holding my breath. Then I heard a footstep. And another. Xun had fallen for the bait.

Clutching the metal rod in my good hand, I circled the stack of tires. I peered around them and spotted Xun, back to me, creeping toward the noise he'd heard in the corner, about four big strides away. I figured I could clock him before he spun around and got a shot off.

If I were lucky.

I took a deep breath. *One. Two. Three.* Then I charged forward.

Xun heard me and whirled around. I closed the gap quickly and whipped the metal rod down on his forearm as hard as I could. A sickening *crack*, and the gun clattered to the ground. Xun's face contorted for a moment, then he fell to the ground clutching his busted arm. He writhed on the concrete slab, not able to get up, only enough energy to spew forth a stream of obscenities.

At least I think they were obscenities. I didn't speak Chinese.

TWENTY-NINE

THE FOLLOWING MONDAY, LEE, Artie, and I sat in a back booth at Lee's, finishing up an early lunch. Lee had ordered the usual spread, and we'd have to find a way to burn off an extra two thousand calories somehow.

"How's Rojo doing?" Lee asked.

"Better. Still in some pain, but the doctors expect a full recovery. He'll be playing guitar and jumping around on stage in no time." I'd visited him yesterday, and he was in good spirits.

"Right through his tuchas, huh?" Artie said, breaking open a fortune cookie.

"Rojo insists it's his hip, but it looked like it was his butt that got hit to me." To be fair, the bullet *had* also grazed his hipbone.

"I'm glad this mess is over with," Lee said.

"Yeah. Me too." Freeman's buddies on the force matched Xun's gun to the one used to kill Lin, Chun, and DeManzi. Unfortunately, when they searched Wong Enterprises for more evidence, none of Hao's files turned up. And Hao played the innocent, claiming he knew nothing about what Xun had been up to. Some brotherly loyalty. "How's Margaret?"

"Relieved, I think. Things between her and Hao have been rocky for years, but she never had the courage to move on. Until now. She kicked him out of the mansion and told him she wants a divorce."

Artie clucked his tongue. "Never liked him much."

"Me neither," Lee said. "The Democratic Party honchos want Edward to stay in the race, but having his uncle charged with multiple murders has effectively killed his chances."

"I feel bad for him," I said, and I did.

"It's a tough blow, but he's resilient. Privately, he said he'd run again in two years. Despite this setback, I think he'll have a fine political career. Make us all proud." A dark cloud passed over Lee's face for a moment. "Of course, he'll have to overcome the baggage of having Xun as his uncle."

"Well, if there's one thing about the American public, they like giving people second chances," I said. "What about Patrick?"

"We held an intervention for him. He seemed to get the message, and I think he realized much of what happened was his fault. He said he's going to check into rehab. We'll see how it goes. Following through has always been a problem for him."

"I hope he succeeds. Addictions are tough to beat," Artie said. "He deserves a shot at happiness, even if he is a politician."

"Yes. He's a good kid, at heart. All three of them are." Lee cracked open a fortune cookie and pulled out the slip of paper.

Lee hadn't learned of Joy's misguided blackmail "prank." When I was at the hospital with Rojo after the shooting, I'd pulled her aside. Told her I knew all about her sending the photos. At first she denied

314

it, but five minutes later she was saying how sorry she was, how she'd just been really steamed at her father. After another few minutes of discussion, she'd decided to admit what she'd done to Edward and Hao. Hopefully, that was the last we'd seen of those photos.

"Channing. I owe you for what you did. I thank you, and Margaret thanks you. More than you can know. You're a true friend." A tear welled in Lee's eye, and he blinked it away. Artie noticed, but didn't make any wisecrack. There was a first time for everything, I guess.

I waved him off. "You would have done the same for me."

Now it was his turn to wave me off. He cleared his throat. "This is fitting," he said, reading the fortune from his cookie. "Beware the man who calls for order but has messy backyard."

Artie simply grunted, but I knew it was a grunt of approval for what I'd done for Lee. At least that was how I decided to interpret it.

———

I made a call from the car. "Nicole, this is Channing Hayes. Please don't hang up on me." I figured O'Rourke had filled her in on my deception.

"I should, you know. Pulling that crap," she said, confirming my assumption.

"I called to apologize. It was very wrong of me. I'm sorry."

Several silent seconds ticked by. "It's funny. When we first met, I thought there was something between us. A little spark. I actually thought you were going to ask me out. My mistake, I guess."

"I, uh …"

"By the way, I heard the news about Edward Wong's uncle," Nicole said, reverting quickly into political mode. I guess she wasn't too heartbroken over me.

"Yeah. Pretty bizarre."

"Is the rumor true?"

"What rumor?"

"That Edward Wong is going to run again in two years?"

Rumors were rampant in the world of politics. "Uh, no comment."

"I'll take that as a definite confirmation."

Politicians. "I have one more favor to ask, an easy one. Could you pass along a message to Mrs. Korbell? Tell her the misunderstanding is all cleared up?"

"I suppose I can do that," she said.

"Thanks," I said. "I really am sorry, you know. About what I did."

"All's fair in politics, I guess. At least for some people," she said.

Ouch. I didn't know what to say to that except, "Take care, Nicole."

"Goodbye, Channing."

I clicked off, thinking about what it would have been like to date her. Wearing that pink fuzzy sweater-blouse, with a string of pearls around her neck, she had that preppy-girl thing going. Plus she was very friendly. Plus she was a looker. Plus she smelled good, up close. All those plusses added up to a pretty potent combination. But …

I picked up my phone again and pressed another number. Waited two rings until my call got answered. "Erin? Hey, this is Channing."

"Hi Channing. What's up?"

"Would you like to go out with me, say dinner, next Friday? Then maybe come to the club? You know, like a real date?"

There was a long pause on her end. "Sure. I'd love that."

In my world, a girl in sweats trumped a girl in pearls any time.

———

An hour later, I opened the door to Room 144, and thirty-one second-graders all stopped what they were doing to stare at me.

"Okay, class, quiet down now. Our guest, Mr. Hayes, has arrived," Ms. Bissette said. She recited some kind of cute rhyme and, surprisingly, the talking ceased. I made my way to the front of the classroom, winking at Seanie who sat in the front row, beaming. It wasn't until I was standing by the whiteboard that I noticed Donna, leaning against the back wall, tucked away in the corner. We made eye contact and she mouthed the word, "Relax."

Did my anxiety show? I mean, come on, these were *second graders.*

"Sean, please come introduce your guest," Ms. Bissette said, motioning for Sean to get up. He didn't need any encouragement; he'd popped out of his seat before she'd finished her sentence.

I held out my fist and he bumped it, then faced the class. "This is Channing Hayes. He's a stand-up comic who works with my mom. He's going to tell you what he does and why he's so funny." Sean stuck out his arm at me, like he was showing off a side-by-side refrigerator on a game show. Then he scampered back to his seat.

"Thanks, Sean. And thank you, Ms. B., and the rest of the class for inviting me here today. It's been a while since I was in second grade."

Some kid called out from the back, "Like a century."

The class erupted in laughter.

Heckled by an eight-year-old? I glanced at Donna, who was shaking her head. She didn't want me going after him.

"Like two centuries," I said, eliciting only a couple giggles. Heckler: 1, Me: 0. "Okay, as Sean said, I'm a stand-up comic. My job is to make people laugh. Who thinks that sounds like a fun job?"

All the kids shouted out.

I wondered if Wendell White ever played a second grade. "It *is* a fun job. I mean, what could be more fun than telling jokes and making people laugh?"

"Riding roller coasters."

"Taste-testing ice cream."

"Playing video games."

"So make us laugh," a girl with a ponytail cried out.

"I'll do my best." I licked my lips. Last night, I jotted a few things down and I'd reviewed them in my head on the drive over. "I bet you all like animals, right? And farms? Me too. In fact, I was on a farm last week, and I saw two cows arguing. One said to the other, 'So, what's your beef?'"

Silence. I waited a beat, looked around. *Hello? Hello? Is this thing on?* Against my better judgment, I glanced at Donna. She had her head in her hands. "See, a beef means a problem, and beef comes from … never mind." I was breaking one of the sacrosanct rules of comedy: Never explain your jokes.

I licked my lips again. "So what's a cow's favorite thing to do?" I waited half a beat. "Go to the mooooovies."

A couple snickers. *Dead room.*

I pressed on. "What's a cow's favorite city? Moo York." A few more laughs. "What does a cow drive? A moooving van."

More laughter. The class was starting to warm up.

"This farm had sheep, too. Lots of white, fluffy sheep. Who knows what a sheep likes to do at the pool? The baaaaackstroke." I held on to the *baaa* a good four seconds.

The kids loved that one, but I think I heard a groan from Ms. Bissette.

"What did the musical sheep do? Play in a baaaaand." I glanced at Donna. She gave me a thumbs-up.

"What do dogs like to do? Go for a walk in the bark." I waited for the laughs to die, then forged ahead. "Who did the horse invite over for lunch? His neeiigghhbors."

Now the class was rolling, and I was having fun. Time to cap things off on a high note. "How many cows does it take to write a book?" I paused, to build anticipation. All the kids stared at me, smiles on their faces, waiting to erupt at the punch line. It was moments like these a comic lived for. "Don't be silly. Cows can't type."

Funny what can bring the house down.

THE END

ACKNOWLEDGMENTS

Q: How many people does it take to produce a book?
A: A whole lot!

My sincere gratitude goes to:

Booksellers, librarians, and, of course, my terrific readers.

Dan Phythyon and Ayesha Court, for their invaluable input.

My faithful and insightful early readers: Sam Feigeles, Sue Ousterhout, Mike White. Megan Plyler and Dorothy Patton. Mark Skehan and Doug Bell. The Texas crew: John Stevenson, Jill Balboni, Kim Stevenson, and Samantha Stevenson.

Those who provided me with inspiration along the way: Elaine Raco Chase and Ann McLaughlin. The effervescent Noreen Wald.

Donna Andrews, Ellen Crosby, John Gilstrap, and Art Taylor for their wisdom.

Reed Farrel Coleman and the P. J. Parrish sisters (Kris Montee and Kelly Nichols) for their generosity and kind words.

Basil White, David Bickel, and stand-up comics everywhere.

All my friends in Mystery Writers of America, International Thriller Writers, and The Writer's Center for their support. All my cyberpals on Facebook, Twitter, and throughout the blogosphere.

My wonderful agent Kathy Green for her tenacity and encouragement, among other things.

All the talented people at Midnight Ink: Bill Krause, Terri Bischoff, Brian Farrey, Connie Hill, Steven Pomije, Courtney Colton, Donna Burch, Ellen Lawson, and the entire sales staff.

The best (and most enthusiastic) family a guy could have: Ruth; Karen, Jamie, and Emma; David and Wendy; Susan, Becca, and Phillip; and Lisa, Paul, Samantha, and Malon.

My mom, Bev, and my late father, Leonard, for taking me to the library whenever I wanted.

My children, Mark and Stuart, and my wife, Janet. Love, always.

Thanks!

ABOUT THE AUTHOR

Before Alan Orloff stepped off the corporate merry-go-round, he held a variety of positions at a number of prominent companies, including General Electric, *The Washington Post*, and Arbitron Ratings. In the nineties, he founded Environmental Newsletters, Inc. to help organizations reduce their negative impact on the environment.

Alan earned a B.S. degree in Mechanical Engineering from the University of Maryland and an M.B.A. from MIT/Sloan. He belongs to Mystery Writers of America, International Thriller Writers, and The Writer's Center in Bethesda, Maryland. His debut novel, *Diamonds for the Dead*, was a finalist for the Best First Novel Agatha Award.

Residing in Northern Virginia with his wife and two sons, he's currently hard at work on his next novel.

WWW.MIDNIGHTINKBOOKS.COM

From the gritty streets of New York City to sacred tombs in the Middle East, it's always midnight somewhere. Join us online at any hour for fresh new voices in mystery fiction.

At midnightinkbooks.com you'll also find our author blog, new and upcoming books, events, book club questions, excerpts, mystery resources, and more.

TM
MIDNIGHT
INK

OTHER MIDNIGHT INK BOOKS BY ALAN ORLOFF

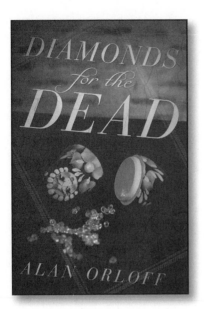